The
DESIRE

Books by
Dan Walsh and Gary Smalley

THE RESTORATION SERIES
The Dance
The Promise
The Desire

Books by Dan Walsh

The Unfinished Gift
The Homecoming
The Deepest Waters
Remembering Christmas
The Discovery
The Reunion
What Follows After

SERIES • 3

DESIRE

A NOVEL

DAN WALSH
AND GARY SMALLEY

Revell

a division of Baker Publishing Group
Grand Rapids, Michigan

© 2014 by Dan Walsh and Gary Smalley

Published by Revell
a division of Baker Publishing Group
P.O. Box 6287, Grand Rapids, MI 49516-6287
www.revellbooks.com

Printed in the United States of America

Library of Congress Cataloging-in-Publication Data
Walsh, Dan, 1957–
    The desire : a novel / Dan Walsh and Gary Smalley.
        pages cm. — (The Restoration Series ; #3)
    ISBN 978-0-8007-2150-3 (pbk.)
    1. Adoption—Fiction. I. Smalley, Gary. II. Title.
PS3623.A446D47 2014
813′.6—dc23   2014009982

This book is a work of fiction. Names, characters, and incidents are the product of the author's imagination or are used fictitiously. Any resemblance to actual events or persons, living or dead, is coincidental.

14 15 16 17 18 19 20   7 6 5 4 3 2 1

About that time the disciples came to Jesus and asked, "Who is greatest in the Kingdom of Heaven?" Jesus called a little child to him and put the child among them. . . . "Anyone who becomes as humble as this little child is the greatest in the Kingdom of Heaven. And anyone who welcomes a little child like this on my behalf is welcoming me."

—Matthew 18:1–2, 4–5

1

Michele didn't know why she'd come here, why she tortured herself this way. The place stirred all kinds of emotions inside her. None of them good.

They were just children playing on a playground. They were just moms chatting on a bench under a tree.

"Watch, Mommy, watch!"

Michele walked along the sidewalk in one of the many shaded playgrounds in River Oaks. It was Friday afternoon. A little boy, maybe three years old, stood at the top of a yellow kiddy slide, facing the moms on the bench. But Mommy didn't watch. None of the women did. They just kept yakking away.

"Mommy, watch me!" He stood there a few moments more.

One of the women glanced his way. Long enough to say, "Great, Sammy," then back to her little group.

Sammy looked at her, waited, then went down the slide.

How could she do that? What could she possibly be talking about that mattered more than her son? Some new sale at the mall? Some new coupon deal on the internet? Michele watched Sammy land softly on his rear end, stand up, and brush the sand off his pants, then run around to the ladder again. Sure enough, when he got to the top: "Mommy, watch!"

This time, his mother only looked, then offered a dismissive wave. Back to her friends, who received the fullest measure of her attention.

I would watch you. If you were mine, I would watch every single time. And listen to every word you said, whether it mattered or made no sense at all.

As Michele reached a picnic table at the other end of the playground, the little boy went down the slide again and looked over at his mom when he stood. He registered no disappointment, none that she could see. It was amazing how resilient and forgiving children were at that age, and even older. At the school where she taught kindergarten and first grade, she saw that resilience all the time. Due to cutbacks and having almost no seniority, she could only work part-time, which left her afternoons free.

She counted five children on the playground. Three boys, two girls. All preschool age. Two babies in strollers over by the moms. So many kids for three ladies. *Aren't they the lucky ones?* They looked to be her age, maybe a few years older. Must have married young like she had. Probably waited a year then started popping babies out at will, one right after the other.

How nice for them.

And look, they brought them to the playground to play. Such good mothers. But how good were they really if they could blot their kids out of their consciousness so completely?

Her anger stirred. *That's what happens when things come too easily. They don't mean as much.* Like the way her younger brother Doug treated his little red Mazda, the car her parents had bought for him when he got his license. He'd been back from college this past weekend, and the car, as usual, was a mess. And Doug, as usual, was oblivious to it. She and Tom, her older brother, never had a car handed to them like that. They had to work for their beat-up used cars all through high school, come up with the money for their gas and insurance by themselves.

"Mommy, come push me." Another little boy stood on a tire swing, trying to shift his body weight back and forth. He didn't weigh enough to generate any motion. "Mommy?" he cried out again.

"I can't right now, honey," one of the other women said. "Ask your sister."

"She's not big enough."

Michele waited for the mother's reply, as did the little boy on the swing. She didn't answer. She did laugh extra hard at something the woman at the far end of the bench said. Michele wanted to scream, or at least say something. Really, she wanted to walk out to the playground and push the little boy herself.

Wouldn't that get their attention?

Her cell phone rang. She lifted it out of her purse. It was her mom. Should she answer it? Generally, she enjoyed talking with her mom, but they weren't on the same page about this issue. Her mom tended to side with Michele's husband, Allan. Their opinion was simple: not getting pregnant after a year of trying wasn't that big of a deal.

But it was a big deal to Michele, a very big deal.

What if her mom asked Michele where she was or what she was doing? Should she lie? That wouldn't be right. She answered on the third ring. "Hi, Mom, what are you up to?"

"Hey, Michele, I'm just doing some shopping for our big Sunday dinner. Doug will be coming back from school, and of course—"

"Two weekends in a row? Isn't that some kind of record?"

"I know," her mom said. "Of course, Tom and Jean and the kids will be here, and so will Charlotte. Even Audrey Windsor is coming."

"Mrs. Windsor? Haven't seen her in a little while. How is she doing?"

"I'm not sure. I think she's okay. Your father talked to her. She called a few days ago saying she had something important to talk to him about, so he invited her to the dinner."

"I wonder what it is," Michele said.

"I have no idea. I'm just calling to make sure you're still coming."

"I am. But remember, Allan's not home yet from his mission trip to Africa."

"When does he get home?"

"Tuesday night. He's flying in to the Orlando airport."

"We'll miss him. We'll have you guys over some night soon after he settles in to hear all about it."

"That sounds good. So should I come right after church on Sunday?"

"About an hour after. But not much later than that. You know how your father is. He wants to eat as soon as we sing the closing song."

Michele laughed.

"Well, I better go. Talk to you soon."

Michele put her phone back in her purse and turned to face the children on the playground again. The situation was the same. The children playing and laughing, occasionally calling out to their moms for attention; the moms' attention still mostly focused on each other.

It was sad.

But as upsetting as it was seeing these children taken for granted, Michele was aware of a peculiar conflict inside. Another part of her longed to be sitting right there under that tree with the moms, chatting away.

A few minutes later, when tears welled up in her eyes, she knew she had to move, to do something else, anything. She pulled out a tissue and dabbed her eyes, then gathered her things. As she did, she noticed a slim, brown-haired girl a few yards away, standing by a tree, looking right at her. She wore jeans and a baggy pullover sweatshirt, which seemed odd to Michele. It was quite warm out. As Michele looked closer, she understood why. The baggy sweatshirt did a poor job of hiding the fact that the girl was pregnant. When she saw Michele noticing, she looked away.

Michele pulled out her keys, but she did it too fast, and they fell to the pavement. Bending down to pick them up, she heard footsteps behind her and turned. It was the girl who had been standing by the tree.

"I couldn't help but notice you looking at the kids on the playground." She had a slight accent, maybe New York. "And how it made you cry." She hesitated a moment. "I've seen you here a few times. I've been coming too. But I don't think for the same reason. Mind if I ask you a question?"

Michele restrained a sigh. Had she not dropped her keys, she'd be on her way to the car right now.

2

I was just getting ready to go," Michele said.

The girl sat down. "I can see that. This won't take long. You don't even have to tell me your name."

That sounded odd. But Michele couldn't just get up and walk away. It would be too rude. She relaxed her grip on her purse. "What do you want to know?"

"I guess . . . well, maybe two things. Why were you crying? And why do you come here to watch little children play?"

Michele didn't want to answer either question. Not with a complete stranger. But the girl looked right into her eyes. She seemed totally sincere. "Why do you want to know?"

The girl paused. "I get it . . . Answer a question with a question. You don't want to tell me. It's okay. You don't know me."

Tears welled up in the young girl's eyes. She blinked them back, turned her attention to the kids on the playground.

"I'm sorry," Michele said. "I just wasn't prepared to talk about what you want to know. It's deeply personal. You know that, right?"

The girl looked at her again. "I know. I forget sometimes, not everyone says what's on their minds like me. It's just . . . I have a big decision to make pretty soon, and I'm looking for answers." She looked back at the children. "They're really cute at that age. Not a care in the world."

"I know," Michele said. "Is your big decision about . . . the baby?"

The girl smiled. "Now look who's getting personal."

"I'm sorry, I didn't mean—"

"It's all right. Yeah, it's about the baby. I'm actually past due." She looked down at her belly. "I don't mean with the baby, with this decision. The baby's not due for two more months."

Michele could hardly believe the girl was seven months pregnant. She would've guessed five. "You don't look like you've gained a pound over what the baby weighs."

"The doc agrees. He'd like me a little fatter. Not fatter, but you know what I mean. Guess it's my genes. My girlfriends back in high school used to hate me, 'cause I never gained any weight."

"Where are you from?"

"Long Island."

"I guess your genes also affect your looks. You don't look old enough to be out of high school to me."

The girl smiled. "Just graduated last year. Came down to Florida a little after that. Long story. Not a happy one." The smile disappeared.

She had a cute face. She looked even prettier when she smiled.

"So what did you want to ask me?"

"It's just, I've been coming here off and on the last month. I've seen you here quite a few times."

Michele had never noticed her until today.

"Each time I come, you're staring at the kids, watching them play. Not in a creepy way. You always look so sad. Most of the time, I see tears in your eyes before you leave. Guess it just made me curious. I keep trying to figure out what your story is."

Michele sighed. Strong emotions began to stir. She turned to face the kids again. "I want to be . . . like you."

"Like me?"

Michele looked back at her. "Pregnant. I want to have a baby. But I can't. At least not so far."

"How long have you been trying?"

"We've been trying a little over a year. My husband and I. His name is Allan." Why did she say that? They weren't using names.

"A year's not very long, is it?"

Michele could tell by the tone of her voice, she was trying to sound comforting. But it wasn't comforting. Almost everyone said that. Couldn't they see it was an annoying thing to say to someone in her situation? "It's a long time when you want it more than anything else in the world. It's a long time when you're doing everything you can to get pregnant, and it doesn't happen. When nothing you try works. Then you see it happening to everybody else but you. Even to women who don't want to get pregnant." Immediately, Michele regretted that. "I'm sorry. I really wasn't thinking about you." She actually had Jean, her sister-in-law, in mind. She'd gotten pregnant with their last baby while she was still on birth control, when Tom was still out of work.

"That's okay. I certainly wasn't planning on this. I was just being stupid."

"See, that's what I mean," Michele said. "It's not fair. God allows girls who don't even want babies to get pregnant, then says no to people like me." She couldn't help it; the tears wouldn't stop.

The girl pulled out some tissues from her sweatshirt pocket and handed them to Michele. "I never used them. I just brought them in case my allergies acted up."

Michele wiped her eyes. "Thanks."

"You're right. It doesn't seem fair. I don't know what God's thing is when it comes to babies and who gets them. Well, I mean, who gets pregnant. Who gets them is another matter. That's kind of my problem, where I'm stuck at the moment."

Michele suddenly wondered, was that what this girl was getting at? Was she looking for someone to adopt her baby? "I'm not really interested in adopting a baby right now."

"What?" the girl said, looking confused.

"You said you were stuck, about who gets babies. And you said you were making a big decision. I just thought—"

"That I was asking you?"

"I guess."

The girl smiled.

Once again, Michele was struck with how pretty she was when she smiled. With a new hairstyle and some makeup, she might even be called beautiful.

"No," the girl said, "I wasn't hinting at you taking my baby. My big decision is whether to become a single parent or give my baby to this adoption agency, one I found out about at this clinic that's helping me. They gave me all these assignments to help me sort it out, and I think I know which way I'm leaning, but I'm still not 100 percent sure. It's such a big deal. It's my baby's life, where she's gonna spend the rest of it."

Now Michele understood. "I guess the answer to your question is . . . I come here to dream. I'm dreaming of the day when I'll have my own baby and I can bring him or her to a playground like this." She looked back toward the children.

"But I can promise you, when that day comes, I won't be sitting on a bench ignoring them, chatting with my friends. I'm going to be right out there with them every single minute." Michele needed to stop. She could feel a rant coming on. "So why do you come here?"

Tears appeared again in the girl's eyes. She quickly looked away. "I guess to help me convince myself, to help me close the gap on those few remaining doubts about what to do with my baby."

"You're leaning toward adoption then?"

The girl nodded. "I could never give her this, a life like this. A neighborhood like this. A playground like this. Have you seen the cars in the parking lot? I parked mine in the street two blocks away. It's complete crap. I'm not even married. I've got a terrible job and no future. They could film episodes of *Cops* in my apartment complex. A lady from the adoption agency told me that almost all of their couples have nice cars, nice houses. They're married, and they have good jobs. They check all this out before they approve them. And they're all Christians. They've all been praying, sometimes for years, for a baby just like mine, because they can't have one on their own."

She released a heavy sigh. "That's what I want for my baby. What she deserves. It's not her fault God stuck her with me." This time, there were too many tears to blink back.

Michele reached out her hand. "What's your name?"

The girl pulled out another tissue and dabbed her eyes. "Christina. My name's Christina."

— 3 —

It was Sunday afternoon at the Anderson house on Elderberry Lane in River Oaks. All the leaves were in the table to accommodate the additional family members and friends. It reminded Michele of a scene from a Hallmark holiday movie, minus the Christmas decorations. A little early for that in mid-September.

All the Andersons were present, except Uncle Henry and Aunt Myra and Michele's husband, Allan, who technically wasn't an Anderson. Michele missed him terribly. She was becoming less a fan of his short-term mission trips to Africa. For one thing, she hated being so disconnected. When he was home, they talked every day; he would even call her at lunch.

She looked toward the far end of the table, the place where Uncle Henry and Aunt Myra usually sat in big family gatherings. They were traveling out West on a two-month trip in their little RV. But Charlotte was there, sitting next to her mom, talking up a storm. Her New England accent in full bloom.

At the other end of the table next to her father sat Audrey Windsor, looking regal and refined, as always. Michele thought she looked like a character straight out of *Downton*

Abbey. She had come earlier to talk with Michele's dad about something, but Michele didn't know what. Whatever it was, it put an interesting smile on her dad's face. She also noticed he kept looking down the table at her big brother, Tom.

Michele was sitting in the midsection of the table, next to Doug and across from Jean, Tom's wife. Tom sat next to her and was busy feeding the baby. Michele and Jean had become close friends over the past year. Even though Michele envied Jean's ability to get pregnant so easily, she loved her dearly. Jean was totally on her side and very sympathetic toward Michele's situation. She knew how much getting pregnant mattered to Michele and told her she prayed for her every day.

"So Tom," Michele said, "how are you liking your new job? How's it feel to be an IT guy again?" Over the last year, Tom had finished his schooling and finally got his coveted IT certification. He hadn't found an IT job until a few weeks ago.

"It feels great," he said. "It's taken a little getting used to working eight to five again. Especially having to put a tie on every day."

"But he'll get used to it just fine," Jean added.

Tom smiled. "Yes, I will. But I miss working at the Coffee Shoppe. It was a totally different atmosphere than any job I ever had. If only it paid more, I might have considered staying."

"Was it a big difference?" Michele asked.

"A huge difference," Jean said. "Almost double the pay."

"Wow."

"And," Tom added, "at the ninety-day mark, we'll get full benefits. So yeah, I can get used to this again."

"How far do you have to drive every day?"

"Twenty minutes. Way better than when I worked at the bank. Now I miss the rush hour traffic completely."

"Allan hates driving in bumper-to-bumper traffic," Michele said. "Maybe more than anything else in the world." She looked at her watch. It was 1:30. What was he doing now? It was already nighttime there in Ethiopia.

"Someplace you have to go?" Doug said.

"No," Michele said. "Just counting down the hours till Allan and I can talk again."

"When's he going to call?" Jean asked.

"Not until midnight."

"Midnight?"

"Well, it won't be midnight for him. It'll be nine in the morning, tomorrow morning. There's a nine-hour time difference."

"That's so strange," Doug said. "He's living in the same moment as we are, but in a totally different world. So it's, what, 10:30 at night for him now?"

Michele nodded. "And it's not a pretty world where he is. Those poor people live in more poverty than you can imagine. I've seen pictures and videos. It breaks my heart. I can't even look at them very long or I'll start to cry." That was one of the things that had attracted her to Allan—his willingness to give his time away so freely to others. But she wasn't so keen on this now as she had been back then.

"But I still don't get why he has to call you so late," Tom said from across the table. "Cell phone service is so cheap now, even international long distance."

"Not in Africa," she said. "Allan said it's crazy expensive there. We're not even connecting by cell phone. We're using Skype. For some reason, internet service works a lot better than cell phone service. But even that doesn't work very well, if you ask me."

Jean set her glass down. "I'm surprised they even have the internet over there."

"I know, but they do. Allan says it's not up all the time. It can go down for three to five days at a time." She looked at her watch again. "I hope it works tonight."

"Why so late?" Jean said. "Aren't you teaching school in the morning?"

Michele nodded. "We don't have a choice. Allan said the internet connection is the strongest in the morning. Well, *their* morning. The times that work best for me don't work for him. He either can't get through at all, or it takes forever to say things back and forth. We tried it once, and it was awful." Michele wanted to stop talking about this.

"So what's he doing over there this time?" Doug asked.

"Who wants coffee?" Michele's mother stood at the end of the table, counting the hands.

Michele raised hers, hoping this coffee call was enough to change the subject.

It wasn't.

Doug leaned toward her. "So what's Allan up to in Africa these days?"

"You really want to know?"

"I asked."

"He's got a blog about it, if you want the link, with lots of pictures and videos."

"Maybe I will look at it . . . later. But can't you just give me the highlights?"

"Sure. I guess the main thing is reaching out to orphans. That's the focus of their trip, all these street kids in Addis Ababa. There's so many of them, thousands, I think."

"Addis Ababa? Sounds like a town from Aladdin."

"From the pictures I've seen, it's nothing like the scenes from that movie."

"How'd their parents die?" Doug said.

"Mostly from AIDS, some from other things. But no one takes care of them. It's not like here at all." Images from Allan's pictures and videos started flashing through her mind. "They live in tiny little shacks and beg all day. Most don't even go to school."

"That's horrible," Jean said. She looked at her children, Carly, Tommy, and Abby, the baby. "I can't even imagine that."

"You should see those videos. Or maybe you shouldn't. I couldn't get the images out of my mind for days after I did."

"That's pretty heavy." Doug looked at the spread of food laid out on the table. "They've probably never seen anything like this."

"It must look like heaven to them," Tom said.

For the next few moments, no one said a word. Michele felt that same guilt feeling she always felt when this subject came up. One of the hardest parts of her conversations with Allan was the unavoidable small talk. *How are you doing? How are things going? What did you do today?* Allan would answer, and the things he said were equal parts horrifying and heartbreaking.

She didn't know how he did it. She understood how he got talked into going the first time. But why did he keep going back?

Her mom, who had been in the kitchen for the last several minutes, walked back into the dining room. "Coffee's on. Who's ready for dessert?"

— 4 —

ADDIS ABABA, ETHIOPIA

It was hot and muggy, even at 1:00 a.m. Allan tossed and turned on the lumpy bed in the modest bedroom of an equally modest guesthouse. Street noises sailed through the open windows at constant but irregular intervals. But these weren't the causes of Allan's insomnia. He'd grown used to these things in the first few days of his trip.

Allan couldn't get the images he had seen earlier that day out of his mind. Not just the sights but the sounds . . . and the smells.

He thought he'd seen it all before. This was his fifth trip to Africa in three years. His third to Ethiopia. Extreme poverty, the wholesale lack of basic goods and necessities, broken down or nonexistent roads . . . he had seen all of these things plenty of times. Allan knew you didn't get used to it if you were from America, no matter how many times you came here, but the shock value wore off after the first few days. You couldn't function or fulfill your mission if you let it get to you.

But nothing Allan had seen thus far prepared him for what

22

he had seen today, about fifteen minutes outside the city in a little village named Korah.

→ →

8:30 A.M.—THE DAY BEFORE

Allan and his friends were just finishing their breakfast when Ray Jenkins walked in all excited. Ray was a full-time pastor, in charge of evangelism and missions at the church Allan and Michele belonged to back home. Ray was leading this trip, but he had unofficially made Allan his right-hand man. Beside Ray stood a short African man, who Allan guessed was a native Ethiopian. A troubled expression on his face caught Allan's attention, since it contrasted with Ray's smile.

Everyone stopped talking. They had been expecting Ray to lay out their marching orders for the day. "Guys, let me introduce my new friend here. This is Henok. Met him last night after our outreach meeting. We stayed up talking for hours. He has some amazing stories to tell about where he grew up. It's not far from here. There are hundreds of orphans living there. Right, Henok?"

Henok looked around nervously, as if concerned someone might be listening. "Yes," he said quietly, with a strong African accent. "Many orphans there. Many lepers and elderly too. Many people with AIDS."

"Henok and his wife have been trying to start an orphanage for two years," Ray continued, "but they lack the funds and resources. They actually adopted a little boy from there themselves."

"But our home is very small," Henok said. "There are so many more who need help. Our hope is to get a bigger home and rescue other children."

Allan started tensing up; he didn't know why. Well, he knew one reason. He wasn't nearly as adventurous as Ray. Ray seemed fearless, willing to go anywhere or do anything if there was even the slightest chance of reaching people for Christ. Allan was just getting used to the routines they had established on this trip, and they only had a few more days to go before they flew home. He wondered what new adventure Ray had in store this time. "Is this what we're doing today?"

"I wasn't thinking all of us," Ray said. "At least not right away." He looked at Allan and said, "I was thinking you and I could go check this place out. See if we think it might be a fruitful place to spend our last few days as a team."

Allan smiled. Inside, his stomach was still tensing up. "Sure, Ray. I'll go," he said as he stood.

"Ed," Ray said, "why don't you lead the guys back out and pick up where we left off yesterday until Allan and I get back?"

"You want to meet back here?" Ed said.

Ray looked at his watch. "Sure, how about 12:30 for lunch? Henok, we can get back here by then, right?"

Henok nodded. "No problem. The village is only about fifteen minutes from here."

"Great," Ray said. "Then that's our plan. How much time before you're ready to go, Allan?"

"I'm ready now." Technically, that was true. He was ready on the outside. What he wanted to do was suggest Ray let him and Ed switch places.

"Then let's go."

The rest of the men stood, and each one, in turn, shook Henok's hand. Allan noticed he was actually smiling by the time they finished. But Henok's smile faded as they made their way through the tables and out to the street, where their car and driver awaited.

Allan's smile had faded well before that.

◆ ◆

Allan had grown used to driving through the streets of Addis Ababa by now. Parts of the city were quite modern. Large commercial buildings were beginning to appear. More of them with each trip. Lots of construction was under way. Plenty of paved roads. There were still far more people walking to their destinations than you'd ever see in a US city, and far more merchants selling fruits and vegetables along the curb. But Addis Ababa definitely gave the appearance of a city trying to find its way into the mainstream.

Still, unmistakable poverty abounded. Even more so the farther they drove from the center of town. After five minutes, the paved roads disappeared, and things became very bumpy.

The driver did his best to follow in the ruts created by a large garbage truck ahead. Ray sat up front with the driver; Henok and Allan sat in the back. Henok sat on the edge of the seat, leaning forward, answering Ray's questions. "So the village is named Korah?"

"Yes," Henok said. "Korah."

Ray asked the driver, "Have you ever heard of this place?"

"Yes. It is a terrible place. People from the city never go there. It is where we dump our garbage."

"It's the city dump?" Allan asked.

"Yes. You will begin to smell it long before we arrive."

"After you are there awhile," Henok said, "you get used to the bad smells."

"I don't agree," the driver said. "The smell stays in your nose for days, and on your clothes. It is a town of lepers. It is where they have always sent the lepers, for many years. Many with AIDS are there too."

Allan looked at Henok. "Didn't you say last night that you grew up there . . . in Korah?"

The driver shot Henok a look through the rearview mirror. A sad look came over Henok's face, and he slid back in his seat. Allan realized he had asked the wrong question. Henok was clearly embarrassed.

Henok looked out the window. "Yes, I grew up there. But that is not who I am anymore. I escaped."

"Do any of your family members still live there?" Ray asked.

"Yes." Then a long pause. "Some do."

5

As they got closer to Korah, the driver began to get visibly nervous. Allan noticed Henok was sitting fully back in the seat now, mostly looking out the window. He wore a distant expression on his face, as though seeing different things than what everyone else saw.

"Is there another way in?" the driver asked Henok. "I don't believe the guards will let us in the front gate with these Americans."

"Yes," Henok said. "Take a right up here, just past that cluster of bushes. It's a narrow dirt road."

"More narrow than this?" the driver asked.

"Yes. And you must drive slow, even slower than we've been driving on this road. With the rain we've had these past few days, there will be many ruts and mud puddles. Follow the road around the big mountains of garbage you see out the window. It will lead to the back way. We can sneak these men in there, no problem."

"Why do we have to sneak in?" Ray asked. "All the people we've met in Addis Ababa have been very nice to us."

"This is a place of shame," the driver said. "The government would not want Americans to see this."

"But every country has garbage dumps," Ray said.

"Yes, but not like this," Henok said. "You have never seen anything like this."

After the driver made the right-hand turn, they saw many people walking on either side of the road, different ages, all dressed in rags. Many were women and children wearing blank stares; most were barefoot. Some carried dirty white bags and sticks with hooked ends. Allan began to see rows of the most pathetic little shacks as the road widened up ahead. He had seen impoverished areas in Africa before, even in Addis Ababa. Those places were like middle-class subdivisions compared to what he saw now.

The strong odor that had been coming in the windows was now almost unbearable.

"How long have these people been living here?" Ray asked.

"Many years," Henok said. "Since before I was a child. And before we came, the lepers were here. Long ago, a king banished all the lepers to this place. Mainly to die, away from everyone else. They still come here to die. But then this became the place where all the trash was brought from the city. Trash means food for the hungry. So, the orphans and widows began to come in search of food."

"This is what they eat every day?" Allan asked.

"It is all they have to eat," Henok said. "Without it, they would starve. You'll see as we get closer. The garbage and dump trucks bring the fresh trash, and the people swarm all over it, picking through the piles to find bits of food and little things they could sell in the market. That is why they carry these bags and sticks." He was pointing to a cluster of young boys walking by. "They will sort through the garbage for hours, putting anything they find in those bags. When they are full, they will carry them back to their homes—these little shacks you see—to feed their families." Tears filled his eyes. "That was me just a few years ago. I was like that boy there." He pointed to one young man hurrying to catch up with the rest.

"You were responsible to feed your whole family?" Allan asked.

Henok nodded. "Me and my two brothers. There were seven of us living in one room. It's not far from here."

Allan hadn't seen any strong, older men. "Henok, where are the fathers?"

"There are no fathers," he said. "That is why the widows and children and the elderly come here. This is their only hope."

They drove a few moments in silence. Out the side window, Allan saw a little boy maybe six years old sitting against a broken sign. Next to him, a dirty white bag, half full. He pulled something out of it, smiled at the sight, and held it up. It looked like a crunched-up yogurt container. He straightened it and, with his left index finger, began scooping out little bits left inside. His eyes closed as he swallowed the few remaining bites, then he licked his lips. When he opened them, he looked right at Allan and smiled even wider. You'd have thought he'd just eaten a chocolate sundae.

A little farther down, the road narrowed again. They drove past another row of shacks made of mud and sticks with rusty metal corrugated roofs. A woman squatted outside one, arranging bundles of rotten bananas in neat rows. A few still had small sections of yellow, but they were mostly bruised and blackened. Allan couldn't imagine eating even one.

"Pull over here," Henok said. "We must walk from this point."

"I will stay here with the car," the driver said.

As soon as they left the car, they were surrounded by children. All of them smiling, as if they hadn't a care in the world.

"You are like celebrities," Henok said. "They almost never see a white man."

Instantly, Ray began touching them. Rubbing their heads, patting them on the shoulders. Allan began to do the same, but he didn't want to. He had secretly hoped they would remain in the car the entire time. He felt a growing revulsion inside and a fear of catching something contagious. *Lord*, he prayed, *help me be more like Ray.*

Suddenly, Ray bent down and picked up one of the children, a little boy, and carried him in his arms. "And how are you today, young man?" he asked. The boy giggled and smiled.

Other children began lifting their arms toward Allan, wanting him to do the same. A part of him felt intense compassion for them, but another part raised a red flag. *This isn't safe. You'll catch some serious disease. You don't have immunities for this place, or these people.* After these thoughts, a wave of nausea hit him. He took a deep breath, but the smell was overwhelming. Allan suppressed all this and picked up a little girl who had been staring at him the entire time. She hadn't said a word.

She had the biggest, brightest eyes, and she was light as a feather. She couldn't be more than three or four years old. "You have the prettiest eyes," Allan said. He pulled three Hershey's Kisses out of his pocket and showed them to her. She seemed puzzled, so he opened one partway. She smelled it, then opened it the rest of the way and popped it in her mouth.

The look on her face was priceless, and her smile melted his heart.

6

As Henok led them through an opening at the back of the dump, Allan buried his nose in his forearm against the stench. Ray did the same. Henok kept walking forward. As they followed, Allan was certain he'd lose his breakfast any moment, but somehow it stayed down.

Henok turned and noticed the difficulty they were having. "I'm sorry. I forget how it is for those who never come here. We can turn back."

Allan was happy to hear that, but Ray said, "No, keep going. We need to see this."

Allan had seen—and smelled—enough.

"Are you sure?" Henok said.

"Yes," Ray said. He set the little boy down. "I can't carry you anymore. I'm afraid I'll drop you." They were standing before a massive heap of garbage about thirty feet high, and it was clear Henok intended them to climb it.

Allan released the little girl. The boy took her hand and led her away, but he did not leave the dump as Allan expected. Instead, he led her around the base of the hill several yards away, then they both began to climb.

"What's he doing?" Ray asked.

"Come back," Allan said. "Don't go up there." The children looked at them for a moment but continued to climb. "Where are they going?"

"To get food," Henok said matter-of-factly. "It's what they do every day."

"Children that young?" Ray asked.

Henok didn't answer. He took a few steps up the base of the hill, then stopped. "We must be very careful as we climb. It is extremely dangerous. Do your best to follow my handholds and footsteps."

"It doesn't look that steep to me," Ray said. "If the children can do it . . ."

"That's not the danger," Henok said. "There are many needles buried in the trash. If you fall, and one pierces your skin, you could catch AIDS or TB or many other bad things. My eyes are trained to spot them. So do as I do and go only where I go. Once we're over this hill, you should be all right."

The men climbed single file. Allan had a thought and almost said it. How about if he stayed at the bottom of the hill until they got back? But he kept following Ray. As they neared the top, he kept hearing beeping sounds. Lots of them. When they reached the crest, he saw the source. Bulldozers spread throughout the dump were moving massive piles of trash. And garbage trucks of every size were dumping more piles here and there.

They looked across acres and acres of dark gray garbage, as far as the eye could see. The scene on the ground offered little contrast to the overcast sky. Hundreds, maybe thousands, of people wandered through the rubble. Children, mothers with babies tied to their backs, the elderly, teens, and lepers, all holding big bags, poked and sifted through the garbage. Crowds were especially thick around the bulldozers and garbage trucks. Mingling among the throng were dogs and goats and so many birds.

All Ray and Allan could do was stand and stare. Both had lowered their arms and were no longer covering their noses. The smell was just as nauseating, but it seemed inappropriate to be so obvious, an insult to these poor souls who had to live and forage for their food here every day.

Henok motioned for them to follow. They carefully walked down the hill toward the same group of people the little boy and girl had joined, all of them digging through a fresh pile of trash left behind by a small blue garbage truck. Allan couldn't take his eyes off the little girl. She had squatted down and was imitating everything the boy did.

"Is that her brother?"

"No," Henok said. "She has no brothers or sisters. But he looks after her when she is near."

Allan noticed something then. There were no fights. No pushing or shoving. No one grabbed anything out of anyone else's hands. He looked around. It wasn't just with this group. He didn't see anyone acting aggressively anywhere else, either. Back in America, people regularly blamed big-city violence and crime on poverty. But look at the poverty here. It was so much more severe. A different league. Yet everyone seemed almost polite, even the children.

Ray said to Henok, "You seem to know that little girl's story."

Henok nodded his head. "I knew her mom. She grew up here in Korah. We were . . . friends. One day she was working all by herself, and a well-dressed man came to the dump and promised her work not far away. He said he'd pay good money. I wanted to stop her. I yelled for her, but she was too far away. The man took her to his house and raped her, then he brought her back and tossed her to the ground."

"That's terrible," Allan said.

"Yes." Henok sighed. "She got pregnant from that. After she gave birth, she got sick with TB. A few months later, she died, leaving her little daughter here by herself."

"She's an orphan?" Allan asked. "No one looks after her?"

"Yes," Henok replied, "she is an orphan, but she has a grandmother. She lives in another part of the village. I knew where, so before I escaped this place, I brought the little girl to her. But her grandmother isn't capable of feeding her, so she comes here to get her food every day like everyone else."

Allan walked over to the girl. Henok and Ray followed. She saw him and looked up. He smiled, and she returned the smile. That was when he noticed she had two big dimples. Picking her up again, he said, "I wonder what your name is."

"Ayana," Henok said. "Her name is Ayana. It means 'beautiful blossom.'"

"That is a lovely name, Ayana," Allan said, gently touching the tip of her nose with his index finger. Instantly she smiled again. She spoke her first word, but Allan didn't understand it.

"She said hello in Amharic. That's the language she speaks, the language most of the people here speak."

"Can you say it again?"

Henok repeated it. Allan tried to say the word, but judging by both Ayana's and the little boy's reaction, he muffed it badly. But it caused them both to laugh, so it was worth it.

Henok said something else that made Ayana laugh then began a brief conversation with her. "Ayana is very curious about white people. She mentioned her grandmother. I think she wants you to meet her."

"Yes," Ray said. "We'd love to. Can she take us there?"

Henok suggested Allan allow him to carry Ayana as they walked to her grandmother's, so they could get there faster. Henok already knew the way. It wasn't far, maybe a ten-minute walk. They came to a small hut, like so many others, made of mud and straw and not much else. But she did have a metal roof over her head. Some of the others nearby didn't even have that.

They stepped inside a single room with a dirt floor, approximately eight-by-ten. The grandmother seemed startled to have company. Perhaps, Allan thought, even more so to see white men. She slowly got up and greeted the men with a typical Ethiopian kiss: once on the right cheek, then the left cheek, and one more kiss on the right. She said something to Henok in Amharic.

"She wants to make us coffee to honor us for visiting her home. It will be safe, the water is boiled."

The old woman pointed for the men to have a seat on her bed. There were no chairs in the room. She began roasting some coffee beans over an open fire. Once the beans were roasted and put into a bowl, she put a pot of water on the fire. While the water boiled, she ground the coffee beans by hand, smashing a stick into a bowl. After she finished, she served the coffee to the men. Over the next several minutes, she and Henok talked. He occasionally paused to fill them in. They learned she was born in Korah, the daughter of lepers.

"Both her parents were lepers?" Ray asked.

Henok nodded. She told them that life had been very hard. She never knew from one day to the next if there would be enough food. Even today. People from the city treated you badly if you lived here, she said, as though you were no better than the garbage in the dump. Most of her family had already died. All she had left was Ayana, and she was terribly afraid of what would happen to Ayana after she died.

When they had finished their coffee, Henok looked at the time. "We had better get going."

"Would you ask her if we can take pictures?" Ray said. "Of her and Ayana."

Allan bent down and playfully swooped Ayana off her feet. "There are those precious dimples," he said.

Henok asked her about the pictures, and she said that would be fine. It was too dark inside, so they stepped outside to take them. For most of the shots, Allan held Ayana. When they were done, he almost didn't want to let her go. Ray asked if they could pray for the grandmother and the little girl, and she happily said yes.

After the prayer, they hugged and said good-bye. As they walked toward the car, Allan looked back at them standing there next to their little mud hut. This was all they had. All they would ever have. This was their present and their future. It felt so wrong.

Ayana looked right at him. She lifted her little hand and waved.

7

Allan had finally fallen asleep. The images of Korah kept haunting him whenever he closed his eyes. He kept seeing that last moment, when Ayana's tiny hand waved goodbye as he walked away. He'd accidentally overslept. When he awoke, he quickly pulled himself together and hurried to the breakfast café to meet the rest of the team. The men had maneuvered the tables in a semicircle around Ray, who was talking as they ate.

"Allan," Ray said, "I was just about to send someone after you."

"Sorry, guys. Had a hard time getting to sleep last night."

"Quite a few of us did," Ed said. "That was rough." He was referring to how they'd spent yesterday afternoon. After Ray and Allan had made it back to Addis Ababa to meet with the team for lunch, they had all agreed to change plans and spend the rest of the day in Korah.

Allan had almost declined. He could've easily cited an upset stomach or even a headache, because both were true. But he went. This time, he didn't see Ayana or the little boy they had met that morning. But he'd continued to look for her throughout the afternoon.

"Go grab some breakfast and join us," Ray said. "I'll hold off what I was going to say till you get back."

Allan walked past the small buffet and threw some breakfast things on his plate, unsure if he'd eat them. He took the empty seat the guys had left for him next to Ray.

"We didn't get too far," Ray said. "Everybody just talked about how much the dump affected them."

"It's affecting me now," Allan said. "I feel an overwhelming sense of guilt just looking at this plate of eggs. This would be a king's feast to everyone out there. And seeing those kids . . ."

"Believe me, Allan. We all feel the same way." Ray sipped his coffee. "I'm thinking the trip to Korah yesterday was the reason we came here."

"But what can we do?" Ed said. "There are thousands of people there, and it's been like that for so many years."

"I asked Henok how many people lived there," one of the other men said. "I don't know if this is accurate, but he said a hundred thousand."

"Whatever the exact number, it's a massive amount," Allan said. "The worst part is how many of them are kids." The group paused. Allan forced down a few bites.

"I know the numbers are huge," Ray said. "It's hard not to be overwhelmed. Standing at the top of that hill of garbage, looking down on it all. How can you not be? But I kept thinking, I've got to do something. I can't 'unsee' everything I've seen. There's got to be something we can do for those kids. Even if we could only help a few of them, it would be something."

Ray stopped a moment. Allan figured it was to let what he'd said sink in. It worked, at least for him. The problems at Korah were too massive if you looked at the whole thing all at once. So don't look at the whole thing; look at *one* thing. What was the one thing he could do?

"So here's my idea," Ray said. "Let's help get Henok's orphanage going. It will be a small operation at first. I'm sure Henok will help us get it set up locally and even be willing to run it."

"But we're flying back tomorrow," Ed said.

"I know. So we have to make today count. Yesterday afternoon, we forgot the video camera. I know you guys got some videos from your cell phones, but I'd like to go back out there and spend the rest of the day intentionally capturing footage we could use back home. Something we can polish up enough to show people at our churches, to help them grasp what's going on here. I know I can get my church behind this. I'm sure most of you guys are going home to a church that'll be expecting a trip update. What if we could show them a video about Korah, especially about the orphans? Talk up the idea. See if we can get some fund-raising started. Things here are way less expensive than in the States. And Henok's a pretty sharp guy. We can work with him by emails and Skype, help things move along with government officials."

Sounded like a great idea to Allan. Everyone was nodding their heads.

Ray put his hand on Allan's shoulder. "I was thinking of Allan here, maybe he can be our point man once we're back home."

"But I've got a full-time job," Allan said. "I can't really travel much. I'm using vacation time for this trip, and I only get so much of that."

"I'm not thinking you'll need to travel," Ray said. "Once we get things to a certain point, we'll probably need to come back here. But I'm not thinking of you driving or flying around to a bunch of churches back home. More of a behind-the-scenes kind of thing. Some tasks on the phone, some emails. Helping to coordinate what the other guys are doing in their churches."

Allan felt relieved. "I suppose I could do that."

"Great. We can talk about this some more while we're out there today. Let's get our stuff together. I'll go find Henok and brief him. He already said he could go out with us again today. Then let's meet out by the curb in thirty minutes."

"Can we make that forty-five?" Allan asked. "I told my wife I'd call her at nine. Haven't talked with her for a few days."

"I'd like to call home too," Ed said.

"Sure," Ray said. "Let's meet in forty-five minutes then."

— 8 —

Michele was nodding off.

Normally, when she had to work the next morning, she'd be asleep by 10:30. But Allan had said he'd contact her tonight on Skype, if at all possible. He was almost thirty minutes late. She was beginning to doubt it would happen. Communication was the worst part of these trips. No, the worst part was him being gone every night and her being left alone.

Was there a best part?

She forced herself to think about all the good he was doing. He was helping people. Lots of people. Orphans and widows and sick people and hurting people and people who had almost nothing. She was sitting in an upscale townhome in River Oaks, in a nicely decorated and spacious master bedroom suite. From her soft, upholstered chair, she could see into the bathroom. There was a garden tub with whirlpool jets. She barely used it anymore; it was a nightmare to keep clean. But there it was, and she could use it whenever she wanted.

Allan had talked to her once about the bathroom situation of most of the people in Ethiopia. Halfway through, she had to make him stop. The images in her mind were so revolting.

She stared at the computer screen, waiting for the little icon to activate, indicating Allan was on the line. *Please, Allan . . . please call.* She heard a beep and jumped. But it wasn't him. It was her cell phone on the nightstand. Apparently informing her the battery was fully charged. She stood up and walked to the bathroom to wash her face with cold water.

Five more minutes. She would give it five more minutes.

As she turned off the faucet, she heard that familiar chime from her laptop. She dried her face and hands and ran to the computer. There was Allan's beautiful face staring back at her. She clicked the button to accept the call, and the picture instantly enlarged. "Can you see me? Can you hear me?" she asked.

"I can. Man, are you a sight for sore eyes. I haven't seen anything that beautiful since . . . since I left you at the airport."

It was so good to see him. But something in his eyes . . . she could tell he was struggling with something. "You look good. A little tired maybe. Your eyes look kind of puffy. Are you sleeping okay?"

"I was until last night. Had a real hard time for some reason. Well, I guess I know why." He looked away, offscreen.

"What's wrong? What happened last night?"

He looked back at her. "Just some stuff we saw yesterday. Had a hard time getting the pictures out of my mind. I'll tell you about it when I get home."

"Would it help to talk about it? I'm here if you want to talk about it now."

"I don't think so. I'm going back out there again in just a few minutes. Maybe seeing it all again will help take the sting away. If we talk about it now, it might mess up your sleep. It's midnight there, right?"

"A little after," she said. "I can see it's daylight there from the window behind you. That's so strange. I still can't get used to the time difference. It's tomorrow for you already."

"I know. One more day and we start the long journey home. I can't wait to see you."

"I love you so much," she said.

"I love you too."

There was a long pause, which rarely happened in their conversations. "What's wrong, babe? You seem . . . off somehow. Are you just worn out?"

"I'm sure that's part of it." He looked away. When he looked back at her, he said, "No, that's not it. Not really. I'm sure it's this place."

"You mean Addis Ababa?"

"No, the place we visited yesterday."

She noticed something then. He was looking right at her, but it was as if he wasn't seeing her anymore. He was seeing something else, in his mind. "Tell me about it."

"No, I'm sorry. It can wait. Tell me about you. How are you holding up, with me being gone again on one of my trips?"

She had to be careful or she'd slip into a faraway stare too. This wasn't the time to talk about her baby woes. Rather, her lack-of-a-baby woes. "Nothing much going on here. You missed a big family dinner today after church. Doug was even there."

"Again? That's two weekends in a row, isn't it?"

"It is."

"Wonder what he's up to?"

"I don't think he's up to anything," she said. "Maybe he just misses us."

"Maybe."

She knew why Allan had his doubts. The family was seeing less and less of Doug over the past twelve months. He had just finished up his freshman year and was beginning his sophomore year at Flagler College in St. Augustine. He was staying at a dorm on campus, but the college was only a ninety-minute drive from here. Before he'd left for college, he had vowed to drive home most weekends. That lasted maybe a month.

"Guess who else was at the dinner?"

"Who?"

"Audrey Windsor. Remember her?"

"Sure I do," he said. "The lady who taught your dad how to dance."

"That's her. She called Dad this week saying she had something big to discuss with him, so he invited her to Sunday dinner."

"You know what it was?"

"I don't. Not yet, anyway. When the kids went down for a nap, I went out shopping with Jean for a little while. As we walked out the front door, I saw Audrey in Dad's home office, still talking. Dad was clicking away on his computer, working on some kind of spreadsheet."

Allan laughed.

"What?"

"I guess you really are curious."

"Well, we haven't seen her very much the last few months. She did say it was something big. And then they're in there talking about it for hours. She was just saying good-bye when Jean and I came home from the store."

"Well, maybe your mom can tell you what it's all about tomorrow."

"I'm definitely going to call her when I get home from school."

Allan glanced at his watch.

"Do you have to go already?" she said.

"In a few minutes. But I'm also thinking about your bedtime. You're teaching school in the morning. I know how hard it is facing those kids when you haven't had enough sleep."

That was definitely true. But she didn't want him to go. "So you and your team are heading out to that place again? Whatever it is?"

"Korah. It's a little village about fifteen minutes from here."

"Well, at least it's not very far."

"It's not. But it's nothing like Addis Ababa. Even the worst parts of town are way better than anything there."

There was that look again, like he wasn't seeing her anymore. "What's it like?" He didn't answer for several moments. "Allan?"

"I'm sorry."

"It must be awful."

A long pause. "It is. I've never seen anything like it."

From the pictures and videos Michele had seen of other places, that was really saying something. "Not on any of your trips?"

"Nothing even close."

She wanted to help him, to be there for him. But maybe he was right. Maybe she shouldn't hear all about this place right before bed if it was that bad. "What's it called again?"

"Korah," he said. "They call it Korah."

9

Marilyn Anderson sat on the sofa and watched as her husband, Jim, came hurrying out of their master bedroom doorway. He was getting ready to leave for an appointment, but he seemed to instinctively know she was too exhausted to get up and kiss him good-bye. She was grateful she had the day off from both of her weekday occupations: her part-time job at Odds-n-Ends and her volunteer work at the Women's Resource Center.

He walked toward her, bent down, and gave her a kiss on the cheek. Her mind drifted back to yesterday's dinner after church.

Only half the crowd had left after coffee and dessert. By then, it was late afternoon. The rest hung around long enough to heat up the leftovers around six. Michele had stayed until well after dark. Marilyn felt bad for her daughter. She was clearly down and missed Allan something awful. Marilyn had spent a good deal of energy simply trying to lift Michele's spirits. After Michele left, the house still wasn't quiet, of course, since Tom and his family lived upstairs.

They had been living there for a year now, since they had been forced to unload their house in a short sale. She loved having them here, especially loved getting to spend so much time with her grandkids. But she could never fully relax until they were in bed. Jean did her best to give them some sense of separation, making as much use of the upstairs as possible.

"Will you be gone all day?" she asked Jim.

"Actually, no. I was only going to take a half day. Maybe a little more than half. If you're able to, I'd like to take you out for a little bit around midafternoon. Maybe go for a walk down by the river or get a cup of coffee."

"Really?"

He looked upstairs for a moment, making sure they were alone. "I have some pretty big news to share with you."

Marilyn sat up straight. "Is it about what you and Audrey Windsor were talking about yesterday?"

"It is." He looked upstairs again.

"Can you tell me—"

Her phone rang. Jim was closer, so he picked it up. "Hello? Excuse me? Oh yes. She's here. What's that? I see . . . just a moment, let me see if she can come to the phone." He pressed the mute button. "Hon, it's Arlene from the Women's Resource Center. Do you want to take it?"

Instantly, Marilyn shook her head no, then felt a strong impression God wanted her to say yes. Or maybe it was just guilt. She waved for Jim to hand her the phone. "Hello, Arlene?"

"Marilyn, could I ask you a huge favor? I know you're off today and I wouldn't call you at home like this normally, but something pretty important has come up. Do you have a minute?"

Jim kissed her on the cheek, whispered, "See you around 2:30," and waved good-bye as he opened the door to leave.

She waved back then gave Arlene her undivided attention.

"About an hour ago," Arlene said, "I got a phone call about

a young girl we've been counseling for several months. Her name is Christina. She's going through a really tough time right now."

"I think I know who she is," Marilyn said, "but I've never met her."

"I got Christina to agree to meet me down at the center," Arlene said. "I'm wondering if you could possibly join me there. I'd really appreciate it. I don't want to lose this girl. She's in such a vulnerable place right now."

Marilyn held her cell phone a few inches away from her face, closed her eyes, and released a sigh. Now she wished she hadn't taken the call. She was aching for rest. What Arlene was asking hardly seemed like a restful thing. "There isn't any other time we could meet her?" Marilyn asked. "It has to be today?"

"I'm afraid so," Arlene said. "Christina's mentor, Megan . . . you know Megan."

"I do."

"Megan was supposed to meet with her today. In fact, this was supposed to be their last time together. Last week, Megan got a call from her sister saying their mother was very sick. She asked if Megan could come up there soon to help. She'll probably be gone for months. She hated leaving all her girls but felt she had no choice. Yesterday, Megan's mother took a sudden turn for the worse, and she had to leave this morning to fly up north. That's what has Christina so upset. At least that's part of it. She was hinting about pulling out of the program altogether until I told her I'd meet with her myself. I'd be the one doing most of the talking today. But if you could be there, and she got a chance to meet you, I think it would reassure her she's not going to fall through the cracks."

"When would I need to be there?"

"We're meeting in my office in just over an hour."

An hour, Marilyn thought. Everything inside her wanted to say no, but again, she felt this tug that God wanted her to do this. "Okay. I can do that."

"Oh, thank you. I'm so glad you said yes. I'm going to call Christina right away and tell her. I'll see you in a little while." Arlene sounded excited.

At least one of them was.

◆ ◆

Christina pulled into the parking lot of the Women's Resource Center and stared at the front door through the windshield of her '98 Ford Taurus. The windows were down since the A/C didn't work. Barely anything in this car did. It had all these fancy buttons and gadgets, but most of them didn't do a thing. She guessed their purpose was to remind her of still more things she couldn't afford.

She really didn't want to come here today. Ms. Ryan had talked her into it. That's right, Arlene. She wanted Christina to call her Arlene, which she found hard to do. Arlene was a real lady, refined and—what was that other word? Dignified. Refined and dignified. Not the kind of person she felt right calling by her first name. She was sure Arlene had asked for that courtesy to better identify with her, make it seem as if their lives weren't so far apart. But the gap was huge, and using first names wasn't going to close it.

Arlene was nice enough, though, and Christina had decided to give this thing one more try. It really upset her losing Megan. They had been meeting together for over three months now, every week at least. Christina felt like she could really trust Megan, could ask her anything, and Megan would answer her straight up.

Megan had quickly become like the mother Christina never had. Well, Christina had a mom, biologically speaking, back home in New York. But Christina had seen enough moms on TV shows and movies to know how far offtrack her childhood had been.

"Mom" was living with boyfriend number four, and that count was just in the last three years. Number four, like all the rest, hit on Christina whenever her mother wasn't looking. She'd had enough of it. "Mom" hadn't even tried to contact her after she'd been gone a month, even though Christina kept sending her notes about where she lived now.

But Megan had fit the mother role nicely. Christina had actually begun to believe Megan truly loved her, in a motherly sort of way. Megan had said she did many times, and Christina was finally beginning to believe it.

And now Megan was gone.

Christina knew she had good reason. Megan's mom was dying, all of a sudden out of nowhere, Megan had said. She hated to leave Christina stranded like this, but she had to fly home and take care of her. Of course she did. Christina knew this.

It didn't help any.

She looked up, noticed a nice car pull into one of the open spaces by the front door. An attractive brunette got out, and it wasn't until she turned to face the parking lot that Christina realized she knew this woman. Well, she didn't really know her. But she recognized her as one of the regular volunteers. Christina had thought she could've been a fashion model when she was younger. The attractive lady walked to the front door just as Arlene came out to greet her.

No way, Christina thought. Was this her new mentor? Both women turned to walk inside, but Arlene stopped to look once more at the parking lot before closing the door. Christina wanted to duck, but she wasn't fast enough. Arlene saw her sitting in the car. She smiled and waved.

Well, Christina had better get out and give this thing a try. She had promised Megan this morning she would.

10

The three women sat down in the counseling room. That wasn't what the Women's Resource Center called it, but that's what it was. It had a warm ambience, though, more like a small living room than an office. Marilyn couldn't tell by the look on the girl's face who was more nervous about this meeting, her or Christina. The nervous tension provided one benefit: she was now wide awake.

Christina was a petite little thing, very cute in a rough sort of way. So far, they had only exchanged polite introductions, but Christina's New York accent was quite pronounced. Marilyn tried not to stare, but several times she glanced down at the obvious bump in Christina's belly. What had Arlene said, that she was six or seven months along? She couldn't be more than eighteen or nineteen years old, her son Doug's age.

Arlene had mentioned that Christina had just recently made up her mind to choose the adoption path for her baby, which Marilyn thought was courageous. Christina looked way too young to be a mother. Marilyn thought about the total absurdity of Doug becoming a father right now.

Arlene opened up Christina's file on the coffee table. She

had another one just like it in her hand. "Again, thanks for coming, Christina. We really are sorry you couldn't stay with Megan as your mentor until your baby is born. Megan hated doing this to you. You know that, don't you?"

"I know," Christina said. "She didn't have much choice."

"I read over your file this morning," Arlene said. "Including all of Megan's notes. I'm giving this copy to Marilyn to bring home, so she can get up to speed on all the things you and Megan had talked about." She handed the manila folder to Marilyn. "Is there anything you want to tell Marilyn in person about your situation?"

Christina shifted in her seat. She looked uncomfortable. "Not a whole lot to tell. Like an idiot, I moved in with my boyfriend—who I didn't really love, by the way. I just did it to save money. My roommate had just moved out. I was gonna lose the place in a few weeks, so when he suggested we live together, I said yes. Then, continuing to behave like an idiot, we started sleeping together. You'd think I would know better. I wasn't on the pill, and he was too lazy to—well, you know. So it happened, I got pregnant." She paused to take a swig of bottled water. "What can I say? I wasn't very bright."

"You don't need to keep putting yourself down," Arlene said. "We're not here to judge you."

"Oh, I know that. Everyone in this place treats me well. Way better than I ever got treated out there. I'm not putting myself down. It's just a fact. I guess the biblical word Megan used was being a fool. Same difference. I know God's forgiven me for the mess I've made of things. Megan said God sometimes has to put people in tough places to get their attention, make them aware of how much they need him. I try to look at it that way . . . that God used all this to bring me to Christ. I was a million miles away from God a few months ago. But that doesn't change the fact that I was an idiot for letting it happen."

Marilyn couldn't help but smile. There was something refreshing about this young girl's honesty.

"Could you tell Marilyn and me a little about how you came to the adoption decision?"

"Sure. It's not complicated. I've been thinking about it a long time. It's just, I'm not ready to be a mom. That's pretty much the whole story. I don't want my baby growing up the way I did, or worse. Megan gave me these papers to read about both choices, adoption or single parenting. And I guess you could say, I did some of my own research. It's not that I don't love my baby. I do. But it came down to deciding what's best for her instead of what's best for me. This baby will not be better off with me, and that's just a fact. Not at this point in my life."

"Megan said you were pretty committed to this option," Arlene said. "Do you struggle with your decision at all? Is there anything you'd like to talk about?"

"I think Megan covered all the bases. I did struggle a lot at first, but then God did something that helped take my struggle away."

"What was that?" Marilyn asked.

"I started visiting a children's playground in River Oaks. I went several times."

"Do you live in River Oaks?" Marilyn said.

Christina laughed. Then she looked at Arlene, as if to say "Is she kidding?" "Not hardly. I can't even afford to eat in River Oaks. No, I went there because I know that the type of couple who will adopt my baby could probably afford to live there. Anyway, this last time I went, I see all these kids playing, having a blast. Across the way on some bench under a tree, all these moms are laughing and talking. But closer to where I was, there was this other girl sitting by herself at a picnic table. She was maybe twenty-five. I've seen her there a few times. It's always the same. She just stares at the kids. Her face always looks so sad. This time when I looked back at her, I saw tears running down her face. Normally, I would've left her alone, but for some reason I felt like I should talk to her. So I did."

"What did you find out?"

"She was crying because she and her husband couldn't have any children. They had been trying like crazy for over a year. We got to talking a little while. The thing was, it became crystal clear to me. This couple had the kind of home a baby should be raised in. With a father and a mother, people who can afford to take care of a baby and are ready to be parents. For them, it's the right time. But this—my life right now? It is so not the right time."

"What's the status of your baby's father?" Arlene said.

"There is no status. He was a loser then, and he's a loser now. He wanted me to have an abortion. No way I was going to do that. I know it's legal but, to me, it's still wrong. I knew that before I gave my life to Christ. But he said that's the only way he'd stay with me, if I got rid of the baby. So I got rid of him. But before he left, he said he'd sign any papers he needed to for the adoption. He's all for anything that lets him off the hook." She took another swallow of water and repositioned herself on the upholstered chair. "But see, that's the thing . . . now I'm in a jam. A big one." She sighed heavily and started fidgeting with a pen.

"What's the matter?"

"I can't afford my place anymore. I'm really trying, but he used to cover half the expenses. The rent's due in three weeks, and a week after that, the utilities. I can't keep up. I don't make near enough to cover it."

Arlene looked confused. "But I thought the adoption agency you signed up with is going to help you with living expenses."

"They will . . . some. But I did the math; it's not enough. And if you saw my place, it's nothing fancy. It's not even in a nice part of town. If I don't find a roommate soon, I'll be out on the street."

She had this tough New York persona, but Marilyn noticed real fear in her eyes.

"Don't you have any savings?" Arlene said. "Can your mom help out?"

Christina looked away. "No, I don't have any savings. And you must have missed it when you read that file, the parts about my mom. Otherwise, you wouldn't be asking that question."

"I'm sorry," Arlene said. "I did read that. I just forgot."

"No problem," Christina said. "God'll do something, right? That's what Megan would say. Doesn't look good right now, but . . ." She sighed.

"I do believe God will take care of you, Christina," Arlene said. "How may not be clear to us at the moment, but you're right to put your trust in him. And you know what? I believe he's already picked out the perfect place for you, and it's definitely not out in the street."

Tears welled up in Christina's eyes. "Megan texted me some Bible verses to look up this morning. They kind of say that too. I'm trying to have faith. Gets hard when we talk about it, though. Three weeks seems so close, and so far I don't have any options."

Suddenly, she did.

An idea popped into Marilyn's head. A crazy idea. Not the kind of thing she'd ever think of. And certainly not the kind of thing Jim would ever approve.

Or would he?

Oh, how she wished he would. She certainly couldn't bring it up here until they had talked. Then she remembered, she and Jim were supposed to talk this afternoon.

11

The meeting with Christina and Arlene had continued for another thirty minutes. It seemed to end much better than it had begun. Christina sounded a little more encouraged. She had even accepted Marilyn's invitation to join her for lunch on Wednesday. She hoped to have her idea approved and ready to share by then. With something this big, Jim would definitely need some time to think about it, if he went for it at all.

As she reached her car in the parking lot, Marilyn heard the unmistakable sound of a car trying to start unsuccessfully. She followed the sound and soon realized it was Christina's car. She was trying to start it over and over again, but it was no use. Marilyn knew precious little about cars, but on those last two tries it sounded like the battery was dying. She heard that sickening click-click-click sound. Arlene's car had just left the parking lot. She didn't see anyone else who could come to Christina's rescue.

Right after the meeting, her sense of exhaustion had returned. But she put her keys back in her purse and walked over to Christina's car, just as Christina got out. "That doesn't sound very good," Marilyn said.

"No, it doesn't. Piece of junk. It did the same thing yesterday when I was leaving the restaurant where I work."

"What did you do to get it going yesterday?"

"Nothing. I don't know a thing about cars. But a guy I work with came out and got it going using jumper cables. He said my battery was dying and I better get it replaced."

"I have jumper cables," Marilyn said. "I've never used them myself but—no, wait a minute. They're in my husband's car. I'm not sure if he's home yet, but we only live five minutes from here."

"You live in River Oaks?" Christina asked.

"We do. We've lived here for almost fifteen years."

"Must be nice."

She said this with a touch of sarcastic envy. Marilyn let it slide. "It really is. Maybe after lunch on Wednesday, we can stop by the house."

"Really?"

"Sure. If it's nice out, we could even go for a swim."

"You have a pool?"

"We do, and a privacy fence around the backyard. None of the nearby homes have windows that can see in, so it really is private."

"Sounds nice, but I think I'll pass on the swimming." She patted her stomach. "Believe me, nobody wants to see this body in a swimsuit. So, you think your husband will bring those jumper cables? I've gotta be at work in an hour."

"I'll call him right now." Marilyn hoped Jim could help. She knew he would if he was free. As she pulled her cell phone out of her purse, she had a thought. What if God had set this up on purpose? To give Jim a chance to meet Christina in person before she sprung her big idea on him when they talked?

◆ ◆

Christina couldn't help it, she was starting to like this lady. Even though everything about her said she came from money.

Her clothes and rings, her hair and car. Just the fact that she actually lived in River Oaks was intimidating. Who lived in a place like this? It was the land of make-believe. Christina would never invite anyone back to where she lived. Not even if she'd cleaned it for a week. But Marilyn had a kind face and gentle eyes.

While waiting for her husband to come—Jim, she called him—they had kept the conversation light. Marilyn kept asking her get-to-know-you questions but did it in a way that didn't seem nosy. She was actually pretty easy to talk to.

Ten minutes later, a gorgeous Audi sedan pulled up. A nice-looking older guy and an extremely good-looking younger guy about Christina's age got out. Suddenly, she regretted not fixing her hair or doing her makeup before coming here. And she became very self-conscious of her baby bump. The older man walked up and gave Marilyn a quick hug. Must be Jim.

"Christina, come over here and let me introduce my husband and son."

Christina walked over to the group.

"This is Jim, my husband. And this is Doug." She looked at her son. "I didn't think you'd still be here."

"I'm heading back to school right after this. Dad took me out to lunch first. Can't pass up a free meal."

Everyone shook hands. Doug had the best smile. Maybe the best smile on a guy Christina had ever seen.

Jim popped the trunk and walked around to the back of his car. "I hear someone needs a jump start."

"Yeah," Christina said. "I guess my battery's dying. I really appreciate you doing this. I have to be at work in about forty-five minutes."

Jim carried the jumper cables to her car. "Well, this won't take five," Jim said. "The problem is, if your battery is dying, this will get you to work, but it will just die again by the time you get off. Doug, can you move my car into position so I can hook these up?"

"Sure, Dad."

Christina thought that might be the case. But what was she gonna do? She didn't have the money for a new battery.

Jim opened the hood of her car. "Can I have your keys?"

"They're still in the ignition."

Marilyn walked up. "I'm guessing by our earlier conversation, you don't have money for a new car battery."

"Not unless they're five or ten bucks."

"Jim," she yelled, "how much are car batteries?"

From inside the car, he yelled back, "It depends. Could be seventy or eighty dollars, maybe more. Why?"

Christina's heart sank. Marilyn walked back and talked quietly with Jim. A few moments later, Jim and Doug got both cars running. Doug unhooked the jumper cables and closed the hoods to both cars. Jim and Marilyn walked over to her.

Jim spoke first. "Here's what I'd like to do, Christina. Doug is going to drive Marilyn's car back to the house. Okay, Doug?"

"Sure. My car's parked there anyway."

"Christina, you follow us to a nearby auto parts store, so we can buy you a new battery. We'll have the whole thing done in plenty of time for you to get to work."

"I . . . I can't let you do that."

"Of course you can. Marilyn tells me you've recently become a Christian, right?"

"A couple of months ago."

"Well," Marilyn said, "that's what Christians are supposed to do. Help each other if they can. You need the help, and we're able to help, so that's what we'd like to do."

"I'll pay you back, as soon as I can."

"No, you won't," Jim said gently. "This is a gift. You don't need to pay us back. We better get going if we're going to get you to work on time."

"I don't know what to say. No one's ever done anything like this for me before."

Marilyn put her hand on Christina's shoulder. "We're happy to do it. Just follow us to the store."

Christina got into her car and closed the door. Doug smiled and nodded to her as he drove off in Marilyn's car. Jim and Marilyn got into the Audi and began to pull away. She got right behind them.

"Thank you, Jesus. Thank you." It was all she could say.

She tried to block the next thought before it fully formed. It was about their son, Doug. The way he looked at her. That beautiful smile followed by a different look when he noticed her stomach. She hated being pregnant so much just then. Not the baby. It wasn't the baby's fault.

She hated herself, for being so stupid.

12

Marilyn was surprised at how much energy she had. She wasn't the least bit tired anymore. They had just gotten Christina safely on her way with the new car battery. Christina was so excited, before she'd left she had given Marilyn a hug and said, "Are we still on for lunch Wednesday?" Marilyn assured her they were.

After Christina left, Jim reminded her about that talk he wanted to have about "something big" and wondered if they still had time to talk. Marilyn smiled and said she had something big to go over with him too. She had just gotten out of the car and was waiting for him to join her on the sidewalk in Riverfront Park.

He reached for her hand. "I was so glad we could do that for Christina," he said. "I feel really good inside."

"I was just thinking the same thing," Marilyn said. She took his hand, and they walked toward the river. "So, looks like we both have something big to discuss with the other. Who's gonna go first?"

"I know it's supposed to be ladies first, but do you mind if I go?" Jim said.

Marilyn was actually glad he wanted to talk first. Her idea was so crazy; she had no way of knowing how Jim would react. She didn't want to spoil this wonderful mood and bring their walk to an abrupt end. "Sure, I don't mind."

"Well, you already know it's about what Audrey and I talked about on Sunday."

"You two were talking for hours," Marilyn said.

"We had a lot of ground to cover."

"So what is it? I can tell by your mood it's a good thing."

"It's a very good thing. For us, but even more so for Tom and Jean."

"I knew it. You kept looking at them at the dinner table. I was sure it had something to do with them." Marilyn couldn't begin to imagine what it was.

Jim looked out at the river then back at her. His smile had grown even wider. "How would you like to have the house all to yourself again? Well, I would still be there."

"I don't understand. Is she asking Tom and Jean to move in with her?"

"No. She's asking if Tom and Jean would like to buy her house."

"In River Oaks?"

Jim nodded.

"That cute little bungalow house with the dormers? The one where you learned how to dance?"

Jim nodded again. "That's the one."

Marilyn couldn't believe it. "But how? She's moving?"

"She is. Her older sister's health is deteriorating, and Audrey wants to move in with her to take care of her. She said it looks like this will be a permanent move, not something temporary. So she's decided to sell the house. She prayed about it and wanted to see if it might be possible to sell it to Tom and Jean." He kicked a stick out of the way just in front of her on the sidewalk.

"But how could that work? Isn't their credit shot from what happened with their house?"

"It's not totally shot, but I'm sure it's way too soon for a bank or mortgage company to consider something like this. But that's not an issue. That's what took so much time, working out the details with Audrey. She wants to hold the mortgage. It would be a good source of income for her every month, and even giving Tom a great deal, she'd get a better interest rate than she'd get from a CD or money market account."

"Can Tom and Jean afford it?"

"It'll be a little tight for the first year or two, but I've been helping him with his finances over the last year, so I know where they're at. She's willing to drop the price for a quick, no-hassle sale to a level I think they can handle. And she says she's watched everything that's happened with them since Tom came clean last year after hiding when he lost his job. She's been impressed with how hard he's worked to finish his schooling and pay down their debt. She started asking me about it a few months ago. I didn't realize at the time why she was so curious. But she's been thinking about it for quite a while, about selling the house, I mean. Her sister's illness just helped her to decide now was the time. I still have to ask Tom and Jean about it—"

"Are you kidding? They'll love it. Jean and I talk quite a bit. She feels pretty bad about how long they've been living with us. Just last week, we talked about this over coffee, saying that now with Tom's new job, he'll be bringing in a lot more money. They discussed finding an apartment. I told her not to be in a rush about it, we're fine. But I could tell, the thought of buying a house didn't even occur to her."

"I'm sure it didn't," Jim said. "Apart from something like this, I don't think they'd be in the market for several years."

They walked hand in hand in silence a few moments. Marilyn was so happy. Tom and Jean would be so excited.

They came to a bench in the shade facing the river. "Let's sit here," she said. "There's such a nice breeze."

Jim sat beside her. "Okay, your turn. So . . . is it a good thing or a bad thing?"

"No, it's good. I think you'll think it's good." Marilyn said a quick silent prayer. "Speaking of good, you know that good feeling you said you got a little while ago after helping Christina with her car?"

Jim nodded.

"In a way you could say my idea is a way to feel that good all the time, for the next several months, anyway." She smiled.

Jim shook his head and returned her smile. "Okay, what's this about?"

She took a deep breath; she had to get her thoughts under control. Sometimes when she got nervous she could just rattle on. This was too important. "At my meeting with Christina and Arlene, I found out a lot more about Christina's situation. She comes from a really messed-up life, up in New York. I'll tell you all the details sometime, and it will just break your heart. She's down here now without any family and wound up getting pregnant by some guy she was living with, whom she describes as a total loser. He's out of the picture completely now. But because he is, in a week or so, she'll have no place to live. She's working and getting some financial assistance from the adoption agency that's working with her, but it's only enough to afford a dumpy apartment in a not-very-nice part of town."

"So she doesn't live in River Oaks," Jim said.

"She couldn't even think about living in River Oaks."

"So what's your idea?"

"I'm thinking of Doug's place," she said.

"The garage apartment?"

"Yes. Doug's been here the last two weekends, but you know he's hardly ever home. Once he gets back in the rhythm of going to class every week, we probably won't see him again till Thanksgiving. The apartment is fully furnished, and I'm pretty sure it won't cost us a thing. Between her job and the money she's getting from the agency, she'll be able to cover all her own expenses. I really think God might be the one who put this thought in my head. But I'm not trying to pressure you. I'm really not. I know he has to put faith in your heart for this too."

Jim sat back on the bench and took a deep breath. She tried to read his face but couldn't. She felt a strong urge to keep talking, to keep selling him, but she held her peace. A young mother walked by, pushing two children in a stroller.

After she passed, Jim said, "I am open to this. I want you to know that."

This sounded like his introduction to shooting the idea down.

He stopped talking a few moments, as if thinking through his words carefully. "It's just such a big deal. I mean, having Tom and Jean living with us is one thing, but we don't really know this girl at all. It's going to be a major adjustment adding a total stranger to the mix. I don't know . . ."

"Well, here's one thing," she said. "The apartment over the garage really is self-contained. It's totally separated from the main house. It even has its own kitchen. I'd be able to look after her better, with her living there, but it's not like she'd actually be living with us."

"That's true." Jim's face lightened up slightly. "I suppose it would be more like renting the place out."

"That's what I was thinking."

"But I'd hate to do anything Doug would interpret as us pushing him away. I did my best at lunch to really appeal to him to keep coming home on weekends as often as possible."

"Were you careful about the guilt thing?" Marilyn asked. "You know I don't want him coming home just because he feels guilty."

"No, I was careful. I just made it about how much we enjoy seeing him, how much we miss him when he's not there." He thought about this. "Well, guess I got a little guilt in there."

"Just a little." Marilyn smiled.

"So, I'd really like to talk with him first."

"That's fine," she said. "I'm having lunch with her on Wednesday."

"I'm sure I can talk this over with Doug before then. And I really am open to this, Marilyn. I mean that. It's just . . . it's such a big thing."

— 13 —

Michele had been nervous standing in the main lobby of the Orlando International Airport, staring down the hallway as incoming passengers came through the gate area. It was Tuesday, late in the afternoon. Allan's return route from Africa had been such a hodgepodge of different flights, even different airlines, with long layovers in large airports; she was afraid he wouldn't show up on time.

But her fears had quickly dissipated when she saw his beautiful smile peeking out from behind a small crowd of women dressed in business attire. He looked exhausted, more so than he usually did coming home from these trips. They hugged and kissed, then hugged and kissed some more. She couldn't help it; she started to cry. It just felt so good being back where she belonged, standing inside his strong arms.

They had gotten through the baggage claim process with little trouble. Miraculously, all of his bags had made it intact and were all there to greet them on the baggage conveyor belt.

Now they were almost home. They had just driven through the main entrance to River Oaks. Allan was in the passenger seat. She had kept the conversation mostly light, considering the almost dazed expression on his face. She was somewhat used to this from his previous trips. The jet lag was significant. It was four in the afternoon here. For Allan, it was one in the morning. The biggest jet lag she had ever experienced was three hours coming back from California.

Beyond this, she suspected his fatigue had more to do with culture shock. She watched his eyes as they drove home from the airport. She remembered that look from previous trips. It was as if he was seeing these very familiar buildings and places for the first time.

"Are you okay?" she asked.

"Just tired," he said. "I'm sure that's it."

"Are you sure? You're always tired when you come home from one of these trips. But you seem . . . different. Did anything happen since we talked the other night?"

He looked at her, then reached out his hand and stroked her cheek softly. "Not especially. Some things definitely happened. But not bad things. We went back out to that place I was telling you about."

"Korah?"

"Yeah. Spent the whole last day there." He shook his head, as if not believing the memories he was obviously reliving. "You can't imagine it, Michele. I want to tell you about it, all about it. I might just need a few days to catch my breath."

"That's okay." She squeezed his hand. "I'll still be here in a few days. What was the first thing you ate when you got back on American soil?" Maybe changing the subject would help.

He seemed to think a moment. "I don't remember. A sandwich, I think. Yeah, turkey and swiss cheese. It wasn't very good, or maybe I just wasn't that hungry. I still have half of it in my brief bag."

This was different. Normally, he would get all animated talking about how wonderful it was to finally be able to eat a decent meal again. He wouldn't even care that it was airport food.

"These places," he said as they drove through the first big neighborhood in River Oaks, "they're like castles. It's like a fairyland. Like that place right there on the corner." He pointed to a house not much different than the family house on Elderberry Lane. "After what I've been seeing in Korah, I can't get my mind around the idea that one family lives there." He almost sounded like he had a slight tone of disgust in his voice. He looked at her. "I saw places, little one-room shacks, where nine people lived. At night, they were packed in like sardines. Dirt floor, rusty tin roof. No streets, just mud."

She didn't know what to say. What should she say? Should she apologize? It felt almost appropriate. They continued driving through street after street of the most gorgeous homes and yards America could produce. River Oaks. Home sweet home. "Do you think . . . this is wrong? That people shouldn't live in places this nice?"

"What? No. That's not what I'm saying. I don't think it is, anyway. It's just so hard seeing these people—not the people here—in Korah, I mean, living with nothing. Absolutely nothing. And there's not even the hope that someday their situation will improve. I talked with one old man. I thought he must be seventy or eighty. It turned out he was fifty-three. He'd lived his entire life there. I don't think he could even conceive of the possibility of life on any street here in River Oaks. I couldn't even find the words to describe it to him. He'd have no reference point."

Allan paused, looking at Michele as she drove. "But the hardest part were all the kids. Hundreds of them. Most of them orphans. Just scrounging around every day, rummaging through dirty, filthy garbage, looking for anything they could eat. The smell was horrendous, Michele. Beyond belief. We not only lost our appetites, most of us felt like we would lose our breakfast any minute. I can't even imagine being hungry enough to eat something I picked out of there."

She made a few more turns. The townhome village where they lived was just a few minutes away. Their neighborhood was still gorgeous, but the homes were much smaller. Maybe seeing them would be easier for him to bear. "Well, are you still glad you went?"

"Yeah, I'm still glad. All in all, it was a fruitful trip. I'm sure we'll be going back there. Maybe just back to Korah. Ray said he believes that discovering that place was the whole purpose of our trip."

"What do you think?" She tried not to sound too enthusiastic. She was actually a little discouraged to hear him already talking about wanting to go back.

"I totally agree. As hard as it was. Nothing else we did on that trip even comes close to the significance of those last few days in Korah." He turned toward her in his seat. Not just his head but his whole body, a new look of excitement on his face. "The guys . . . well, the guys and I . . . we decided we *have* to do something. None of us felt right seeing all of that and just walking away. We couldn't live with ourselves if we did."

She didn't like the sound of this. "Like what?" She turned left down the little driveway that ran behind their section of townhomes. She could see their place just up ahead.

"Michele, we're going to help this man we met build an orphanage there."

"What?"

"An orphanage. Just a small one at first. But we spent most of the plane ride home figuring it out. It can work, Michele. It really can."

"You're saying we here. Who's we?"

"Me and the rest of the guys."

"What's your role in this supposed to be?"

"Ray's going to be the point man, in charge of all the fund-raising and kind of be the spokesman. He's asked me to take care of all the logistics here at home. The administrative stuff."

She pulled into the driveway. His face was all lit up.

Her heart was filled with dread.

14

Later that afternoon, Allan lay down for a nap. He had hoped to stay awake through the evening then go to bed early, around nine. His body wouldn't cooperate; it thought it was two in the morning. Before he conked out, he had asked Michele to please get him up in an hour, two at the most. He wanted to get over this jet lag in the next day or two before he had to go back to work.

They didn't talk anymore about his Africa trip or this new orphanage plan, but it was all Michele could think about. He had never come home from any of the other trips in this condition. She didn't know what to call it, but it made her uneasy. He'd been this tired before but never this excited about going back. Usually when he got home, he focused on her, how much he missed her, how much he hated being apart this long. Even how grateful he was to live in America.

There was a gentle knock at the door. Must be Jean, she thought. Tom and Jean were still living with her folks, so she only lived a few blocks away. She and Jean had become close over the past year. Michele had invited her over for a cup of coffee.

Well, for coffee and to talk.

Michele opened the door. "Hi, Jean. The kids aren't with you?"

Jean stepped through the doorway and gave Michele a hug. "No, Mom is watching them. When you said Allan had gone down for a nap, I knew that wouldn't last long if I brought the kids. I can't stay long. Maybe just long enough for one cup. Your parents asked us to eat dinner with them tonight."

They walked through the hallway and into the kitchen. "You guys eat together quite a bit, don't you?"

"We do, but your mom hinted that tonight was going to be very special. Some kind of surprise."

Michele fixed their coffee. "Well, thanks for coming on such short notice."

"Don't need to thank me. I love coming here, especially without the kids. Can we sit outside on the patio? There's a beautiful breeze blowing through."

"Sure, I was thinking the same thing."

As they carried their coffee past the stairway, Jean said, "Probably better to meet out there too, so we don't wake Allan up. Especially if you wind up saying something funny. You know how ridiculously loud my laugh can be."

"I don't think even your laugh would make any difference right now. A wrecking ball could hit this place and he'd still stay asleep. I also don't think there's much chance of me making you laugh in this conversation." She opened the patio door.

"Uh-oh," Jean said.

"It's not that bad. It's just not that funny, either." She walked around the table and sat in the shade.

"Did something happen on Allan's trip? Because other than how lonely you normally get when he's gone, you seemed fine on Sunday." Jean sat down next to her.

"I don't know," Michele said. "It's probably just me being moody. This whole thing about not getting pregnant."

"So I guess that was a false alarm last week when you were a few days late?"

"As always."

Jean reached her hand across the glass table and patted Michele's forearm. "I'm sorry. One of these times it won't be."

"I guess," Michele said. "You'd think I'd stop getting my hopes up so easily after a year."

"Good luck finding that switch."

"What switch?"

"The hope switch. I've never known anyone who could turn that off and on. I think you're being too hard on yourself. This is a big deal. And you're not alone, Michele. I was reading in a women's magazine the other day. One in eight couples deal with infertility. One in eight. That's a lot of people. Millions."

Michele sipped her coffee. "Doesn't feel like millions. Doesn't feel like anybody knows what it feels like. No one ever talks about it, even at church. There's so many kids, and so many moms. So many strollers. Seems like that's all we ever talk about: the children's ministry, what to do with all the kids for this event or that event. The pastor's wife keeps dragging me in deeper, because I'm a schoolteacher. Guess I'm supposed to be great with kids. Even yesterday, she called saying she wanted to meet with me soon to help her evaluate some new children's program."

"Wow," Jean said.

"What?"

"You really are in a pit."

"No, I'm not. It's just—"

"Yeah, you really are."

Michele knew she was right.

"All this time, I thought you liked children," Jean said.

"I do . . . mostly. It's just . . ." She didn't know what to say, what she was really feeling. She had hoped to be having this conversation with Allan. He was normally pretty good at hearing her out, helping her sort through conflicting emotions. But he'd come home preoccupied with his new orphanage plan.

"You're just hurting inside," Jean said. "And that's okay. It's a painful thing. You've wanted to be a mom as long as I've known you. And for some reason, for right now God is saying no. We don't know why. It's only—"

"Don't say 'it's only been a year.'"

"I wasn't going to," Jean said. "I was going to say . . . it's only a matter of time. Just because God is saying no now, doesn't mean he's gonna keep saying no forever."

"I'm sorry."

"It's okay."

They sat in silence a few moments, sipping coffee, enjoying the breeze.

"I really do like kids," Michele said.

"I know."

"Especially your kids."

"I know that too. And I also know you like the kids you teach at school."

"Some of them."

"And the kids at the church."

"A few of them. Most of them." She smiled.

"See, you're already coming around. Have you talked about all this with Allan?"

"He just got home."

"I don't mean in the last hour or so, I mean recently. Does he know how you're really doing with this infertility thing?"

She hated the sound of that . . . her "infertility thing." But it was a good question. Did Allan know? She thought he knew. But did he really? They'd talked about it before. Several times, in fact.

"When was the last time you guys talked about it?" Jean asked.

"A little while ago."

"Like what, a week before he left? A month ago? Does he know about you driving to the playground to watch the kids play?"

"I haven't been doing that very long."

"So, he doesn't know."

"No, he doesn't know."

"How many times have you done that?"

"Just a few." Maybe three or four.

"Are you hiding it from him?"

"What? What a thing to say. Of course I'm not hiding it from him."

"Then why haven't you told him? Oh my gosh, I can't believe this conversation we're having."

"What do you mean?"

"Don't you remember? A year ago you were challenging me for not sharing everything with Tom. Remember? When I thought I was pregnant?"

She did remember. Here she was, doing the very same thing. But why? Why was she holding back from telling Allan all the things she felt inside? She wanted to. A part of her did, anyway. But another part of her was convinced he didn't want to hear it. He'd already made it clear. He'd agreed with her mother.

"What's the matter, Michele? You look as if you're going to cry."

"I just realized why I'm not sharing all these things with Allan. It was a conversation at the house about a month ago, after a Sunday dinner. Everyone else had left. You and Tom had taken the kids upstairs. Allan and I were helping my mom put the kitchen back together. I don't know how we got into it, but my mom was trying to comfort me about this not-getting-pregnant thing. And she brought up that 'it's only been a year' argument, so I shouldn't be that concerned. Allan jumped right in there with her, saying we had all kinds of time, and that maybe I shouldn't be focusing on it so much."

She inhaled deeply and said, "I have such a strong need to hold a child in my arms. My child. I want to press her soft little face next to mine." Her words began to falter. "It's all I think about, Jean. They don't seem to understand how much this matters to me. No one does."

15

An old-fashioned spaghetti-and-meatball dinner, that's what Marilyn had decided to make tonight. She had done all the cooking, but the recipe for the sauce was her daughter-in-law's. That had been a hard concession to make when Tom and Jean had first moved in a year ago. Tom had let it be known, as tactfully as he dared, that Marilyn should let Jean make the spaghetti and meatballs sometime, because her sauce was "out of this world good."

So she did, and it was.

Jean's spaghetti sauce had now become the official Anderson family recipe. And since tonight was their special night, Marilyn had decided to make Tom's favorite dinner the way he liked it best.

It had been challenging at times, but throughout the dinner Jim had stuck to his decision to put off unveiling the big surprise. Earlier, when he'd shared his idea with Marilyn, she absolutely loved it. It would make the whole thing so much more fun.

"It looks like everyone's finished eating," Marilyn said. "Did anyone leave room for dessert?"

Only the kids said they had. Everyone else moaned and groaned and rubbed their stomachs.

"I've got an idea," Jim said. "Why don't we all help Grandma get these dishes out to the kitchen, then go take a walk. It's really nice out. When we get back, we'll be ready to eat that dessert."

Everyone agreed it was a great idea. Ten minutes later, they were walking down Elderberry Lane with Jim subtly leading the way. Marilyn was pretty sure she knew where this walk would take them. Audrey's house was only about six blocks away. The bungalow-style homes were considerably smaller than the homes in their neighborhood, but they made up for it in total cuteness. She and Jim had toured several of them when they first moved to River Oaks. She would've been perfectly happy with several models, but Jim insisted on a much bigger home.

"So how's the new job working out?" Jim asked Tom.

"I'm getting the hang of it. I was a little rusty at first, but it's all coming back to me."

"Do you like the people you work with?" Marilyn asked.

"Mostly. I don't know anybody well yet. Still haven't figured out who to trust yet."

"Don't trust anyone," Jean said. "That's what got you in trouble at the bank job. You can trust your dad and mom and me."

"And me," little Tommy said. "You can trust me, Daddy." His contribution reminded all of them he was getting old enough to start paying attention.

Marilyn realized what they were talking about, the trust issues both Tom and Jean were clearly still struggling with. Tom's previous IT job had actually been stolen from him by a guy he had thought was a good friend. But this "friend" had betrayed him to their new bosses, making himself look good at Tom's expense, and taking credit for many of Tom's achievements. In a way, she was glad Tommy had spoken up, forcing them to change the subject. That passage in Philippians ran through her mind: *Forgetting what lies behind . . .*

They turned right at the stop sign; Marilyn knew they would. One block ahead, the bungalow section began. They walked in the street near the curb. None of the streets between here and Audrey's were busy. The sidewalk was nice but not wide enough for them all to see each other as they talked. Marilyn and Jim definitely wanted to see Tom's and Jean's faces when they broke the news.

They continued on for a few more blocks, talking about this or that, everyone in a relatively good mood. Jim had hoisted Carly around his shoulders. She had both hands firmly gripping his forehead. Tom had done the same with Tommy. Jean was pushing a sound-asleep little Abby in her stroller. Marilyn couldn't help but notice how many times Tom and Jean gazed longingly at the homes as they passed by. Seeing it through their eyes gave Marilyn a fresh appreciation for the wonder and privilege of living in a place like this.

It wasn't just the homes; it was also the parks. They had already passed two of them, perfectly landscaped, manicured, and edged. Each had colonial-style benches strategically placed under shady trees surrounding a bubbling fountain. And she loved the imitation gaslight street lamps. At the far end of the second park was a swing set. Tommy immediately begged for permission to play there. Tom was about to say yes but looked at his father.

"Why don't we stop there on the way back?" Jim said.

"On the way back from what?" Tom asked.

Jim hesitated. "From our walk."

The answer was instantly met with whining from Tommy,

then Carly, whom Marilyn suspected had no idea what the whining was about.

"If you don't stop," Tom said, firmly but gently, "we won't go at all. Grandpa said we'll go to the playground on the way back. You just have to be patient for a few minutes."

"I hate patient," Tommy said.

"I do too," Marilyn said.

"You're not helping, Mom. Say 'Okay, Daddy.'"

Tommy obeyed. Soon his smile returned.

Five minutes more, and they reached Audrey's street. "This looks a little familiar," Tom said.

"I would've thought the whole area around here looks familiar," Jim said. "You and Jean go for walks all the time."

"We do. But we normally don't get farther than that playground we just passed."

"What do you guys usually talk about on your walks?"

"All kinds of things," Tom said.

"Do you ever talk about the future? Like where you might be living a year from now?"

"We've been trying not to do much of that," Tom said. "We know we're kind of stuck because of what happened with the house. Dreaming like that isn't good for my health. But I promise you, we'll be moved out way before then. That's one of the things we were talking about on our last walk. I think in a month or two we should be able to afford our own apartment, let you and Mom have your house back."

Marilyn realized they were coming up to Audrey Windsor's house.

"Oh, I think I can pretty much guarantee you'll be out of our house by this time next year." Jim actually said this with a bit of an edge.

Marilyn knew he was just setting things up.

"We will, Dad. You guys have been really patient with us."

"But I don't think you'll be living in an apartment."

"I don't think we have much of a choice," Jean said.

Jim stopped walking and turned to face Audrey's house. Marilyn walked up and stood beside him. "I disagree," he said. "I think you do have a choice." That same edge again in his voice.

Tom and Jean stopped walking and turned to face his parents. Both of them looked confused. "I'm not following you," Tom said.

A big smile crossed Jim's face. As he turned and pointed toward the house, he said, "Wouldn't you much rather live here?"

"We can't, Dad. I already checked. There aren't any homes to rent in this neighborhood. There's a few in yours, but we're miles from making a rent payment like that."

"Who said anything about renting?"

"Well, we could never buy a house here."

"Who says?"

"The bank says. Or at least they would if we asked. But I know better not to ask. We're at least a couple of years away from—"

"Who said anything about talking with a bank?"

"Dad, what are you talking about?"

Jim walked up to Tom, gently set Carly down. Marilyn saw tears well up in his eyes. "God's been good to you, Tom. To you and Jean."

"I know he has."

"And I believe he's been pleased with how faithful you've been, how you've followed through on all the things you said you would do over the past year. Your mom and I haven't heard either of you complain even once."

"Thanks, Dad . . . but what are you talking about?"

Jim glanced over his shoulder at the house. "This . . . is Audrey Windsor's house. That's why it looks familiar. She wants to sell it to you guys, at a price you can afford, and she wants to hold the mortgage herself."

"No way."

"Yes way."

Tom and Jean looked at each other. They embraced as tears filled their eyes.

— 16 —

It was Wednesday, just before noon. Marilyn was searching for a parking place in front of Giovanni's, her favorite Italian restaurant and café, right on Main Street. That was where she was meeting Christina for lunch. After her talk with Jim this morning, she was even more excited about this.

He had given her the green light for Christina to move into the garage apartment. Doug had surprised him on the phone when they'd talked that morning. Jim had expected at least some resistance to the idea. But all Doug asked was, "Where would I sleep when I came home?" As they thought about it a moment, Doug answered the question himself. "Guess I could just sleep on the pullout sofa bed in your office downstairs." Jim mentioned that Tom and Jean would be moving into Audrey Windsor's place in a month or two. Doug could sleep in one of the upstairs bedrooms after that.

"Yeah, that'll work," Doug had said, and that was it.

Marilyn got out of the car and walked toward the restaurant. Christina's car was right by the entrance. She couldn't wait to share the news with her. As soon as she came through the front doors, she saw Christina sitting in a chair in the waiting area, wearing a pretty blue dress. She really was an attractive young girl. "There you are," Marilyn said, extending her arms for a hug.

Christina hugged back in an awkward way. Marilyn remembered she was from New York. Maybe they didn't hug so freely up there. "You look beautiful," she said. "I love that dress on you."

"Thank you," Christina said.

The hostess walked up to seat them. "Could we sit at one of the café tables outside?" Christina asked. "I've always wanted to do that."

"Sure, no problem." The hostess picked up two menus. "Follow me."

"I like it outside too," Marilyn said.

After they sat, the waitress took their drink orders. Christina looked all around; she seemed mesmerized by the scene. Marilyn wondered if she had ever eaten in a place this nice. "Order whatever you'd like, Christina. My treat."

"Are you sure?" Christina smiled. "Because I'm pretty hungry."

"Well, you've come to the right place. The food here is very good, and they serve lots of it."

Christina opened the menu and began to read, her eyes like a child reading a storybook. She wound up ordering something simple, linguine in a white clam sauce. She said it reminded her of home. Marilyn ordered veal marsala, the lunch portion.

As they ate, Marilyn spent the time getting to know Christina better, steering the questions and discussion away from anything that might make her tense or sad. This wasn't supposed to be a counseling session, and Christina had far too much sadness going on in her life as it was. Marilyn learned that Christina had an older brother named Angelo that she seemed to think fondly of. He lived somewhere in southern California, but they didn't talk that often. She had lived in this area for over a year and had yet to visit a single theme park. "We'll just have to do something about that," Marilyn had said.

Christina liked to garden, but since she'd always lived in apartments, her gardening was restricted to potted plants. Marilyn smiled when she heard this, knowing the wonderful gardening opportunities awaiting Christina on Elderberry Lane.

Christina was going to church every Sunday, but she didn't understand half of what the preacher said. So far, she hadn't made any close friends. Marilyn asked her if she'd like to visit their church this week and, without thinking, invited her over for dinner after. She hoped Jim wouldn't mind this little surprise, because Christina instantly said yes.

After they had finished eating—and Christina wasn't joking; her plate was wiped clean—Marilyn asked for the check. When the waitress walked away, she said, "Christina, do you have to get right back?"

"I'm off the rest of the afternoon. Why?"

"I'd like to invite you back to our house for a little while. It's just a few blocks from here. You could follow me. There's something I'd like to talk to you about."

"I'd love to do that," Christina said. "I've been dying to see what one of these River Oaks places looks like on the inside."

"Wonderful. Let me take care of this check, and we'll be on our way."

"Marilyn," Christina said, "I just have to tell you . . . I can't remember when I've had this much fun. I don't know how to thank you. For this, for fixing my car on Monday . . . for just making time in your life for me." Tears began to form in her eyes. She quickly blinked them away.

"Christina, I've enjoyed this so much. Really, it's been my pleasure."

⟡

Marilyn kept her eyes on the rearview mirror. Christina stayed right with her all the way down the service lane road and onto the garage driveway. "I'm going to pull my car into the garage," Marilyn said through the window. "You can park yours right there."

Christina's eyes were almost popping out of her head. "You live . . . here?"

"We do." Marilyn was aware of a totally different sensation than what she used to feel at times like this. For years, bringing people to the house for the first time was a matter of prestige and boasting, a chance to impress people with their wealth and her gift of decorating. She was so grateful to find how much her heart had changed. Right now, she felt concern for Christina. She wanted to do everything to make her feel accepted.

Marilyn walked toward the back of the garage. "Follow me." For a moment, she thought about taking her upstairs to the garage apartment first, then changed her mind. "I'll show you the main house first."

They walked across the manicured sidewalk and across the pool deck into the veranda. Christina walked slowly behind her, taking everything in, a look of utter amazement on her face. Marilyn unlocked the French doors that led into the great room and kitchen area and turned off the security alarm. "Would you like a cup of coffee?"

"Sure. Do you have decaf?"

"I do. Tell you what, I'll get the coffee started and then take you on a tour through the rest of house."

"You don't mind?"

"Not at all."

A few minutes later, they were walking through the master bedroom suite. "Do you and Jim live here all alone?"

"Well, this is the house our kids were raised in. They're all grown up. My daughter Michele is married and moved out. Doug hasn't moved out completely. You met him on Monday. But he's away at college most of the time. My son Tom and his family are living upstairs, but they'll be getting their own place very soon. It's not far from here."

"I guess this place will get pretty quiet then."

They came out and headed upstairs. "I suppose it will." They continued to walk through all the bedrooms, baths, and loft area, pausing briefly at a window that overlooked the backyard.

"What's that over there?" Christina asked.

"That's the apartment over the garage, where Doug's been living when he's in town."

"Oh."

"Would you like to see it?"

"You think Doug would mind?"

"I don't think so." They came downstairs again. "Why don't you go over there while I pour our coffee? Once inside, you'll see a stairway to the left. It's right up those stairs. Here's a key to the front door."

Christina smiled and walked toward the garage apartment. Marilyn brought the coffee, creamer, sugar, and a little dessert to the dinette table, then sat and waited for Christina's return.

Ten minutes later, she did.

She had spent twice as much time walking through the garage apartment than the time they'd spent walking through the main house. Marilyn smiled. She had a feeling she knew why. When Christina joined her at the table, Marilyn said, "So, what do you think of the house?"

"Are you kidding? It's like a fairy-tale castle."

"How about the garage apartment?"

"It was . . . perfect."

"We thought you'd like it."

"We?"

"Jim and I."

"I don't understand."

"Christina . . . Jim and I have been talking about how we can best help you at this time in your life. You've shown remarkable courage and faith for such a new Christian, despite facing some really tough times."

"What are you saying?"

"Jim and I would love to have you live here, in the garage apartment, at least until your baby is born."

"I don't know what to say . . . Are you serious?"

Marilyn smiled. "Yes. We'd like to rent it to you."

Confusion instantly appeared on Christina's face. "But I can't pay even a fraction of what it's worth. A place like that's got to be out of my reach."

"We don't want you to worry about that. Jim and I discussed it. He'll help you work out a budget, and we'll just charge you whatever you can afford."

"It can't be true."

"It is true," Marilyn said. "We've already talked it over with Doug, and he's fine with it too."

"He is?"

Marilyn nodded. "When he comes home on weekends,

he'll sleep on the pullout sofa in Jim's office, then upstairs after Tom's family moves out."

"Does Doug come home often?" Christina asked.

"Not as often as I'd like. The place is yours if you want it."

"I do. I definitely do!"

17

"Do you want a cup of coffee? It might help you wake up."
Michele stood in their bedroom doorway looking at Allan, who was now sitting up in bed. This was the second day he'd been home from his mission trip, and the second day spent recovering from a nine-hour jet lag. She hoped he pulled out of it soon; tomorrow he returned to work.

"You going to have one?" he asked.

"Sure, we can drink it out on the patio. We'd be in the shade, now that the sun's starting to set."

"Sounds nice. I'll take a quick shower while you make it." He got out of bed and stretched.

She walked over and kissed him on the cheek. "I'm heading downstairs now. Don't get back in that bed."

"I won't. I'll turn the shower on right now."

After giving him another kiss, she headed for the stairs. It was so good having him home. In a few more days, he'd be back to his old self, and they'd be back to their old routines. She reached the kitchen and started the coffee. It was an odd time for coffee; dinner was already in the oven. But if it helped Allan stay awake until their normal bedtime tonight, it was a small price to pay.

They still hadn't had any in-depth conversations yet, the kind Jean had urged her to have about her pregnancy struggles. Partly because Allan had spent the morning and the better part of the day getting caught up on their bills. Before his trip, he had intended to set things up so she could take care of them all while he was gone. That hadn't happened. But Michele knew the real reason they hadn't talked yet.

It was her. She was a chicken.

The very thing she used to hammer her mom about when she'd lived at home, she was guilty of. Being too passive, not speaking up when something bothered her. Is that when this fault had started with her mom? Years ago, when she was first married? Allan was nothing like her dad, at least the way her dad was back then. He wasn't bossy or controlling. Allan was kind, a good listener. He seemed genuinely interested in her welfare and, for the most part, took the initiative to ask Michele questions when he noticed she wasn't doing well.

For the most part . . .

That wasn't happening here, not in this situation. Allan hadn't asked her a single question about her infertility discouragement since that last conversation with her mom in the kitchen, over a month ago. Why? Was he changing too? Slowly becoming dull and self-absorbed like her father had? Did all couples drift into problems like this a few years after they got married? Michele was almost used to hearing women at church, particularly older women, ask "Is the honeymoon over yet?" She would always respond proudly, "Not even close."

Would she say that the next time they asked?

The smell of coffee filled the kitchen. She carried the sugar and creamer out to the patio table, then went back to check on her dish in the oven.

Ten minutes later, they were sitting out on the patio together, enjoying the shade and slight breeze. "What's that good smell going on in the oven?" Allan asked.

"It's that sausage and spinach noodle casserole you love." Michele had stumbled on this dish by accident a few months after their wedding.

"Mmm, can't wait."

"It'll be ready in about twenty minutes. We can eat out here too, if you want."

"Let's do that." He sipped his coffee and looked around their courtyard. "So glad we decided on a town house instead of a house with a yard. I'd hate to have to come home from one of these trips and spend hours getting caught up on yard work."

At the far end of the courtyard was a stand-alone garage, a smaller version than her parents'. But big enough to serve as the base for a cozy one-bedroom apartment just above it. They had discussed renting it out someday, but not until Michele had gotten pregnant and stopped teaching altogether. They might need the extra money then. Now they liked the privacy.

"Looking at this scene," he said, "and being here with you . . . it's so dramatically different than what I was seeing and doing just two days ago. I still can't get the images out of my mind."

"I'm having a hard time getting the smells out of your clothes."

"I'm sorry. I wanted to do a load of laundry that last day before I packed, but it didn't work out."

"That's okay. I'm just running everything through a second time with a little ammonia."

He looked at her. "But you know, all those people in Korah, they can't ever escape the smell. It's a hundred times worse being there than what you're smelling on my clothes. Can you imagine it? They're smelling that smell right now. Talking about it, I can almost smell it again."

"This trip has gotten to you more than the others did."

He thought a moment. "You're probably right. I wish you could've seen it, Michele, especially the kids. Hundreds of them. Maybe thousands. I think they're the reason I'm still kind of stuck emotionally."

"Well, you better get unstuck pretty soon. You're heading back to work tomorrow." Michele regretted the way that came out.

"I'll be okay," he said. "I scheduled some light duty the first few days, since I've done this now a time or two. I know it takes a little while to get back up to full steam." He took another sip of coffee. It didn't seem he'd noticed her slight frustration.

Turning in his seat toward her, he said, "So how about you? How have you been holding up since I've been gone?"

"I've been . . . okay. I hate how bad the communication is. You know that's the worst part of it for me. It's like the Stone Age. Do you realize we only talked five times the whole time you were away?"

"That's just Africa. They're still so far behind. But you know it's getting better, right? My first trip, when we were dating, you remember that? We couldn't find an internet connection anywhere, and the cell phone coverage was terrible."

Saying that didn't help. "I know. But it's still crummy."

"One of these times it'll be better," he said.

That didn't help, either. Reminding her of his plans to go back again someday. Probably someday soon, if he got his way.

"Did anything big happen while I was gone? Anything you didn't get to tell me over the phone?"

"Nothing too big. Something's going on with Tom and Jean. I don't know what yet. It's supposed to be some kind of surprise."

"A good thing, a bad thing?"

"I think a good thing. Mom and Dad were supposed to tell them last night over dinner. I thought somebody would call me today and let me know, but they didn't."

"Well, why don't you call them, Jean or your mom?"

"I will, after dinner. But that's the only thing that went on out of the ordinary. Oh, Ray's wife wants to talk with me. She called while you were gone."

"Julie? What about?"

"She wants me to help her evaluate a new children's ministry program and maybe train some of the workers if we wind up using it."

"That's good, right? Weren't you wanting to get a little more involved?"

"I guess." She really had said that. For some reason, though, she wasn't that excited about it now.

He leaned forward and reached for her hand. She gave it to him. He gave a little squeeze. She squeezed back. "Something else is bothering you," he said. "What is it?"

Should she tell him? Was this a good time?

Her phone rang. "It's my mom."

Saved by the bell.

— 18 —

H i, Mom," Michele said. She stood up and pointed toward the house, letting Allan know she would take the call inside. He nodded and smiled, then turned his eyes back on the courtyard and his attention, no doubt, to memories of Africa.

"I'm sorry," her mom said, "I just looked at the time. We're not eating for a couple of hours. But I just called you at dinnertime, didn't I?"

"Not a problem. It's still in the oven. I can't talk long, but I can talk a few minutes."

"Just stop me if you need to go."

"So, what's up? How did your big surprise go last night with Tom and Jean?"

"It couldn't have gone better. It's one of the reasons I called. Did you see Audrey Windsor talking with your dad on Sunday?"

"I did. And I figured it must have something to do with Tom, because Dad kept looking at him while they talked. But I haven't been able to figure out what."

"Looks like your brother and his family will be moving out of our house fairly soon."

"Really? What's going on?"

Her mom spent the next few minutes filling her in on the news about Tom and Jean suddenly being able to buy Audrey's house. "I'm so happy for them. This is so wonderful!" Michele was almost yelling. "I wish I could've been there to see their faces. You told them right there in front of the house? What a clever idea."

"It was your dad's. I was just gonna tell them over dinner."

Her father still continued to surprise her. "When is all this supposed to happen?"

"Your father said it should only take about a month or two."

"Is that all?"

"Cutting out the real estate agent and mortgage company gets rid of most of the red tape."

"So how are you doing with this news? With Doug back at school, you guys really will be empty-nesters. Are you still looking forward to it?" Michele stepped into the kitchen and turned on the oven light. Good, the casserole still had a few minutes.

"Well . . . we won't be, not exactly."

"What do you mean?"

"That's another part of the reason why I called. I've got some other news."

The joy in her mother's voice had dropped off considerably. "Is it bad news?"

"No. In some ways, we think it's very good news." But she definitely didn't sound upbeat.

"By 'we,' do you mean Tom and Jean?"

"No, your father and me."

"So, what is this *good* news?"

Her mother hesitated. Michele found herself tensing up.

"To be honest, I meant to call you earlier today, but I've been struggling a little. When this idea first came to me, it seemed totally from the Lord. It's kind of a big thing. Your dad responded so well to it, and even Doug did when we talked to him."

Oh great, Michele thought. They had even talked to Doug before they talked to her—the son who was hardly ever home and mostly disconnected from the family. "What is it, Mom? Would you stop setting it up and just tell me?" A long pause. Michele had gone too far. "I'm sorry," she said. "I didn't mean to say it like that."

"I'm messing this all up, making it way bigger than it is," Marilyn said. "I should have just said what it is from the start. It's just . . . we're not going to be empty-nesters because someone's moving into Doug's garage apartment. Pretty soon, actually. Even before Tom and Jean move out."

This didn't sound so bad. "Who is it?"

"It's this young girl I met. Well, here I go again." A short pause. "The next part is the part I thought you might have trouble with. I want you to know, your dad and I gave this girl the okay without even thinking. I probably should have talked to you first, to make sure you'd be okay with it."

Michele was tensing up again. She reminded herself that her mom was just nervous and that she tended to beat around the bush when she got nervous. This was probably nothing. "That I'd be okay with *what*?"

"With her moving into the garage apartment, where Doug's been living the last two years."

"Why would I *not* be okay with that? Doug's hardly ever home anymore."

"I know," her mom said, "but there's more. I met this girl down at the Women's Resource Center. She's seven months

100

pregnant. She just recently became one of my clients, and we found out she was about to lose her apartment. This way, she'll have a safe place to live until the baby is born, and I'll be able to look in on her."

"Oh." Michele wasn't sure if this new information mattered that much. With all this buildup, she was thinking it should bother her more than it did. "Well, I guess it's a good thing for her that the two of you met."

"So you're okay with it then?"

"I think so. Is there some reason I shouldn't be?"

"I just thought that you might, you know, because you . . . you haven't been able to get pregnant yet. And you've been trying all this time. We've talked about how much it bothers you how easily some women who don't even want children get pregnant, or can't take care of them. And other women like you are totally ready to be moms and want children desperately, but can't."

Michele heard the patio door open and turned. Allan was coming inside. "I remember talking about that, and when I do think about it, it does bother me. So I try not to think about it very much."

"See, that's what I'm talking about," her mother said. "Having this girl living in the garage apartment, won't her presence constantly force you to think about it? Every time you see her? Every time you come over for a visit? Especially in these next two months. She's really showing now, but in a month she'll be even bigger. A month after that, the baby will be here."

Allan walked past her and motioned that he was heading upstairs to wash his hands. Michele nodded. She was actually glad he was out of earshot, so she could speak more freely. "Mom, I don't see it being too much of a problem. I see pregnant women all the time at church. Quite a few of my students' moms are pregnant. Just as many push little babies in strollers. I think I can handle this. Are you thinking she'll want Allan and me to adopt her baby? Is that what all this is about?"

"No, I don't think that has anything to do with this. She's planning to go through an adoption agency anyway. I just didn't want to cause you any pain. I know how hard this whole thing's been on you. I didn't want to do anything to add to it."

"That was very thoughtful. But let me put your mind at ease. I'm really okay. Well, most of the time I am. Allan and I haven't really begun to explore all the medical things available for couples going through what we're dealing with. Actually, that's the next big conversation I want to have with him. I'm just waiting till he recovers from this trip. But I'm not even thinking about adoption right now, so hanging around this young girl shouldn't cause any more pain than usual. At least that's how I'm seeing it now."

"I'm really glad to hear that, Michele."

"We keep talking about 'this girl.' What's her name, anyway?"

"We're really supposed to keep that confidential. But I guess that's kind of silly if she's going to be living here with us. I think you'll really like her once you get to know her. She's a little rough around the edges, but she's very sweet."

"And her name is . . ."

"Her name's Christina."

—19—

For the first half of their meal, Allan did most of the talking. This was largely because Michele kept asking him questions. She did her best to avoid questions about Korah, the dump site where he'd spent his last two days. Whenever he talked about Korah, she became uncomfortable. It wasn't so much the things he'd said, which were hard to hear. All of it was hard to hear. It was the emotional effect it had on him. She was trying to get him back on track; back in the present, not stuck in Korah.

This tactic didn't work. At some point, he stopped eating, stopped talking, and just stared at his plate.

"What's the matter?" she said.

"Nothing. I was just thinking . . . this casserole tastes way better than it looks."

"Hey!" She slapped him in the arm. "I worked hard on that."

"You know what I mean," he said. "Look at it. The green noodles, the gray sausage, and what is that mixed in? Cottage cheese?"

"I thought you liked it."

"I love it. Every time you make it, I eat two helpings. But

look at it. You've got to admit, it lacks a certain . . . visual appeal."

She'd never thought about it before. "So you don't think I should make this dish when we have friends over?"

"Maybe good friends. Very good friends." He smiled.

This was nice. By the look on his face a moment ago, she was expecting him to say something dark and dismal, not make a joke. Maybe he was coming out of it.

"Even as bad as it looks," he said, "any one of those kids I saw in Korah would see it as a feast." That gloomy look reappeared as he shifted his eyes off her and back to his plate. "You can't believe the things they eat, Michele. It boggles the mind. I kept thinking if I was in their shoes, I don't think I could do it. I'm serious. I think I'd just have to starve. It was that bad."

She didn't know what to say. She felt like anything she added would just keep this unpleasant thread going. "Maybe the next time you go back, you can make it for them." What a stupid thing to say. What was she thinking?

"I wish I could. They certainly wouldn't mind how it looks." He took another bite, then another.

It was time to change the subject. "I almost forgot Tom and Jean's big news." She spent the next five minutes telling him all about it. Then she spent another five minutes telling him about Christina moving into Doug's place over the garage. She left out the part about having met Christina before at the playground. Why open that can of worms? She did mention that Christina was seven months pregnant. Allan asked if that was going to be a problem for her. She told him she didn't think so.

For a few moments, neither of them said anything. Before the conversation could drift back to Korah, she said, "I did some research while you were gone."

"Really, on what?"

"I guess you'd call it our . . . infertility problem."

"Is that still bothering you?"

Was he kidding? Did he really just ask her that? "It's probably fair to say I think about it at least ten times a day."

A shocked look came over his face. "You're not kidding."
She shook her head no.

"So it bothers you a lot. I had no idea. How long has it bothered you . . . that much?"

"It's not something that just started recently, Allan. I think it's bothered me since about the second month we started trying. And it bothers me more and more each month that passes by." She set her fork down. Suddenly, her appetite was gone.

"We haven't talked about it in a while. I guess I just figured things had eased off."

That's what she thought he'd thought. "We haven't talked about it because you haven't asked. And because the last time we talked, you and Mom made it pretty clear that someone who'd been trying for *only* a year had no business being as concerned as I was."

"Did I say that?"

"Kind of. You were both trying to tell me a year of trying to get pregnant wasn't such a long time."

Allan's eyes and eyebrows suggested he was trying to recall this moment. "I think I remember the conversation you're talking about. We were in the kitchen with your mom, right?"

Michele nodded.

"My recollection is that we were trying to comfort you, not make you feel bad or guilty."

"I guess I missed that message. I don't recall feeling very comforted after."

He reached his hand across the table. "I'm sorry, hon."

"And you never even asked me about it later. Tonight is the first time we've talked about this subject since then."

"Are you sure?"

"Oh Allan, of course I'm sure. I've wanted to talk about it a dozen times."

He set his fork down too. "Why didn't you let me know? Give me some kind of sign that you were struggling this much?"

She didn't know whether to yell or to cry. She remembered something Ray had shared with them during their premarital counseling. How unspoken words can form walls that get thicker and thicker over time and cause much more pain than if the couple had talked things through right away. Her mom and dad's marriage had been in a crisis at the time. She felt her mom was partly to blame because she hardly ever spoke up when her father did something that hurt her. By that time, their wall seemed like the Great Wall of China.

Tears slipped down her cheeks as she whispered, "I guess I was wishing you were more like you were before we married. You always seemed to know how I was feeling. It was like you could read my facial expressions or tone of voice. You already know how much I've wanted to be a mom. We talked this out before we got engaged. You said you wanted kids just as much as I did. Ever since I was a little girl, besides getting married, being a mom's the only thing in life I ever really wanted."

She wiped her tears with her hand. "Haven't you even noticed the depression I go through every month when that day comes, and it's obvious I'm not pregnant . . . again? I've wanted you to ask me about it and pray with me. Maybe help me find Scriptures to encourage me. Or just hold me close and tell me it will be okay, and say someday soon our baby would come."

The words hung there in the air between them. For several moments, he didn't answer. He just kept staring at his half-eaten plate of spinach-noodle casserole.

When he did look up, she could see that tears had welled up in his eyes. He got up from the table, walked around to her side, and held her. He gently kissed the top of her head. "I'm so sorry, Michele. So very sorry."

~20~

It was all happening so fast.

Christina had hated this dingy apartment from the first day she moved in. She walked through the handful of rooms to make sure she hadn't left anything she might care about later. Once she had given the key to the manager, there was no coming back. He'd made that clear. First thing tomorrow morning, his maintenance crew would come through and clean everything out. Everything would go to Goodwill or the dumpster.

She was betting on the dumpster getting the bigger share.

The apartment had come unfurnished, except for a few odd chairs in the living/dining area. She had added a wobbly dinette table with two metal folding chairs (her ex-boyfriend had actually pulled these out of someone's trash pile). In the bedroom, the same decor. In the center of the floor, a double bed mattress—no box spring. In the corner, a fake-wood chest of drawers—no mirror. One end was actually propped up by three bricks, making it one inch higher than the other.

An image of the garage apartment she was moving to flashed through her mind. Stepping out of the bedroom, she shook her head in fresh disgust. "This is so awful." Back in the living area, she slowly spun around the apartment. "Thank you, Lord, for delivering me from this place."

Shutting the front door behind her, she felt such relief. Marilyn had told her all the furniture in her new apartment was staying. Doug was coming back this weekend to gather up the few things he'd left behind, but everything else she had seen when touring the place was hers to use for as long as she lived there.

Bending forward, she locked the front door . . . for the last time. "This is so wonderful," she said aloud. She walked down the steps toward her car, wondering if she'd see Doug at church that morning. She hoped so. Marilyn had invited her to join the Anderson family afterward for dinner. Then she could move into the apartment. Starting today, she would be a resident of River Oaks.

River Oaks. She couldn't restrain a smile.

Her car started right up, compliments of the new battery. Another Anderson family provision. She glanced at the seat beside her then at the floorboard. She reached behind her, pulled out an empty Walmart bag, and started cleaning up. From now on, this car would be parked in a garage on Elderberry Lane. It had better start looking the part. Right then, she decided to spend the five bucks and drive through the car wash. She had enough time before church began.

She turned around in her seat to back up her car, noticing the smattering of small boxes covering the backseat. All she owned in the world. But that was okay. God was giving her a fresh start. Half this stuff might go in the dumpster too in the next few days. Even looking at it now, she saw a number of things that were much too ugly to fit in that adorable little place.

She put her foot on the brake and typed the church address into the GPS app on her phone. She felt a little nervous about visiting a new church, but just a little. It couldn't be worse than the handful of churches she had visited nearby. No one would miss her in any of those places, that's for sure. No one had even attempted to reach out to her.

She drove out of the apartment complex then down the road toward River Oaks without looking in the rearview mirror a single time.

◆ ◆

Christina pulled into the crowded parking lot of the high school where the church met, following the directions of several men wearing bright orange vests. People of all ages were getting out of their cars and making their way toward the auditorium. They all looked pretty happy.

She parked the car and wrestled with whether to wear her sweatshirt or just carry it in. Now that she had reached the seven-month mark, she was usually too hot, and it did a lousy job of hiding her . . . *bump*.

She lifted herself out of the car and began walking behind a nice young family a few yards ahead. Mom, Dad, a boy, and a girl, both preschool age, and a baby in a stroller. *This is what a family looks like. This is what I want for my baby.* God meant for babies to be in families like this one. She was doing the right thing. Adoption was the right choice.

For her, anyway.

As she neared the double set of glass doors, she began scanning the crowd for Marilyn, who was supposed to lead her to where the rest of the family sat. She began feeling edgy and realized why. At the last church, each of the official greeters by the door had done the same thing: smiled, extended their hand, noticed her pregnant belly, noticed she was alone, and noticed there was no ring on her finger. Then the same look in their eyes. She couldn't quite name it, but it sucked all the welcome out of the air.

But here, that didn't happen.

Oh, a few of the greeters noticed she was pregnant, but that was as far as it went. The joy in their eyes remained. She didn't feel judged. She felt . . . welcome.

"Christina, over here."

She looked toward the voice but didn't see Marilyn. Lots of other people. A few seconds later, she felt a gentle tap on her shoulder.

"There you are." Marilyn gave her a hug. "I love that dress on you."

It was the same dress Christina had worn at the restaurant. "Thanks. This place is crowded."

"Especially just before the service begins. The pastor said when we get our own building, we'll make the lobby much bigger, so people can stand around and chat without bumping into each other. Come on, I saved you a seat right next to Jim and me." They started walking toward the auditorium doors. "Tom and Jean and the kids are here. So are Allan and Michele. They're a few rows back. But you'll get to meet them at dinner."

"Is Doug here, or did he—"

"Yes, Doug's here. Right next to Jim."

They walked into the auditorium, which was a little darker except by the stage. The worship band began to play, and everyone stood. The music was fairly loud with a strong beat. People started clapping. Marilyn led her toward the left and down a side aisle. "Just a few rows more," she said.

The vocalists up front began to sing. Christina recognized

the song. It was one of her favorite worship songs on the radio. In fact, the band sounded just like the group on the radio. The people began to sing.

"Here we are," Marilyn said.

Christina looked down the row and recognized Marilyn's husband Jim, who was clapping and singing. Doug stood next to him, not clapping, but he was singing. At least, she thought he was. People leaned back to let them by. As they got closer, she looked up at Doug again. Even better looking than she remembered.

He noticed her, smiled, then looked back toward the stage. Suddenly, she felt self-conscious. *Stop this.* She had to put any thoughts of him out of her mind. That wasn't why she was here. Anyway, with the way she looked, who she was, and who *he* was . . . it was obvious he'd have no interest in someone like her.

◆ ◆

After the closing song and prayer, everyone stood up and began to file out of their seats. Marilyn turned to Christina. "So, what did you think?"

"I really liked it. All of it." She really did. She wasn't saying that to get in good with Marilyn. "I really understood what the preacher was saying. Parts of it felt like he was talking right to me."

"I know," Marilyn said. "That happens to me every week. Come on, I want to introduce you to my other kids. Well, they're not kids. They're older than you. There's Tom and Jean right over there."

Christina followed Marilyn a few rows back, closer to the exit.

"Christina, I want you to meet my oldest son, Tom. This

is his wife, Jean." Christina shook their hands. "They have three children, Tommy, Carly, and little Abby."

"Which reminds me," Jean said. "I've gotta go get them out of children's ministry. It was nice meeting you, Christina. You're coming to Sunday dinner, right?" Christina nodded. "Then I'll see you there."

"And here's Allan," Marilyn said. "My daughter Michele's husband." Marilyn looked all around. "Where's Michele?"

"She ducked out already. She's got a quick meeting with Julie, to go over some new thing with the children's ministry. But we'll both be there for dinner." He reached out his hand. "Nice to meet you, Christina."

"Julie is Ray's wife," Marilyn said. "He's one of the pastors. You'll like Michele. I'm sure of it."

They stood around a few seconds. Christina looked back to see if Jim and Doug were coming. They were. She thought Doug was looking at her, but he quickly looked away.

21

Michele did her best to suppress her emotions, but it wasn't working.

She knew Julie, Ray's wife, would be there any minute. She had to pull it together. They were meeting in one of the classrooms down the hall from the main auditorium. It was pretty much empty. All the parents had already come and collected their children. The teacher's assistant, a girl about fifteen, was over in the corner putting supplies back in big blue plastic containers.

Michele sat on a chair closer to the door, trying to recover from the horrible words the teacher of that class had just said to her. The middle-aged woman had already left, saying she had some big family celebration to get ready for. Whatever got her out of the classroom.

How could the woman be so cruel and thoughtless? She'd said what she said with a smile on her face, as though passing on a compliment. Michele had recognized the woman as a regular in the church but couldn't remember her name. She seemed to know Michele and at least some of Michele's situation.

"Hey, Michele, sorry I'm late." Michele looked up into

Julie's kind, smiling face. "I was trying to get here but kept getting stopped in the halls."

"That's okay. I've only been here a few minutes."

Julie sat in the chair next to her. She was holding a white notebook. "This shouldn't take but a few minutes," she said. "The introduction chapter in the notebook does a great job explaining itself. I've read it over, cover to cover, slowly. Ray didn't have time to read it because of the trip, but I briefed him pretty thoroughly over coffee yesterday. We're both excited about this."

The enthusiasm in Julie's voice helped to clear the emotional fog for Michele. "What's it about?"

She handed Michele the notebook. "Let me share the basic concept with you first. We don't hate the children's ministry curriculum we're using now. But Ray and I have been talking, and we're thinking maybe we could do better, especially with the elementary-aged kids. The biblical content is pretty light in what we're using now. In some ways, it's just Christian babysitting. That might be okay for the younger kids, but we're thinking we can accomplish more with the older ones. So I've been on the lookout for a new curriculum that's still kid-friendly but also gets them in the Word a lot more."

"So what can I do?" Michele asked.

Julie pointed to the notebook. "We're hoping you can tell us if you think this material connects well with the older kids in children's ministry."

"I suppose I can do that. How much time do I have?"

Julie stood up, so Michele did too.

"You've got lots of time. We couldn't even think about ordering this until after Thanksgiving. Our new semester begins after the Christmas holiday."

That was a relief. The two women walked to the doorway. "By the way," Julie said. She looked up and down the hall to make sure there was no one nearby. "A few weeks ago in our prayer group, you asked for prayer about some problem you're having getting pregnant. I know a little bit about that if you ever want to talk."

Michele couldn't help it; she burst into tears.

"Oh no, what's the matter?" Julie said gently. "Did I say something wrong?"

They stepped back into the classroom. "It's not you, not what you said." Michele opened her purse and pulled out a tissue. She sat back in the chair. "It's something somebody else said."

Julie sat beside her. "Who? What did they say?"

Michele shook her head. She didn't even want to repeat it.

"Was it Mrs. Harden? The woman teaching in this class-room a little while ago?"

Michele nodded, wiping her tears. "How did you know?"

Julie released a frustrated sigh. "I've had some complaints about her before, and some run-ins with her myself. She's not the most tactful person."

"I'll say." Michele looked up into Julie's face. "I don't think anyone has said anything more hurtful than what she said to me a few minutes ago. I don't remember if she was in that prayer meeting, but she obviously knew I've been trying to get pregnant for almost a year." Michele paused, trying to regain her composure. "She said it so calmly, like it was just nothing at all."

"Oh, Michele . . . I'm sorry. What did she say?"

"She said, pretty much just like this . . . 'Well, don't worry about it, dear'—she was talking about me not being able to get pregnant—'God is in control. He knows what he's doing in these things. Sometimes he doesn't let women get pregnant because he knows they wouldn't be good mothers.'"

"What!" Julie shouted. Her face instantly became angry. "You've got to be kidding me."

"I'm not."

"That is the most ridiculous thing I've ever heard. You know that's just a lie, Michele. I'm serious. It's a complete lie."

Michele knew on one level it had to be, but it still hurt so badly. First, hearing it, then saying it again just now.

"I am . . . so . . . angry right now," Julie said. "I just want to . . . no, I'm a pastor's wife. But you know, Christians can be the most insensitive people on earth sometimes. That is such a ridiculous and ignorant thing to say, on so many levels." She touched Michele's arm. "Michele." Her voice became calmer. "I am so sorry someone from this church said something like that to you. I don't think that. Ray doesn't. I can guarantee you none of the other pastors or wives think that. I'd be surprised if anyone else in this entire church thought a thing like that. Because it's *not* true. Our faith is based on what Christ said and the things he taught his disciples. He *never* said anything like that. I've got to do something about this."

"Oh, please don't do anything," Michele said. "I don't want to turn this into a big deal."

"But it is a big deal," Julie said. "I don't want someone who thinks that way—and doesn't even have the good sense not to say it out loud—to be turned loose in our children's ministry. I'm sure Ray will feel the same way. Of course, he'll want me to calm down quite a bit before I do anything. But honestly, I can't let something like this slide."

Michele stood up. "Well, I'm glad to hear you say this. Although I really don't want to make any trouble."

"You're not making trouble, Michele. I'm just so sorry

you had to experience something like that, in church of all places. Are you going to be okay?"

Michele assured her she would. She looked at the clock on the wall. "I really better go. Got a big Sunday dinner to get to."

As she walked to the car, she remembered that Christina would be there. When her mom had mentioned this a few days ago, Michele said it didn't bother her.

Now, for some reason, it kind of did.

—22—

Michele and Allan drove out of the church parking lot and turned right toward River Oaks. "Do you need to go home first," Allan asked, "or can we go straight to your folks'?"

"I'm okay, let's just go straight there." Michele was doing a little better since that awful experience with the children's ministry teacher. Hearing Julie's strong reaction definitely helped. That wasn't how God felt about her, and it didn't have anything to do with why he hadn't allowed her to get pregnant yet.

"What's wrong?"

"I'm okay," Michele said.

"Did your meeting with Julie go well? You seem a little upset."

"The Julie part of the meeting was fine. It's what happened before that."

Allan stopped at the light. "You mean during the service?"

"No. When I first got to the classroom, before Julie got there."

Allan looked confused.

She didn't really want to tell him; it was so upsetting. But she knew their relationship wouldn't get back on track if she didn't start communicating more, right when things happened. So she told him everything: what the teacher said, the way she said it, and Julie's reaction.

His eyes became angrier than she'd ever seen them. "What's this lady's name?"

"Why do you want to know?"

"Because . . . that is the most ridiculous, horrible, thoughtless thing I've ever heard anyone say. I want to know who this lady is."

"Julie said it, but I don't remember. Mrs. Hardy, I think. Or Harding. But Allan, I don't want you to confront her."

"Why not? Someone has to. Someone that heartless needs to be confronted." He glared straight ahead, but he obviously wasn't seeing the road.

"The light turned green," she said. "Julie's going to talk to her, or else Ray will."

"Did she say she would?"

"Pretty much. Please tell me you'll talk with Ray before you say anything to the teacher. If they're willing to handle it, I think you should let them."

Allan took a deep breath. His eyes softened a little. He looked at Michele. "I'm so sorry she said that to you. You know that's completely not true, right? There's no way that's why you haven't gotten pregnant yet."

"I know."

"It's like she was born without a tact gene," Allan said. "I know a guy like that at work. He just says whatever he thinks, regardless of how ignorant it sounds or who might be hurt by it. You can tell by the look on his face, he's clueless. He has absolutely no idea how inappropriate and offensive his comments are."

They turned into the entrance of River Oaks. "Well," Michele said, "what that teacher said may be an extreme example of insensitivity, but I think a lot of people, even people in our church, don't really understand how painful this thing is. The whole reason this incident happened illustrates the point."

"What do you mean?"

"This lady apparently overheard something I said a few weeks ago at a prayer meeting. That's why she knew I was struggling with infertility. The thing is, I wasn't asking for prayer about our infertility problem. I was asking for prayer for your trip to Africa, that God would keep you safe and bring you home safe."

"How did the conversation get from there to infertility?" Allan asked.

"Insensitivity," she said. "A lack of discernment. Take your pick. Do you realize how many times I've asked for prayer for something, and someone in the group inevitably starts praying for me to get pregnant? Half the time, I'm not even thinking about it until they bring it up. Then for the next several minutes, everyone's focusing on me and my inability to get pregnant. Some of the women will come up after we stop praying and ask me how I'm doing, or tell me some story about someone they know that has the same problem."

Allan smiled. "I think they're just trying to be caring when that happens."

"I'm sure they are," she said. "But that doesn't help me at the time. It makes me not want to pray in a group anymore. I mean, if I was struggling with this specifically and I asked for prayer, that would be different. But I've had people praying for me to get pregnant when I had that bronchial infection a few months ago and couldn't shake it."

Allan laughed. "I'm sorry. That's not funny."

Michele sighed. "It just seems like Christians don't know what to do with this, or how to treat people dealing with this problem." They were driving through the cute downtown area of River Oaks now. Elderberry Lane was just a few blocks away. "I got another one of these today." She pulled a small white envelope out of her purse.

"What is it?" he asked.

"An invitation . . . to a baby shower. It's like torture, going to those. Pretending to be so happy as they open all the gifts. Listening to all the moms talk about their delivery stories. All the while I just sit there, smiling, nodding."

"I'm sorry, Michele. Who's the shower for?"

She opened the invitation and read aloud. "The friends and family of Mrs. Samantha Durbin are happy to announce . . . I'm not even sure I know who that is."

"I think I know the Durbins," Allan said. "Not very well. But you don't have to go to that one, Michele. It's their first baby. I think the church has a policy to invite all the women when it's the first baby. But they know not everyone's going to go."

Michele looked out the window. They were in her parents' neighborhood now. "I don't think I will. Maybe I'll send a small gift along."

They drove in silence a few moments. Michele spoke first. "Jean said something interesting the other day."

"What's that?"

"She read that one in eight couples struggle with infertility. She wanted me to know I'm not alone."

"*We're* not alone," he said.

She wanted to believe him, that they were going through this together. She'd felt all alone in this for so many months now. At least he was trying. He reached his hand toward her. She took it and gave it a gentle squeeze.

"If that statistic is for the country as a whole," Allan said, "I'd say it's much higher than one in eight within the church. I think church people are trying to have kids more aggressively than the culture at large. It might be more like one in five."

"Either way," Michele said, "seems like a lot more people struggle with this than you would think. For some reason, we tend to suffer alone. I can think of two other women I know in the church who can't seem to get pregnant. Both have been trying longer than me. We don't even talk to each other. Not very often, anyway."

They turned onto Elderberry Lane. "Maybe you should."

"Should what?"

"Talk to these other women. There's probably a bunch of other women in the church who are dealing with this. We're up to about three hundred people now. Based on that statistic, even with the one in eight number, that's almost twenty women in a church our size. If it's one in five, you're talking almost thirty."

Could that be possible? "I don't know. I'm not sure I want to do something like that."

"Like what?"

"Start some kind of women's ministry or support group. I don't even like to think about it." Talking about it openly would make it feel more real, or like she was giving in to defeat or giving up hope.

"I was just thinking of you talking with those two." Allan pulled up to the curb near her parents' house. "Looks like everyone's here. Wow, even Doug. Three weekends in a row. Wonder what's going on."

Michele recognized all the cars. All except one.

23

It was like being in a movie.

That's what it felt like to Christina. Sitting around the Anderson Sunday dinner table. Everybody talking, several conversations going at once. People passing food; people asking other people to pass food. Listening to family jokes, being the only one who didn't get them. The dad, Jim, sitting at one end of the table; the mom, Marilyn, to his left. None of them seemed to realize how unusual this was. Didn't people stop doing this, like, decades ago?

But she loved it. Every bit of it.

She especially liked that no one made her feel strange. Marilyn had introduced her before they'd sat down, though it seemed everyone already knew who she was. They all said hi, some other nice welcoming thing, then life went on as usual and Christina was allowed to be a part of it.

There were two empty seats in the middle. Christina understood they belonged to Michele and Allan. She had met Allan at church. Marilyn said they should be here any minute. Doug sat next to Allan's empty chair. He had been polite to Christina, but that was about all. It was hard to stop looking at him, but she had been relatively successful. Of course, they had only been sitting for ten minutes. In any case, no one seemed to notice her looking at him, especially Doug. She knew this because every time she did look, his eyes were somewhere else.

"When are you heading back to St. Augustine, Doug?" his brother Tom asked.

Doug took a roll and passed the basket down. "About an hour after dinner. I got my stuff together in a couple of boxes by the apartment stairs. Once I'm gone, the place is all yours, Christina." He smiled at her.

"Can't wait," she said. "I mean, till it's mine. Not can't wait till you're gone."

"I know."

"Did you strip the bed?" Marilyn asked Doug. "And scrub that bathroom real good? The way I taught you when you first moved in?"

"I did better than that. I not only stripped the bed, I put the dirty sheets and pillowcases in the washer and put fresh ones back on the bed. And the bathroom is so clean, you'd never know a guy had been there."

Christina smiled. The bathroom was probably cleaner than the one in her old apartment. "That's very kind of you, Doug."

"No problem."

"Think you can help her get her stuff up the stairs after we eat?" Marilyn asked.

"I was planning on it."

The front door opened. Everyone turned and started greeting Allan and Michele. A few of them stood, so Christina did too. But she stayed back by the table.

Michele . . . she looked way too familiar. She seemed to look at Christina the same way.

Marilyn walked Allan and Michele toward her. "Allan,

you met Christina at church. But you weren't with us at the time, Michele. Well, this is Christina."

Michele stuck out her hand. "We've actually met before, Mom. In a way." She looked at Christina. "Remember, that day at the playground?"

"That's where it was. I knew you looked familiar." Oh my, Christina thought. She's the woman who was crying as she watched the kids play, because she can't have kids of her own.

"What playground?" Allan asked.

"Just one in River Oaks," Michele said. "Well, let's get seated. I'm starving."

"We haven't started eating," Marilyn said. "We're just yakking and dishing out food." She took her place at the end of the table.

After everyone sat again, Doug said, "Any chance we could say the blessing before Michele and Allan get their food?"

"Yeah, go ahead," Allan said.

"All right," Jim said. "Let's pray."

Everyone reached for each other's hands and closed their eyes. Before she closed hers, Christina saw Tommy stretch and reach for his sister's hand. So cute. Then Jim prayed a nice, short prayer. She didn't remember all of it, but she felt especially blessed when he spent a few moments talking about her. It was hard to fathom. He was thanking God for *her*, for God bringing *her* into *their* lives? Everyone said amen and started eating. She wished she could have been a little bolder. If anything, she was the one who should be thanking God for them.

When she opened her eyes and looked around the table, three people were looking back at her: Doug, Marilyn, and Michele. Michele's look was the only one that troubled her, and only a little. The other glances were light and friendly.

Michele definitely had something going on behind those eyes.

✦ ✦

Michele wasn't really starving. She had just said that to change the subject. She still hadn't told Allan about her trips to the playground. It wasn't as though she'd been doing anything wrong. So why hadn't she told him?

Christina certainly looked a little different than she did that day. She looked better. Cleaner, happier, and definitely more . . . pregnant.

"How much more time before your baby is due?" Jean asked.

"Six or seven weeks," Christina said.

Michele wondered if she'd made a decision about whether to keep the baby or not. This wasn't the right time or place to ask such a thing. And really, it was none of Michele's business.

Allan passed her the plate of roast beef. "So you two met at the playground? Was that while I was on my trip?"

"What trip?" Christina said.

"A mission trip to Africa."

"Yes," Michele said. She took one slice of beef and set the plate down in front of her.

"Which playground was it?"

Why did he care? "The big one. The one closest to the downtown area." She didn't look at him, thinking he might get the hint and drop it.

"I was there trying to think through a pretty big decision," Christina said.

"Which decision is that?" Doug asked.

"Doug, don't be nosy," Marilyn said.

"I don't mind. Whether or not to keep my baby and raise

her as a single parent or put her up for adoption, let a married couple be her mom and dad."

"Wow," Doug said. "That's a biggie."

"It is. Biggest decision I ever made."

"Sounds like you've already made it."

"I have."

"Well?"

"Christina, you don't have to get into all that here," Marilyn said. "Doug, don't be so curious."

Michele wanted to know the answer too. She couldn't tell if her mom was trying to protect Christina's privacy or to signal her not to discuss the situation over the dinner table. She got her answer quickly, when her mother's eyes instantly shifted to Tommy and Carly. Probably wasn't the best dinner conversation for little ears.

Christina leaned toward Doug and said quietly, "I'll tell you later if you really want to know." She looked up at Michele and smiled, then back at Doug. "But talking with your sister that day at the playground really helped me."

Michele quickly looked at Allan. He had definitely heard this exchange.

24

By the end of the family dinner, Michele had to admit . . . she liked this Christina. She didn't seem to always know how much or how little to say. She had plenty of opinions but didn't share them in a way that said you must be stupid if you didn't agree. And she had a good sense of humor, bordering on the sarcastic side. She knew enough to play it safe. By the look in her eyes, Michele was sure she was holding back plenty.

It was safe to say, half the laughter at the table followed something Christina said.

Michele thought it was odd; Christina wasn't like anyone else in the family—didn't think like anyone else, didn't talk like anyone else, seemed to view life from a totally different vantage point—yet at the same time, she fit right in.

Her mom was certainly enjoying having Christina there, or maybe she was just relieved. Doug seemed to be enjoying having her there too. As the meal went on, he seemed to be paying more and more attention to Christina. At one point, Michele thought she saw that certain look in his eye. He had only ever brought one girlfriend home, so she couldn't be sure.

Whatever may or may not be happening on Doug's end, she definitely detected interest on Christina's side. Christina looked at Doug *that* way at fairly consistent intervals through-out the dinner. Michele didn't know her little brother too well, but from what she did know, she would be surprised if Doug could overlook Christina's . . . *condition.*

The only awkward moment in the meal came a few minutes ago when it came time to clear the table. The women all got up to help, including Christina. Marilyn, in a voice filled with kind, maternal concern, said, "Oh no, Christina, you better stay put in your condition."

Christina looked so embarrassed; her face blushed instantly. She looked at Doug, then down at her big belly, as if wish-ing she could will it away. She recovered her composure and replied, "Mrs. Anderson, you're so thoughtful. But really, I'd like to help. Besides, did you forget I'm a waitress? I do this kind of thing every day."

"I did forget."

"Christina," Jean said, "I'm afraid you're going to have to get used to being mothered if you live around here."

"You mean smothered," Doug said.

"Hey," Marilyn said.

Doug laughed. "I meant it in a good way. As in smothered with love."

Christina stood up and piled Doug's plate and silverware on top of her own and walked them toward the kitchen.

"Oh, I almost forgot," Marilyn said. "Speaking about your waitress job, isn't it back in Sanford, closer to your apart-ment?"

"It is." Christina set the plates down by the sink. "I didn't really think about that when you invited me to live here. I'll eat up all my tips in gas." She looked around the kitchen and at the family members walking by. "But I can find another waitress job. I wouldn't turn all this down because of that."

130

"How set are you on staying a waitress?" Marilyn asked.

"Are you kidding? I hate it. Especially now. My back kills me at the end of every shift. But I can't do anything else."

"I doubt that," Jim said as he carried in the main meat dish. "I'll bet there's lots you could do."

"I know of one other thing you could do," Marilyn said. "If you want to, I mean. I didn't even tell you this yet, Jim."

"Do what?" Christina said. "You mean like another job? A not-waitressing job?"

Marilyn nodded, smiled. "Right here in River Oaks."

"No way."

Marilyn nodded again. Michele figured it out before her mother even said it.

"How would you like to work with me? At a little shop on Main Street called Odds-n-Ends?"

"Emily's leaving, isn't she?" Michele said. "She told me at church. She's leaving town to go back to college."

"That's right."

"Is Emily someone you work with?" Christina asked.

"Yes, and the store owner goes to our church too. Her name's Harriet. I asked her if she would consider interviewing you for Emily's job."

"And what did she say?"

"She said if I trusted you enough to invite you to move into our garage apartment, she didn't even need to interview you. You could start this week."

"Really? I can't even believe this," Christina said.

"Like I said, smothered with love." Doug walked by, carrying what was left of two side dishes. He was actually helping to clear the table.

"How much of a notice do you need to give your boss?" Marilyn asked.

"How long? For him, not much."

"Two weeks?" Marilyn said.

"More like two days. It's not a nice place. He tells us at least once a day: 'You think I need you? I don't need you. I got fifty people waiting in line for your job. Now get back to work.'" She said it like a New Jersey mobster.

"Oh my," Marilyn said. "That's awful."

"No," Christina said. "That's not awful. That's what he says when he's being nice. I can't repeat what he says when he's being awful."

"I wouldn't give a guy like that two minutes, let alone two days," Doug said.

"Maybe you're right." Christina looked at Marilyn. "Tell the owner I'll start whenever she wants me. Tomorrow even. I'll just call my boss and tell him to call up one of those fifty people standing in line."

Marilyn was so excited, she hugged Christina in a full Mom-embrace. Michele noticed a slight delay in Christina returning the hug. But she did hug her back and kept telling her how thankful she was.

Just then, Allan walked into the kitchen holding his cell phone. "Say, hon, just got a call from Ray. He was wondering if I could meet him for a quick cup of coffee. He said some big things are happening with the orphanage plan and wants to go over them with me. I guess he wants me to start working on them soon or something. Is that okay?"

"You mean now? You're going to meet him now?"

"Well . . . yeah. If it's okay. You know what's gonna happen here. You guys'll clean up like you always do, get the coffee on. Eat dessert a little while after that. I won't be long. I'm too full for dessert anyway."

What could she say? She wasn't okay? But she didn't want

to say it. He was right about the routine. But part of the routine was him being there with her, sitting next to her, drinking coffee at the table as everyone talked and joked around. She also wasn't crazy about all this Korah orphanage stuff coming back into play. It had been so nice the last few days having the old Allan back. She could tell by the look in his eyes, he was already halfway down the road on his way to meet Ray.

"So, is it okay?"

"I guess," she said, as unenthusiastically as she could.

"Love you." He pulled her into a hug and kissed her forehead.

25

When Allan pulled up to the Starbucks in the River Oaks downtown area, he passed Ray's car parked along the curb a few stores down. He found Ray sitting outside in the café area, tapping something into his iPad. Allan looked at Ray's coffee cup and said, "Hey, Ray. I'll get mine and be right there." Ray looked up and waved.

When Allan joined him, Ray set his tablet aside. "Just sending a quick reply back to Henok."

"How's he doing?"

"Extremely well."

"You sounded pretty excited on the phone," Allan said.

"Things are really starting to come together over there. A lot faster than I expected. Life getting back to normal for you?"

"Mostly. Took me a little longer this time than usual."

"Korah?" Ray said.

Allan nodded. "We were only there a couple of days, but I can't get the images out of my head."

"Me neither." Ray picked up his cup. "This time I don't think we're supposed to."

"What do you mean?"

"I mean, I don't think the Lord wants us to let this one go. That's what usually happens on these short-term mission trips. You know how it is. We go over there, do some good for a few weeks. It messes with our minds a little, the whole culture shock thing. Coming face-to-face with the kind of suffering and poverty other people live with every day. Then we come back to the good ol' U-S-of-A with a whole new sense of appreciation for everything God has given us. For a little while. Maybe we stop grumbling . . . for a little while. In a few weeks, the whole thing fades to the margins as real life kicks in and our routines take over."

Ray had pretty much summed up his experience after every other mission trip.

"Once that happens," Ray continued, "it's pretty much out of sight, out of mind until the next time we go over there. *If* we go over there."

"But that's not happening this time," Allan said.

"Not for me. Sounds like not for you either. And I've heard from all the other guys on the team. They're experiencing the same thing. I think it's seeing all those innocent kids, seeing what their life is like. The effect is so much more powerful."

"They were at the dump again today," Allan said. "Another long day spent poking through all that garbage for something to eat." A flash went through his mind of that young boy pulling a crumpled yogurt container out of his filthy white bag, swirling his finger around inside, licking it, then looking up at Allan with that satisfied smile. Ayana's big beautiful eyes came to mind next. How had her day gone? Did she remember him? Then one more picture . . . the scene he had just left on Elderberry Lane. The Anderson clan sitting, yet again, around a large Sunday feast. Thankful, grateful to God. Their biggest concern was trying not to eat too much.

All these images happened in seconds, followed by a strong desire to hold little Ayana again. To see her at that Sunday table, maybe sitting next to Tommy and Carly. Laughing, drinking, eating. Trying to learn good table manners, acting just like cousins.

Cousins? Listen to him. But that's how the thought came to him.

"You're there now, aren't you?"

Allan looked up.

"It's been happening to me too," Ray said, "ever since I got home. Julie's starting to get a little upset. Either her or one of the kids will say something that triggers a flashback, and I'll just go back to Korah. Completely tune them out."

Allan shook his head. "It's not good. I don't want to sour Michele on this. I wish there was some way to involve her more, so that this wasn't just my thing." He took a sip of his latte. "What I really wish is that she'd come with me sometime."

"Then you'd both be staring off into oblivion, tuning each other out," Ray said.

Allan smiled. "Maybe. But at least we'd be doing it together."

"I think one way to cure this distracting stare is to do more than just think about it. We need to *do* something. That's why I wanted to get with you today. That is, assuming you're still willing to be point man on this thing."

Allan thought about some of his recent conversations with Michele. Was being the point man still a good idea? "I am, but I'm not sure I remember the details of what you had in mind." What he did recall didn't seem like it would be all that time-consuming.

"I'm thinking of you being more like the project manager.

You're good at flowcharts and organizing things. I've been making some notes since we got home. I just sent them to you as an email attachment. It's all the different things I can think of that need to be done for this orphanage plan to happen. Not things done by you, but by everybody, including me. I've also asked all the guys to start emailing you, not just me, with updates as we go. I'm mainly going to be working on the fund-raising side, which is already going way beyond my expectations."

"Really? What's happened?" Allan knew that none of their great intentions would ever come about without solid funding.

"For starters, Henok is really on top of things. I can tell he's made this job one. He says the government over there is wide open to the idea. They want to see a proposal for the whole thing. The initial plans, the long-term goals, how we expect to pay for it. He told them this project probably won't cost them a dime. He's hoping to secure some local funding, but the majority of the money will come from churches here."

"And how's that part going?"

"That's the other positive development. Joe got that video put together. I haven't seen it yet. But he said it's incredible. He's going to upload it to YouTube, so all the churches represented by team members can get an idea of what we're talking about. Our church elders are meeting this week. They've already agreed to put funding for this orphanage on the agenda, and I'm going to play the video for them at the meeting."

Allan sat forward in his chair. "They've already agreed to fund the orphanage?"

"Not yet. They've agreed to evaluate it, see if we want to make it a part of our mission budget this year and, if so, decide on how much. But I know once they hear what I have to say and watch this video, they're going to get behind this thing. Part of the reason I need you to get working on this is to help us nail down the costs. Until we hammer out a game plan, we won't know what kind of income we'll need to keep up with expenses. But God's really put faith in my heart that it's all going to come together."

This was exciting news. Allan was so glad to hear that the elders were responding so positively to this. "I think you're right. Once they see this video, how can they not want to help?"

"So what do you think? You still willing to run point on this?"

This definitely sounded doable. Ray was right; Allan was good at organizing things. He could do it in his spare time and not cut into his time with Michele much at all. Then a new thought . . . Michele had to see this video. It wouldn't be as powerful as being there, but it would make it easier for her to grasp why all this was so important to him. Allan nodded. "Sure, Ray, I'll do it."

Then he wondered if Ayana would show up anywhere on the video. He wanted to see her again. But even more, he wanted Michele to see her.

26

Christina was stuffed, which made the already bloated feeling she had just being seven months pregnant even worse. But she didn't care. Nothing could take away the excitement she felt being moments away from getting the key to her new apartment.

Her new apartment in River Oaks.

What would her mother say if she saw her now, living in a place like this? One of the last things her mother did say when Christina left her in New York with her latest boyfriend was, "You go down to Florida and I guarantee you, you'll be homeless or else a prostitute before you know it." Always a source of encouragement, her mom. But Christina didn't want to think about that now.

She walked out of the main house into the backyard and stood under a shaded patio facing a gorgeous pool. The whole backyard was beautifully landscaped, like a scene out of a magazine. To the right was the cozy garage apartment. She remembered the living room had a nice view of the pool. Looking the way she did, she had serious doubts whether she'd be using it before the weather changed and it got too cold.

Just to be able to see it every day would be something. To

be able to walk outside in the morning, every morning, and see what she was seeing now. To walk across the lush green grass and onto the stone patio surrounding the pool and sip coffee at the wrought-iron table. It would even make decaf bearable. To enjoy the beautiful garden areas outlining the pool, the tall white fence and the garage. Marilyn had said Christina could work in the garden as often as she wanted.

It was like a dream.

"You ready?"

She turned toward the voice. It was Doug. She hadn't heard the door that led inside to the apartment steps open. "You mean to get my stuff upstairs?"

"Yeah. Got my stuff all loaded into the car. I'm all yours."

Wouldn't that be nice, she thought. No, stop. "We've got to go to the front of the house. My car's parked in the street."

"I tell you what," Doug said, "how about we switch? I'm heading back to school right after this. I'll go pull my car around to the front of the house, and you drive yours into the open parking space in the garage. That way, I won't have to walk so far carrying your boxes."

"That's a great idea. But after you leave, how will I get my car in and out of the garage?"

"I'm glad you mentioned that. I'll talk to my dad. I think he has a spare garage door opener somewhere in the house. I'd give you mine, but it's built into my rearview mirror. They just plugged in some kind of code to get it to recognize our door."

"Okay." How exciting, her own garage door opener. Her car had never spent a night indoors. Of course, it hardly belonged next to the two cars in there now. But still . . . starting today, she would be parking her car in a garage.

"So I'll go move my Mazda now, and you go move your

car." Doug turned to head back inside. "But hey, if you see my dad in there, ask him about that door opener. Once I leave, you won't be able to close the big door without it."

"I will." She hurried back into the house. Tom, Jean, and the kids were upstairs. Michele and her mother were watching something on TV, looked like a Hallmark movie. She didn't see Jim anywhere.

When Marilyn looked up, Christina told her what they were doing, then asked, "Is Jim still here?"

"He just laid down for a nap," Marilyn said. "Why?"

Christina told her about the garage door opener and what Doug had said. "But I can get it later."

"He can't be asleep yet," Marilyn said. "I'll go see. Even if he is, I think I know where it is." She got up. "Could you pause it, Michele? I'll be right back. You go take care of what you need to, Christina. If I find it, I'll bring it out to you."

"I don't want to interrupt your movie," she said. "You can just leave it on the counter near the back door there, and I'll get it after." Christina walked across the living room and out the front door.

◆―◆

After they'd switched the cars, it took Doug less than fifteen minutes to carry all her stuff up the stairs. He wouldn't let her lift a thing.

"You do realize," she said, "I loaded all that stuff into my car by myself this morning. And I carried it down some rusty metal steps, not this plush carpeting."

"That's because I wasn't there," he said.

"Guess that smothering thing runs in the family," Christina said. Of course, when Doug had used that phrase earlier, he'd included the words "with love" on the end. That wouldn't quite work here. But she sure did love being treated this way. Seeing the muscles in his arms and back flex carrying those boxes up the stairs did nothing to lessen the growing attraction she'd begun to feel for him.

She knew there was nothing to it on his end. He was just raised right. All she had ever known were guys raised totally wrong.

He looked at the pile of boxes in the center of the living room. "How about I move these into the rooms where they go? Might as well put me to work while I'm here." He looked more closely at them. "I don't see any rooms written down."

"Doug, it's not that big of a project. I really appreciate your help. Seriously, I mean that. But I can take it from here." She walked into the kitchen. "You look like you could use a cold drink. I haven't had any time to shop, and I'm not sure the tenant who lived here before me left anything good in the fridge."

He laughed. "I doubt it. I heard that guy was a total loser."

She opened the refrigerator. It was empty. "Well, at least it's clean."

"Don't worry about it, I'll get something in the house when I say good-bye to my folks." He walked toward the stairwell, then turned. "Say, Christina, you don't need to answer this if you don't want to. Maybe I am being nosy like my mom said at dinner. But you were talking about that big decision you made recently about your . . . baby, when my mom cut you off. You said something about my sister, Michele, helping you make it. Mind telling me what it was? You know, whether or not you're keeping the baby?"

She didn't mind answering this question and even remembered telling him he could ask her about it later. For some reason, she wanted to know *why* he wanted to know. What

142

was fueling his curiosity? But she couldn't think of how to ask him. She walked toward him and sat on the edge of the sofa. "I don't think it's nosy to ask. I was about to tell you before. I've decided to place my baby with an adopting couple."

A surprised look came over his face.

"Did you figure I was gonna keep her and raise her myself?"

"So you know it's a girl?"

"They told me after I had an ultrasound a few appointments ago."

"Doesn't that make it even harder . . . giving it up. I mean, giving *her* up?"

"You mean, knowing it's a girl makes it seem more real, like I'm giving up a real person versus an *it*?"

"I guess. I mean, I know it's real." He shook his head. "*She's* real. I was just thinking it might make it harder to let her go."

"It wasn't a big thing for me. I mean, I know it must be for some people, the way they use words. Like calling an unborn baby *it*, instead of saying *he* or *she*. The clinic I went to before going to the one where your mom works does abortions. I didn't go there for that, just to see if I was pregnant or not. They did free tests there. They called babies *it* all the time. Either *it* or *fetus*. The unborn fetus. I hate that term. It's a baby. They use words like *it* or *fetus*, because then they don't have to face the fact that they're talking about ending the life of a person, a little baby."

Doug walked over and sat on the edge of an upholstered chair. "I was watching a video during some prolife weekend at the church. Our youth group was serving refreshments. It was a few years ago. They were showing this doctor who performed abortions, but he also delivered babies for patients who wanted to keep them. I thought that was really odd. But even weirder than that, they showed how he changed what he called the baby when he was talking with the mother, based on whether she was having an abortion or keeping the baby. If the mother was having an abortion, he called it a fetus. If she was planning to keep it, he called it 'your baby.'"

"See," Christina said, "that's exactly what I'm talking about. It's a baby. It's always a baby." She patted her stomach. "That's what's in here, a baby. Whether I keep her and raise her as a single mom or let another couple, a married couple, raise her as their own, she's always a baby."

"I like that," Doug said. "I can tell you feel strongly about it."

"I really do. And I think because I do, it was easier for me to make the decision I made."

"You mean giving her up for adoption?"

Christina nodded. Suddenly her emotions began to kick in. She didn't want them to, but she couldn't stop them. Maybe it was just the way Doug said "adoption." She hated how it sounded. But she still knew it was the right thing to do, the only thing she could do.

"Are you okay?" he said.

"Yeah. It's just, I hate being a girl sometimes. But don't think these tears are because I'm not sure I know what I'm doing. I'm totally sure. Talking with your sister helped, and seeing all these other moms at the playground with their children helped. Seeing kids who had moms and dads who lived in nice places, had decent jobs, who were ready to be parents and planning to be parents. That's what a baby needs." Tears fell down her cheeks. "That's what my baby needs. But that's not who I am now. I can't give her that."

Doug got up and grabbed a napkin off the kitchen counter, handed it to her.

"Someday, I want that to be me. I hope God lets it be me. But I want my baby to have that right away, not years from

144

now." She wiped her eyes. "She deserves to start off that way. And this way, I can give her that chance."

Doug stood up. "That's really something, Christina. And if it matters at all, I agree with you. What you said. All of it. And I respect you for it. I really do. It's probably the hardest decision a person can ever make."

— 27 —

Doug had just left. He'd said a pleasant good-bye and see-you-soon. Christina had thanked him again, not just for his help but for his willingness to move his things so she could stay there. He'd said that he was happy to help. He'd even written down his cell phone number then invited her to call if she ever needed his help again.

It was a nice and polite thing to say, but then, it really didn't mean anything. Oh sure, if she was ever in some kind of jam, she supposed Doug might come to her rescue. But he didn't say, "I'll call you sometime." Or, "Let's keep in touch." This wasn't the start of a real friendship, much less a romance.

She got up from the sofa and watched him walk across the backyard into the house. She wanted him to turn around, if only for a moment, and look up at her. He didn't. She didn't really expect him to.

It was as she thought; he was just raised right. She walked to the other window, the one facing the pool. She reminded herself that God had given her a wonderful place to live. That needed to be her focus. This wasn't a guy/girl thing. She looked down at her stomach.

Look what that got you.

◆——◆

Marilyn heard the back patio door open. The movie she and Michele had been watching was just getting good, but she recognized Doug's footsteps coming across the kitchen floor. She knew what was coming: a sad moment. His weekend visit was coming to an end. "You can keep watching it, Michele. I think Doug's leaving now." She got up to greet him.

"What?" Michele grabbed the remote and hit the pause button. "No, I'll wait."

Doug stepped into the living room. "Well, I'm all done back there. Christina's all set. I guess I'll get going."

Marilyn gave him a hug. "Thanks so much for all your help, Doug."

"No problem. She's a nice girl."

"I think so too," Marilyn said. "I really like her. She's made some big mistakes, but she's back on track now, and she's got a great attitude."

"She's definitely got a tough road ahead, but she seems up for it."

Marilyn pulled back from the hug, though she didn't want to let Doug go. "You want to take a soda with you? We've got some cans left in the fridge, ice cold."

"Thanks, think I will." He walked back into the kitchen.

"Oh, I almost forgot," Marilyn said. "There's a plate of food in there for you on the top shelf. Just some leftovers from today. Thought you could heat them up in your microwave back at the dorm. I know it'll be late by the time you get back."

"Thanks, Mom. That'd be great." He opened the refrigerator and pulled out a can of soda and a big paper plate wrapped in plastic. "It's been great getting dinners like this the last three weeks."

Marilyn stood a few steps behind him. "It's been great having you at the table again too. You know you're welcome back every weekend. You won't have to keep sleeping on the sofa bed in Dad's office. Tom and Jean will be moving into their new house soon. You can sleep in one of the beds upstairs."

Doug turned around, looking hesitant to respond. She had to be careful; she didn't want to push him away. She just loved him so much. Having him at home three weekends in a row had been so nice, but it would be like a frustrating tease if things returned to the way they were before.

"I sure do love your cooking, and it's been nice seeing you all more often." He stepped around her and headed back into the living room toward the front door.

Michele got up off the love seat. "Oh no you don't. You're not getting out of here without giving your sister a hug." She met him halfway to the door. "Mom won't say this, but I can. You only live ninety minutes away. Do us all a favor. Keep this new trend going."

"I'll try."

"Really, Doug," she said. "I know classes are starting up again. You'll go back, get back with your friends, and get busy again. But don't forget us. We're family."

"I won't."

"You won't what?"

"I won't forget. Really, Michele, I've gotta go. There's a big storm front coming in from the west. If I don't leave now, I'm going to get stuck in it."

Michele hugged him again. "All right, go on then."

He walked into the foyer.

"I'll get the door for you," Marilyn said. She hurried to get around him and opened the front door, then followed him out to the wraparound porch. His red Mazda was parked in front along the curb. "So what do you think of Christina?"

He stopped at the edge of the porch and turned. "What?"

"Christina . . . do you like her?"

"Yeah, she's nice."

"You two seemed to get along pretty well."

"I suppose so. She's pretty easy to be with. I feel kind of bad for her, though."

"Because she's pregnant?"

"Definitely that. But from things you said, it sounds like she's had a pretty rough life from the start."

"She has. That's part of the reason why your dad and I want to help her. I don't think she's ever been part of a real family before. And she's made really good progress with just a little investment of time."

"That's a pretty brave decision she's making, with the baby. She told me about it upstairs."

"I hope you know I wasn't trying to embarrass you or her at the dinner table."

"I know. It wasn't something we should've been getting into with Carly and Tommy there. But she told me the process she went through to reach her decision. I can't imagine having to make a choice like that."

"I hope you never have to. You know, her problem is . . . totally avoidable."

Doug gave her a look. "Mom, I know."

"I'm just saying . . . you know how the world is now."

"I have no intentions of getting a girl pregnant. That's one phone call you don't have to worry about getting. Okay, I really should get going." He walked to the edge of the porch and looked up. "Look, it's already starting to get dark off to the west."

"I know you have to go. Your sister thinks you and Christina would make a cute couple. If she wasn't, you know . . ."

"Mom, I can't believe you guys are talking like that."

"You think she's wrong?"

"What? Yeah, I think she's wrong." He lowered his voice. "Christina's pregnant, Mom. She's carrying some guy's baby. I don't want any part of that. So, let's be done with this conversation. I like Christina. And I know you guys are trying to help her, but I'm not the answer in this situation. I did say she was brave. She's even . . . pretty in her own way. But you and Michele gotta get rid of any ideas about me and Christina." He thought a moment. "She's going to your church now, right? I'm sure after this situation is over, she'll meet a nice guy there. Start looking in that direction."

She shouldn't have brought this up now. Obviously, she had totally misread his interest in Christina. She had to trust God for Doug, even though it was hard. There were so many temptations at school. "I'm sorry, Doug. I won't talk about this anymore. I wasn't trying to make you feel uncomfortable."

His eyes softened. "Don't worry about it. I better go." He reached forward and gave her a hug good-bye.

28

Michele was just about to call Allan when she heard a car pull up out front. She and her mom were still watching the movie, but for the last half hour, she had been pretty distracted. Allan's visit with Ray was taking much longer than he had said. He was supposed to be home by about the time they had finished dessert and coffee.

That was almost an hour ago.

When she got up, her mom said, "Do you want me to pause it?"

"That's okay. For some reason, I'm just not into this. Allan just got home. I think we'll get going. I feel a nap coming on."

"I'm feeling pretty sleepy too. Maybe it's this movie."

"That and the big dinner and the fact it's Sunday afternoon," Michele said. "Anyway . . ." She walked over to her mom. "Don't get up." She leaned down and gave her a hug good-bye. "Thanks for feeding us, again." Through the window she saw Allan coming up the sidewalk. "Well, gotta go. Talk to you soon."

She did her best to sound upbeat, but she was a little annoyed. Allan probably had a good excuse for being late. As she opened the front door, she reminded herself it wasn't a big deal.

"Hey, babe," Allan said as he approached the front steps. He noticed her purse. "You're ready to go?"

"I've been ready for almost an hour." That came out with more edge than she'd planned.

"I'm sorry. I should've called. Ray and I just got to talking, and I lost track of the time."

Okay, maybe he didn't have such a good excuse. "I'm pretty tired. I already said my good-byes." She came down the porch steps.

"Did Doug already leave?"

They headed back down the sidewalk toward their car. "Yeah. Mom's watching a movie. Dad's asleep. And Tom and Jean are upstairs with the kids. Haven't heard a peep out of them for a while."

"Maybe they're sleeping too," he said. "And Christina?" He opened her car door.

She knew what he was doing. He could tell she was upset, so he was making small talk. "I guess she's settling in the apartment. Haven't seen her since we finished coffee and dessert. Which . . . was quite a while ago." She sat in her side of the car. He walked behind the car and got in the driver's side. *Take a deep breath, try to calm down. This isn't a big deal. Don't give him such a hard time.*

He pulled away from the curb and headed toward their townhome. "Guess this isn't a good time to tell you what Ray and I talked about."

She didn't answer.

"Things are really coming together for this orphanage plan. I figured it would take months for some of the things that have already started happening. Guess I got caught up in the flow. I'd love to tell you about it sometime."

She knew he meant right now. But she didn't want to hear

152

about it right now. She also knew if she didn't hear him out, he'd keep thinking about it the rest of the afternoon and evening. It would sit on top of anything else they did. "Why don't you tell me about it now? Not all the details, just the headlines. You can talk until we get home."

He smiled. That broke the tension.

"Well, you know it's all about the kids, the ones living in that dump called Korah. Ray said all the guys are having the same trouble I'm having reconnecting with life back home. He's feeling it too. I think if you had come on this trip with me, you'd know exactly what I'm saying. They're just living every day in that place, rummaging through garbage to find something to eat. Day after day, week after week, with no hope of it ever changing. I can smell it right now just thinking about it. You can't imagine it, Michele."

And she didn't want to. "We're gonna be home before you know it. You already told me all this."

"Right, well . . . did I tell you about this guy named Henok? He grew up in Korah."

"I'm not sure."

"He's the one who brought us there, the one who told Ray about it in the first place. Anyway, Ray asked him to coordinate everything over there for us. He plans to make him the orphanage director, I think. Once it's all set up. The thing is, Henok emailed Ray a pretty lengthy update. So far, it's all good news. It looks like God is opening a wide door for this thing to happen. The local government is open to the idea, especially when they heard it wouldn't cost them a dime."

"So where's the money coming from?" Allan took care of the bills, but he always went over them with her, once a month. She dreaded the thought of their next financial chat when the tally for all these mission expenses came in. Not to mention the fact that he used up precious vacation time on these trips. Time they could've spent together.

"Our church for one," he said. "Ray said the elders are meeting this week to discuss the idea of our church making this orphanage part of their mission budget. Sounds like each of the other guys on the team are talking to their churches about the same thing. We might be able to pull this thing off with just that level of commitment. Things over there are so much cheaper. That's kind of where I come in."

"What do you mean?"

"I'm going to put together the battle plan, lay out all the different expenses involved in setting up and running this orphanage. That's part of the reason why I was late. Ray helped me hammer out all the different categories. My job is to figure all that out and give the team a bottom line. A financial goal to shoot for. Well, that's the first part of my job."

Allan's face was all lit up. She wished she could share his joy. All she could think about was how much more of his time and attention—his spare time and attention—would go to this. And how much less time and energy he'd have to spend with her.

"Is anything wrong?"

She looked through the windshield. Their street was just ahead. What should she say? "Did you even remember I have a doctor appointment this week?"

"What?"

She could tell by the look on his face, she might just as well have asked if he remembered she was taking a trip to the moon.

"I guess I didn't. Why? Is something wrong? Are you okay?"

Be careful, she thought. It's not his fault. "No, I'm not okay. There's something very wrong with me, or with you. Maybe with both of us. That's why I'm going to the doctor. We can't seem to have children, and we've been trying for over a year. Remember?"

29

That seemed to hit home.

Allan didn't respond but turned his gaze straight ahead. Michele could tell he was a little angered by what she said, but he was doing his best not to react. She didn't like fueling the tension between them, but she had to get his attention somehow. Allan couldn't multitask. He usually gave the lion's share of his heart to one thing at a time. The orphanage was clearly taking over.

They turned onto their street. Still no response. They turned down the one-lane alley that ran behind their row of townhomes. She felt pressure to say something accommodating or conciliatory but decided against it.

He pushed the garage door button, waited for the door to lift, then pulled in. After turning off the car, he turned and said, "Michele, obviously I'm not tracking with you here. I can tell you're upset with me. By the look on your face and what you just said, I feel like I should apologize. The problem is, if I did, it would just be to make peace. I don't feel like I'm doing anything wrong, and with the way you pick up on things, you'd notice that in any apology I'd try to make. So help me understand what's going on here? You know how much these African mission trips mean to me. This isn't a new thing. I've been going there since before we met and all through our engagement. I never hid from you that this is something I wanted to keep doing after we were married. I remember you even saying that it was okay, that my love for missions was part of why you were attracted to me. Do you remember saying that? Because I do."

"I do remember," she said. "And I remember meaning it when I said it."

"But you don't mean it now? You're not okay with it anymore?"

"No, that's not what I'm saying. At least I don't think that's what I'm saying."

He turned the car's ignition partly on, enough to lower the power windows. "Then what?"

What should she say? How did she really feel? "Allan, I think the problem is . . . neither of us considered we'd have a hard time conceiving children. You know how much I've wanted children. I never hid that from you."

"I want them too. We don't disagree on that."

"But in a way," she said, "we do. Not on whether we should have them, or even how many. But you seem content to just let it happen whenever it happens."

"I don't think we have much choice. We don't have any control over what's going on."

"See, I don't agree with that. There are all kinds of medical things to consider. That's what this doctor appointment is about, to start pushing those buttons, find out what's available. If there's a medical reason keeping us from having children, there might be a medical fix."

"Okay, I agree with that. But I don't see the problem. You're going to the doctor. I'm not against it or trying to stop you."

Lord, help me explain this without getting angry. "You're

not trying to stop me, Allan. But you're also not really with me in this. I don't feel your support. I feel alone, like I'm carrying this all by myself. On my radar, it's a big glowing green dot. So big it dominates the screen. I think on your radar, it's a teeny little blip. A dim light that only flickers a few moments at a time, usually after I bring it up, and then it dies out." She looked into his eyes. He was getting this, some of it, anyway. "You know what's the big green dot on your radar? The one dominating the screen?"

He nodded. "Korah."

"Right. Korah and this orphanage. Which I'm sure is a very good thing. And I'm sure those kids need all kinds of help. And I'm sure you'd do a great job helping them. And I feel totally guilty and totally selfish for even bringing any of this up. But I'm the one you married, Allan. I'm the one here every day. I feel terrible about the condition of those kids at Korah, but somehow, I feel they've taken your heart away from what I'm dealing with, and I'm not sure you understand how much I'm hurting now. I haven't been able to tell you about my own pain because I don't want to upset you or stop you from helping those poor kids."

Those rotten tears began to well up in her eyes. "And I don't want to go through this infertility trial alone. I need you to care about this too. Maybe not as much as me, but a whole lot more than you seem to care about it now." She opened the glove compartment and pulled out a napkin.

He reached across the seat and took her hand. "You have no reason to feel guilty for anything you just said. The kids living in that dump are not more important than you are and what you're going through right now. Not to me. I know it may not seem like that right now. Not by the way I've been acting since I got home."

158

He paused, as if thinking through something he wasn't sure how to say. "Some people might think orphan kids eating decent food is a whole lot more important than whether you and I are having problems getting pregnant. But I don't believe that's how God operates. Jesus said the Father knows when a sparrow falls to the ground. He knows how many hairs are on each of our heads. He's got the capacity to care just as much for those kids as he does for you, Michele, and what we're going through here with you trying to get pregnant. I'm the one with the capacity problem. I've gotta figure out a way to care about more than one thing at a time. But I don't seem to know how to do that."

She dabbed the remaining tears in her eyes. "I love you, you know. With all my heart."

"I know," he said. "I love you too. I guess I just need some help figuring out how to love you the right way."

"This is helping," she said.

"Do you mind if we finish talking in the house?" he said. "I'm really starting to heat up sitting here."

"Yeah, let's go inside."

He closed the windows and they got out of the car. Once inside, she saw his countenance change. "What's the matter?"

He set his keys, phone, and spare change on the hutch where he always put them. "It's just . . . at the meeting I had with Ray, I kind of agreed to do all kinds of things to help get this orphanage thing going."

"You know I'm not asking you to drop that, right?"

"I was kind of thinking that was the point of this whole conversation."

Michele laughed.

"What's funny?"

"You. The way you think. You really can't see yourself juggling both of these things at the same time."

"I guess I can't. I haven't been able to so far."

"Well, you're in luck."

"Why?"

"Because you're not a single guy. Because you married me. Remember that thing we learned in premarital counseling, about biblical roles? You know, between men and women."

"I remember we spent one session on that. But I remember the outline was quite a few pages. What are you thinking about?"

"I'm thinking about what God meant when he told Adam that he was bringing Eve to serve as his helper. Remember what the pastor said about that not being what most people think? That God didn't intend for Eve to be Adam's little helper, like some junior assistant. By calling Eve his helper, God was pointing out how much Adam *needed* the help. And that was part of what God meant when he said it's not good for man to be alone. You, my love, are not alone. You've got gifts, and I've got different gifts. And in this situation, my gifts can help you be able to do the things you told Ray you would do. And still have room in your heart to care about me and help me with this infertility challenge."

He put his arms around her. "I like the sound of this *helper* thing. But I don't see how you can fix my problem. I think I'm hardwired this way."

"You are, on your own. But you're not on your own. Not if you let me help you."

"What do you have in mind?"

"I'm going to put on some coffee while you go up and change that sweaty shirt."

He looked down at it. "I think I need a quick shower."

"Even better," she said. "When you come back down, I'll have the coffee ready. We'll sit down at the table and work out a plan. I think what you need is to make time compartments for these things."

"Time compartments?"

"I'll explain more after your shower. The idea is to block out time for the important things and actually write them into your calendar. That way they don't sit around inside your head and clutter things up. We'll figure out how much time you can safely give this orphanage project, and your job will be to live inside the boundaries we set. It's like how we budget the money, only with time." She reached up and kissed him. "Now go get your shower."

"What about your nap?"

He released her, and she walked toward the kitchen. "I'm not tired anymore."

~ 30 ~

Thanks for walking with me," Michele said.

It was four days later, late morning on Thursday. Michele had called in to the school, but they didn't need her today. But she wasn't discouraged. She'd had a wonderful quiet time going over a chapter in the children's ministry notebook Julie had given her last Sunday. She'd been reading it every morning for the last few days and was getting a lot out of it.

"You know me," Jean said, "always looking for an excuse to get out of the house." They walked through a shaded park about midway between Elderberry Lane and Michele's townhome. Jean pushed little Abby in a stroller; the baby was sound asleep.

"Is my mom watching Tommy and Carly?"

"No, they're actually in this little preschool I found. Just till noon. They go three times a week."

Michele continued down the sidewalk. "Well, the reason I wanted to see you is this notebook, the one I talked to you about on the phone. In a way, it's rocking my world." Michele wished she had it with her so she could read some of the things she'd underlined that morning.

"Really? A children's ministry book?" Jean said. They reached a corner in the sidewalk and turned to the right.

"Let's see if I can explain it. This whole curriculum is based on four basic commands. The idea is that there are four main beliefs every Christian should know and own, and these beliefs flow out of four commands. Two of the four are about love. Love God, love others."

"Like what Jesus called the two greatest commandments," Jean said.

"Exactly. I've read those verses and heard teachings on them lots of times. I don't know if I'm just in a different place now or if the stuff in this notebook is just saying everything in a different way. But it feels like I'm reading something brand-new. I wanted to run it by you and see what you thought."

Just up ahead, the trees ended and so did the shade. "Do you mind if we turn around before we reach there?" Jean said, pointing with her eyes. "I don't have any sunblock for Abby."

"Not at all. It's starting to get pretty hot out here anyway."

"So what about the stuff sounds new?"

"For starters, I always thought loving God and loving others were just things I was supposed to do, commands I was supposed to obey. Not that I obey them all the time, but I'm supposed to. It's my job, as a Christian, I mean."

"And this notebook says . . . that's not true?"

"Not exactly. But it says I need God's help to love him and love others the right way. On our own, we don't have the power to pull it off. Including something as basic as loving him and others. That's what humility is all about. Being honest about our weakness and being willing to ask for God's help. Humility makes it possible for us to receive God's grace, and it's that grace that gives us the ability to love the way we're supposed to."

They walked a few steps. Jean didn't respond. Then she finally did. "Wow."

"I know," Michele said. "Doesn't that change things for you? It did for me. It made me think about why I'm not such a loving person."

"Don't say that," Jean said. "You are too."

"No, I'm really not. Not lately anyway. I know I'm supposed to love. And sometimes I try to be loving. But if I'm being honest, it's a lot of work. And I think, for the most part, I'm mostly focused on myself. Like this whole getting pregnant thing. I've been obsessing about this for months. Really, almost a year."

"I wouldn't say obsessing."

Michele stopped walking and looked at her sister-in-law and friend. "Jean . . ."

"Okay, maybe you were obsessing."

"*Were* obsessing?"

"You're not obsessing now," Jean said.

They started walking again. "Okay," Michele said. "Maybe not now but every single day—sometimes every hour of every single day—until this morning. And I've been totally stressed out by it. Which is another new thing the notebook talks about. New to me, anyway."

"It talks about stress? In a children's ministry book?"

"In the part to the parents it does. It connects loving God with living completely free of stress."

They reached the same corner of the sidewalk as before, but this time they turned left. Jean shook her head. "Don't think I've heard that before. Go on."

"The idea is, when we're loving God wholeheartedly— which grace helps us to do—we're finally putting him in the highest place in our hearts. He becomes the object of supreme

164

value. And we start looking to him to meet our deepest needs instead of to other people and other things. And he does. He's the only one who can. Our tendency is to expect things from his creation that only he can give us. When I read that, Jean, I just froze. I think I do that with Allan all the time. I think I'm doing that with this pregnancy dilemma. I've gotten to the place where I can't see myself ever being happy, not until I have a baby. And since that's not happening, and we have no idea when it will, I'm doomed to be constantly miserable. Miserable and stressed out." She was feeling stress just repeating all this.

They came up to a bench situated midway through the park along the sidewalk. Michele sat.

"I think I do the same thing," Jean said. "At least I used to. I still do sometimes, but I think I'm getting a little better at trusting God since our world fell apart last year. That was our overwhelming situation, kind of like you're having now with this baby thing."

Michele was trying hard to remember something she wanted to say. "There was something else I read that got to me. I underlined it twice. What was it? It was something about what causes stress. It was really simple . . ." Then it popped into her head. "I know—the author said stress is the gap between what we expect from God's creations and what we're actually receiving. Since only God can meet our deepest needs, the more we look to people and things to satisfy us, the more gaps we'll have and the more our frustration will increase. Doesn't that seem true to you?"

"It makes total sense to me," Jean said.

"That's how loving God with all our hearts reduces stress. The more we look to him as the only one who can make a difference, the less we look to things that can't truly help us.

The stress goes away because the gaps get closed. God fills our hearts with more love and joy and peace while we wait for our circumstances to get better. With our stress and anger no longer controlling us, we get freed up to care about others instead of always thinking about ourselves."

Jean just looked at her a few moments.

"What?" Michele said. "What are you thinking?"

"I'm thinking . . . that's pretty profound, what you just said. I'm thinking I want to read that notebook."

"So this kind of seems new to you too?"

"Kind of," Jean said. "Not like it's some weird new doctrine. I just never heard it put that way before. It's so simple."

Michele's phone rang, startling them both. Even little Abby began to stir. Michele looked at the screen. "Hmm, that's different."

"Who is it?"

"It's Christina. She just texted me. She wants to know if we can meet this afternoon. She says she wants to talk about something pretty important."

31

Come on in, Christina." Michele stepped back from the doorway to let her in. "That's a cute outfit."

Christina walked down the hall past the doorway leading into the kitchen. "Thanks. Your mom took me shopping at the Women's Resource thrift store."

Michele closed the door and walked past Christina into the dining area. "I know where that is. I volunteered there a few months last summer."

Christina patted her stomach. "I'm getting down to the final stage where nothing fits. I start working at the gift shop this weekend, the one where your mom works."

"Odds-n-Ends," Michele said.

"That's the one. Your mom thought I should have some clothes that didn't look ridiculous on me."

Michele pointed to the dining room table. "I made us some decaf, and this is some crumb cake left over from last night. You can drink decaf, right?"

"I can. Drinking that's been one of the hardest things about being pregnant. Well, that and getting in and out of the car."

Michele laughed.

"I miss my afternoon coffee," Christina said. "I get so sleepy right about . . . now."

"Do you ever take naps?"

"No. I just want this baby to come already, so I can start drinking coffee again." She poured herself a cup. "Thanks for making it, though. That was thoughtful. And this crumb cake looks almost like the kind I used to get in New York."

"That's real butter, in case you're wondering," Michele said. "It's fattening, but I like putting it on the sides."

"I won't tell if you don't," Christina said.

After they fixed their coffee and cake, they moved into the living room. Michele couldn't tell by Christina's demeanor whether she came to talk about something positive or negative. She didn't seem tense.

Christina squirmed a few moments then seemed to find a comfortable position. She took a sip of her coffee and said, "Before I tell you why I'm here, I want you to know I haven't talked to anyone else about this, not even your mom. I know she's my counselor, or advocate, I guess they call 'em, and for the most part, she's been really helpful. But after you hear what I'm gonna say, I think you'll understand why I couldn't talk to her about this. I didn't want to put her in the middle."

That got Michele's attention.

"I prayed a lot about this. I'm still a young Christian, but I gotta go with my instincts, what my heart's telling me to do. And I felt like I'm supposed to talk to you first, before anyone else. I'm not saying that God's saying you've got to say yes to what I'm asking. I want you to. But honestly, I really can't tell if you're supposed to say yes. I've got no instincts on that. I'm thinking, God might speak to you or maybe Allan, not to me."

Michele took a sip of her coffee, attempting to quiet her growing tension. She wished Christina would get to the point.

"Look, I'm sorry. I'm all over the place here. I always do

that when I get nervous. You're not making me nervous. What I've got to say is making me nervous."

Michele was getting nervous now too.

Christina reached for her crumb cake, sliced off a corner with her fork, then stopped. "What am I thinking? I can't eat. Maybe after I get done talking."

"You mind if I do?"

"Not at all. It looks delicious, by the way."

Michele took a bite of the crumb cake, trying to break this tension Christina had introduced into the room.

"Okay," Christina said, "here goes. I'm at a point in my pregnancy where I have a decision to make."

"I thought you already made that decision," Michele said.

"No, not that one. You're right, though. I did make that decision. According to the adoption agency, though, I can change my mind whenever I want."

"Are you thinking of changing your mind?"

"No, not at all. I don't know why I brought that up. The thing is, so far I haven't taken very much assistance from this agency. Less than a thousand dollars, I think."

"Do you have to pay them back, whatever they give you?"

"No, I don't. They made that real clear in the beginning. In fact, if I go through everything, all the way to when the baby's born, and I change my mind, even then they'll still pay for everything. In fact, the woman at the agency said it happens to them all the time. And whenever it does, the birth mom is off the hook. Totally. She said if they made us pay the money back after we change our minds, the courts would say we only went through with the adoption because of money pressure. And that would nullify the adoption, because the decision was made under—what did she call it—*duress*."

"I guess I see that logic," Michele said.

"I figured out that's one of the reasons why adoptions are so expensive," Christina said. "The adoptive couple, the ones who actually get to adopt, wind up paying for all the deals that fell through. Well, *deals* isn't the right word. But you know what I mean."

Michele thought she did. But she still had no idea where Christina was going with all this. "If you don't mind me asking, Christina, what does all this have to do with me? I'm not really seeing—"

"You're right, I'm going into way too much detail. I'm sorry. I should have spent more time in prayer. Maybe I'd have a little more self-control right now. It's just, this is a really big thing."

What is?! Michele screamed inside her head.

Christina stopped, repositioned herself on the couch, took a sip of her coffee, then took a deep breath. "Okay, the thing is, like I said, I haven't taken too much money from the adoption agency. So if I quit them now, I wouldn't feel too bad. It's nothing compared to the amount of money they'd lose if I quit them after the baby was born. You know, if I changed my mind. But still—"

"Why would you think of quitting them?"

"I wouldn't, unless you said yes to what I'm about to ask. Don't give me an answer right away. I'm sure you're going to want to talk to Allan anyway, because it's such a big deal. See, what I've been praying about, what I want to ask you is . . ." Tears instantly appeared in Christina's eyes. "I was afraid this was gonna happen."

Michele quickly got up and fetched a box of tissues from the hutch. She was dying inside.

Christina dabbed her eyes, took another deep breath. "I'll just say it. I'm wondering if you and Allan would want to adopt my baby? After this idea came to me, I looked into it a little bit. If we didn't go through the adoption agency, we could do something they call a private adoption. The big thing with that is, it doesn't cost hardly anything compared to working with an agency. There's just the hospital bills, some lawyer fees, and that's pretty much it. I certainly wouldn't charge you anything. I wouldn't want to make a dime off this." Christina reached for another tissue to stem the tide of a new release of tears.

Michele didn't know what to say. She hadn't expected this at all. Her initial reaction was to say "no, thank you," right here, right now. She still had her heart set on having a baby the old-fashioned way. But she also wasn't ready to say anything now because of the new things she had been learning from the children's ministry notebook. She could tell Christina had something else to say.

"The main reason for this idea is because of my baby, and me thinking about what's best for her. This time I've spent with your family has been like a dream. I didn't even know there were families like this, not in real life. I can't think of a better set of parents than you and Allan. I would have loved to have someone like you for a mom. And if my baby could grow up here, in a place like this"—she used her hands to include the whole downstairs—"with people like you, and have grandparents like your folks, and aunts and uncles like Tom and Jean. What could be better than that? Nothing could."

Christina stopped talking. Now she was looking at Michele's face, staring right into her eyes. Michele had no idea what kind of signals she was sending. She didn't feel anything deep or profound. Mostly she felt . . . confused. She had no idea whether this sudden development was something God was doing or just some fantasy Christina was having.

Christina reached for another tissue. "The way I feel about your family is the hardest part of this whole thing."

"What do you mean?"

"Leaving you all. I know that's what I would have to do if you said yes. It would be way too awkward for everyone if I stayed around. I read about these things they have called open adoptions, where the birth mother keeps hanging around to watch the baby grow up. That's not for me. I'd want to make a clean break, let my baby bond to her new parents, and them with her, without any interference from me. And that would mean . . ." The tears began to flow again. "No more Anderson family for me."

Michele instantly thought about some of the things she had read that morning, about loving God and loving others. What Christina had just offered to do was a perfect example of sacrificial love, a mother's love. God's love.

Now it was her turn to reach for the tissues.

— 32 —

Christina had left Michele's home that afternoon with Michele's heartfelt gratitude for even considering her and Allan worthy of such trust, and with her assurance that they would talk over Christina's offer that night and pray together for God's guidance.

Since then, it had set so heavy on her heart. She could hardly get her head around it; it was such a big deal. She'd actually called Allan to see if he could come home early so they could talk, but he couldn't. He was working with a client right up until five. She'd told him they had something important to discuss, big enough to put dinner on hold when he got home.

He was upstairs getting changed now. Allan had suggested they take a walk. Something about a walk just made listening and thinking easier to do. She got up from her chair when she heard him coming down the stairs. "It's really nice out right now," she said.

"I could use some fresh air," he said. "I hate being shut up in the office all day." Half of Allan's time was spent out in the field. He opened the front door for her. As she walked past him, he said, "So, what's this big news? I can't tell by the look on your face if it's good or bad."

They walked down the sidewalk, holding hands. "It's not really a good or bad kind of thing. It's just very unusual. Potentially life-changing."

They reached the end of their walkway. "Which way do you want to go?" he asked.

"Doesn't matter." They turned right, started walking up a slight incline.

"You're not going to keep me guessing."

"No, I won't do that. I had a visit from Christina today. She texted me this morning saying she wanted to talk about something important."

"Did she come to the house?"

"She did. I wasn't at all prepared for what she had in mind. She wanted to know if you and I want to adopt her baby."

"What? Really?"

Michele nodded. "She's totally serious. She said she's given it a lot of thought. And prayed about it too."

"What brought this about? Do you know?"

"I guess she's reached some fork in the road with the adoption agency she's working with. She hasn't used very much of their money yet, but that's about to change. She said she'd feel guilty if she let them pay for some of the big-ticket items coming up and then pulled out of their arrangement."

"So if we did this," Allan said, "we wouldn't be going through her agency?"

"No, if we did that, it would cost us just as much as anyone else."

"So . . . we'd be doing, what, a private adoption?"

Michele nodded. "I don't know what that involves, since I haven't been looking into adoption, but I guess you just agree to pay the hospital costs and some attorney fees. Whatever it is, it'll be a fraction of what it costs going through an agency."

They walked in silence a few moments. "This really is big," he said. "Bigger than when we decided about the house."

She squeezed his hand. "I know. I did a little checking after she left. If we decide to do this, we'd have to do it soon. There's all kinds of things we'd have to get started on. Lots of paperwork, sign up for a home study. All kinds of things."

"So you're thinking seriously about this?"

"Well . . . yeah."

"I thought you were pretty much against the idea of adopting, until we'd gone through all the medical solutions to you getting pregnant."

"I thought so too. I'm still kind of leaning in that direction, but now I don't know. What if this is something God wants for us? It's so out of the blue. Maybe God put the idea in Christina's heart. If he did, I don't want to shut it down because it doesn't line up with my plans. And when I think about how much it costs to adopt the normal way . . ."

"I've heard over twenty-five-thousand dollars," Allan said.

"Exactly."

They made it to the stop sign at the end of their block. "Want to keep walking?" he asked.

She responded by tugging his arm to the right. There was a nice shady park at the end of the next street. They walked past two more townhomes without a word.

"It's so hard to know what to do," Allan finally said.

"I know."

"This wasn't even on my radar."

"One thing I can tell," Michele said, "Christina's 100 percent committed to placing her baby with an adoptive couple, no matter what. If not us then someone else." Michele thought about one other thing Christina had mentioned. "And she said something else that almost broke my heart."

"What?"

Michele thought about that moment again. "Sometimes I take my family for granted. Even with all our problems, you forget when you've had something all your life, how much it matters to someone who's never had any at all."

"What did she say?"

"She thought about what it would be like—how awkward it would be—if you and I adopted her baby, and she stayed right here like she is now."

That seemed to hit Allan. "Yeah, I guess that would be awkward."

"She thought that through and said she knew if we did this, she'd have to leave our family for good. She'd even move out of the state, so she wouldn't be in the way. She was crying as she said it."

Allan shook his head. "That's pretty heavy. She really loves it here, loves your folks especially." They walked a few more steps. "That would make it pretty hard for me. Thinking we were responsible for basically putting her in exile."

"I don't like that part of it, either. But if I'm being honest, and we decided to do this, I'd be glad she's willing to do something like that. I know it works for some people, but I think it would be hard for me to bond with an adopted baby if the birth mom was constantly involved."

"Is that your gut instinct? You think we should do this?"

She sighed. "I don't think I have a gut instinct about this. Since Christina left this afternoon, I've been spending about ten seconds at a time, going back and forth between being thrilled and scared to death."

Allan laughed, took a deep breath. "I think I'll be joining

you on that roller coaster in a few minutes. This isn't the kind of thing you figure out. And it's not like there's a Bible verse that speaks to it, none that come to mind anyway. We're just going to need to pray, really pray, and ask the Holy Spirit to make it clear. To give us the wisdom to know what to do, and to give it to us in a way that we can understand. When does she need to know by?"

"She didn't say. Just soon."

He looked up ahead. "There's that nice park. Let's aim for the bench under that big oak tree. I don't see anyone around, so let's just sit there and give this whole thing to God. It might take a little while for us to discern what he wants us to do, but I'm confident he'll make it clear."

Michele liked this. It was great being connected with her husband again.

33

Over the next two days, Michele and Allan talked and prayed about this issue. A lot. They hardly talked about anything else. Michele had confided in Jean but no one else. Not even her mom. She hated hiding anything from her mom, but Allan felt they needed to respect Christina's wishes on this. Christina didn't want to bring Michele's mom into the discussion unless they felt pretty certain they were going to say yes.

Michele looked at the digital clock on the microwave then stood and peeked through the window to see if Allan's car was coming down the alleyway. It was Saturday, but he'd gotten called in to work. She didn't know why she was so nervous. Standing there, she thought back to their dinner conversation last night. Allan said he had been searching through the Scriptures for guidance but, for the most part, came up short. He found lots of verses that spoke of God's willingness to direct their steps in general, which did encourage him. Several Scriptures reminded him how highly God viewed adoption, even using the metaphor of adoption to describe how Christians become his sons and daughters.

But Allan couldn't find anything that helped him know for sure whether or not *they* should adopt Christina's baby.

He'd concluded by saying, "I think this is something we're going to hear in our hearts, not our heads. Like I said before, let's both commit to really listen to the Holy Spirit over the next twenty-four hours, and ask him to give us both the same answer."

So that's what they did. They stopped talking about it the rest of the night.

Michele spent most of today getting caught up on housework, which kept her mind occupied. Throughout the day, though, she kept whispering little prayers, asking the Lord to make his will clear.

While she ate lunch, her mind had begun to wonder and dream. When Christina had first shared the idea, Michele was so overwhelmed that it hadn't occurred to her how close Christina was to delivering her baby. Five weeks. That was all.

Which meant, if this idea was from God, Michele would have a baby placed in her arms five weeks from now. She would be a mom. Her torment would be over. On one level, the thought thrilled her. Imagine, not having to wait nine months for a baby but five weeks. Not waiting who-knows-how-long to get pregnant. For that matter, what if it wasn't even possible for her to get pregnant? What if they learned one of them had some physical problem that shut the door completely?

But if this adoption opportunity was from the Lord, she and Allan could have a family now. Well, five weeks from now. But that was hardly any time at all.

This daydream of adopting Christina's baby went on for some time. But it didn't last. As much as she'd wanted it to, it just wouldn't stick. She was more aware of this strong undercurrent in her heart that kept sweeping the images away.

Sometimes with a big decision, her mind would create a pros-and-cons list, and she'd involuntarily go over each side in her head. This wasn't like that. It was like standing in front of a door you desperately wanted to open, but the knob just wouldn't turn.

She heard a noise and looked out the window again. It was Allan; his car had just pulled into the garage. He'd called her on his way home. She had begun to explain things to him but didn't get very far before he was interrupted by another call he had to take. He said they'd talk as soon as he got home.

◆ ◆

"Let's talk outside," Allan said. "Seems like it's cooled down enough." He led Michele out to the covered patio. He was so glad to finally get to talk to her about the things going on inside him, but he was nervous at the same time. What if he'd heard wrong? What if he'd missed what God was telling him? The stakes were higher in this situation than almost anything else they had faced together.

As they sat, he reminded himself that they had prayed for God's wisdom, for God to speak the same word to both of them. It was time for Allan to trust God and share what he had received and hear what Michele had to say.

"You look like you had a rough day," she said. "Anything go wrong?"

"Not really. I think it's just this adoption thing. It's such a big deal. How'd your day go?"

"It was fine. Kept my mind occupied with housework."

"So, does that mean you didn't get time to wait on the Lord?"

"No. I had a good quiet time this morning after you left. Short but fruitful. I prayed off and on throughout the day. I kept waiting for, I don't know, some powerful moment where the Lord would make it so clear, I couldn't possibly miss it."

"That didn't happen?"

"Not exactly."

"Did anything happen . . . to push you one way or another?"

"Oh yeah," she said. "It was just a lot more subtle than I was expecting."

He reached for her hands. "So tell me about it."

"You go first."

He really didn't want to. What he had to say wasn't good. Well, *good* wasn't the right word. What if Michele had heard the opposite message? She seemed so vulnerable right now. The last thing he wanted was to cause her more stress and pain. "Do I really have to? I'd really like to hear what you have to say."

"Allan . . . c'mon. You can just tell me. You're the man. You're supposed to lead."

He took a deep breath. "Okay. But listen, if we didn't get the same direction on this, you don't have to—"

"Allan, just say it."

"I don't think we're supposed to adopt Christina's baby. There, that's it. I can't really tell you why. On paper, it makes perfect sense to say yes. There's no good reason not to say yes. The first part of the day, for most of the morning, I was very positive about it. Whenever I had a spare moment to think, I'd daydream about how our lives would change if this happened."

"I did too. Were they pleasant daydreams?"

"Oh yeah. I loved them. By lunchtime, I was sure the answer was going to be yes."

"Then what happened?" A curious smile came over Michele's face.

Her smile puzzled him. "Then . . . throughout the afternoon, I became aware of something else going on inside. I don't know how to explain it. But it was like I felt this certainty that we shouldn't do this. That we're not supposed to. Then I found myself wrestling with that. But I couldn't shake the certainty. And I realized, I wasn't wrestling with the answer I felt God was sending but with what it would do to you. How much you'd be disappointed."

Her smile grew slightly wider, and her eyes moistened.

"Then when I got in the car to come home, before I even started the engine, there it was. Not an audible voice, like someone sitting in the backseat. But almost. This thought came into my mind as clear as a bell. *This isn't the child I have for you.* I don't know how to describe it, but I knew instantly it was the Lord." He choked up as he said the last part.

Michele's eyes now welled up with tears. But Allan got the sense he wasn't seeing sorrow. "So tell me your story."

"It's amazing. That's all I can say. God is amazing." She slid her chair back and stood. "I'll be right back. I don't know how I thought we could have this conversation without tissues." She walked into the house, leaving the patio door open.

A few moments later she returned. "I had almost the exact same kind of morning. And almost the exact same kind of afternoon. It was like all the joy about doing this completely evaporated. Somehow I knew in my heart, it wasn't going to happen. It wasn't *supposed* to happen. Instantly I could tell, all those happy thoughts and dreams of becoming a mom in just a few weeks were just fantasies. And yet, instead of feeling sad, I felt total peace. Then you know what else happened?"

"What?"

"Even though I knew it meant Christina's baby was not for us, it didn't make me sad. Somehow I also knew there was something else God wanted me to know . . ." She could barely say the next part. "He has *another* child in mind for us."

34

"Come on in, Christina." Allan stood back from the doorway. Michele stood a few feet behind him. After they had reached the decision a short while ago, Allan took the lead and initiated this visit with Christina. Michele was glad. She couldn't imagine handling something like this by herself. He had called Christina, asking her to come over for coffee after dinner.

Michele turned back toward the living room, heard their footsteps following behind her. "I have a fresh pot of decaf made and some cookies. Would you like some?" she asked Christina. She already knew Allan would.

"That would be great, thanks."

"You two go sit down in the living room, I'll bring it out." As she prepared the coffee, Michele was surprised to find she wasn't nervous at all. And she didn't detect any tension on Christina's face. She walked the coffee, cream, and sugar out to them on a tray.

Christina looked at both of them as she stirred half-and-half into her cup. "I guess you guys made a decision about the baby, right? That's what this is about?"

"You like to get right to it," Allan said.

"I'm from New York," Christina said, smiling. "I don't have a choice."

Allan sat forward in his chair. "You're right, that's why we wanted to meet. How have you been the last two days, since you and Michele discussed this?"

"I've been all right. A little edgy but not too much."

"You're five weeks from your due date, right?" he asked.

"That's what they tell me."

Allan sipped his coffee. "Before I say anything else, Christina, Michele and I want you to know how honored we are that you would consider asking us to do something like this. I really mean that. It's a huge thing."

"You're welcome. But after getting to know you, it was an easy decision to make."

"And Michele told me, as part of that decision, you were even willing to move, to leave the Anderson family and River Oaks altogether."

Christina nodded. "I'd want to make it as easy on you as possible. Not just on you but your whole family. I'm the kind of person who'd have to be all in or all out. I think it would be way too awkward if I hung around."

"Michele also told me how much you've grown to love this family, and how hard it would be for you to leave."

Michele looked into Christina's eyes. That got to her. But she held it together.

"I get that," Allan continued. "It's rare these days to find a family as close as they are." He looked at Michele. "I love being a part of it."

"Me too," Christina said. "Well, I'm not really a part of it. Not like the two of you."

"You are a part of it, Christina," Michele said. "I know,

for my mom, you're not just someone she's helping at the Resource Center. She cares about you, a whole lot. I don't know you the way she does, but I already understand why."

"And since you want us to get right to it," Allan said, "I guess one way to say this is . . . you're not going to have to leave the Anderson family once your baby is born."

Michele looked at Christina. It took a few moments for what Allan said to sink in. But it did.

"So you're not going to adopt my baby?"

Allan reached for Michele's hand. "No, we're not. But we'd love to. And I'm not just saying that. Both of us had some wonderful daydreams today as we thought about it. On many levels, it doesn't make any sense for us to say no."

Michele was curious now. She wasn't sure how Christina was doing, but she could tell this news didn't crush her like she thought it might.

"But on one level, it did make sense to say no?" Christina asked.

Allan laughed. "No, that's not what I mean. That's just an expression. It didn't make sense to say no on any level."

"Do you mind telling me how you knew?" Christina asked. "How you knew you weren't supposed to say yes?"

Allan did a good job gently explaining the process they went through to help discern God's will. It only took a few minutes, and Christina listened intently. Still, when he finished, she didn't seem upset about the decision or even show any signs of discouragement on her face.

"Do you have any questions?" he asked.

"I don't think so. I couldn't say it as good as you, but I did ask the Lord to prepare me for whatever your answer was gonna be. I think he did. It wasn't like anything I heard. Not like a voice or anything. But as time went by, especially after you called to invite me here, it's like I already knew what you were going to say."

"I'm so relieved," Michele said. "The last thing I'd ever want to do is hurt you."

"That's nice of you to say."

"Earlier this afternoon," Allan said, "I decided to call the adoption agency you're working with. I didn't tell them about anything we're discussing. I just asked for some information about the kind of screening they put couples through before they approve them to adopt a baby."

"They went over all that with me," Christina said.

"It's a pretty extensive process," Allan said. "I was impressed."

"I know. I'm sure that's part of the reason why I'm not freaking out right now. They're really careful about who they give babies to."

"Yes, they are."

Michele was impressed that Allan had done this. He hadn't mentioned it to her before now. But it was just like him to be so thoughtful, to think through the possible fears and insecurities Christina might have when they said no.

"So you know your baby is going to be placed with a couple that has a very stable Christian home."

"I know," she said. "I think what happened was, whenever I thought about where my baby might end up, based on the stuff they were telling me, I kept imagining her being with someone just like you two. And then something clicked in my head on one of those times, and I thought, why not *you* instead of a couple like you? I remember you telling me, Michele, that you really weren't interested in adopting the first time we spoke back at the playground. But I thought I had to give it a shot."

"Well, we're really honored you did," Michele said. "And you're right, I did say that when we first talked. I still want to try to have a baby the old-fashioned way. Allan and I are going to look further into what that might involve, medically speaking. But I learned something about myself through this situation."

"What's that?"

"When faced with the very real possibility that I could be a mother very soon, I realized I wanted to say yes. It didn't matter to me that the baby wouldn't be mine. You know what I mean, by birth. For hours, I kept thinking about how wonderful it would be to have a child to care for as my own, and I knew right then, it didn't really matter to me if that child came naturally or through adoption. That was a real breakthrough for me. I don't know what God has for Allan and me down the road, but you've helped my heart get to a much better place."

— 35 —

Four Weeks Later

"You poor thing. You didn't have to come in today." Marilyn looked at Christina waddling through the back door of Odds-n-Ends. The store hadn't opened yet.

"I know. I wanted to." She took a few steps down the hall then stepped left through a doorway to set her things down on the lunchroom table.

Marilyn walked her way. As she came closer, she caught a glimpse of Christina's side view. Over the last four weeks, she had gotten so big. "You still have one more week left, right?"

"Six days to my due date, but I think it's gonna be today. Look at my feet. I couldn't even put my shoes on. You think Harriet's gonna mind?"

Marilyn looked down at Christina's flip-flops. Her ankles had completely disappeared. "She won't be in until noon. But I'm sure she'll be fine."

Christina looked up at the clock. It was just a few minutes before nine. "I'm not sure I'll even last till then. I hardly slept at all last night, again."

"Let me guess, multiple trips to the bathroom?"

"Felt like every thirty minutes. I had to sleep almost sitting

189

straight up to relieve the heartburn. It's awful. And the pressure in my lower back feels like the baby doesn't know where the door is."

Marilyn laughed. "You feel her all the time now, I bet."

Christina nodded. "I've been feeling something else this morning too."

"What's that?" They walked into the open store.

"I'm pretty sure I'm starting to have my first contractions."

Marilyn turned around. "Really? Are you sure? You know about Braxton Hicks contractions, don't you?"

Christina nodded, wincing as the baby kicked her left side. "These aren't them. I've already been having them. I read all about it on the internet this morning, and about how the real ones feel. I'm starting to time them to see how far apart they are, but I lost track driving over here."

"They're that close?" Marilyn asked.

"About ten to fifteen minutes apart. I had one while driving and had to pull over until it stopped." She looked at her watch. "So another one is due any minute."

"Christina, oh my goodness. Has your water broken yet?"

"No."

"Come over here and sit down." Marilyn led her to a chair behind the counter. "I'm going to call Michele, see if she can stay here with us. I don't think she's teaching today."

"No, don't do that," Christina said. "I don't want to bother her too soon. Maybe we should wait until they're closer together."

Marilyn walked back to the lunchroom to get her phone. "I won't ask her to come right away. But I'd still like to call her, give her a chance to get ready. She insisted I call her the minute you went into labor." She came back into the store. "This way she can be ready to come whenever we call."

"So, you think I'm in labor then? Officially?"

"I think you could be. We'll know in a little while for sure. If those contractions keep coming, if they come more often and more intense."

Christina slid a small box over and propped her feet on it, then rubbed her stomach. "Were any of your babies early?"

"Doug was, just about a week early, like this. Both Tom and Michele were late. Tom, one week. Michele almost two. Here," she said, lifting her phone. "Let me call her now. I have to unlock the front door in a few minutes."

"It was stupid of me to come," Christina said. "I can't work in this condition. I think I was just afraid of being alone."

"Don't worry about it. But that's why I want to call Michele. I can't leave the store until Harriet gets back at noon. If you need to go to the hospital before that . . ." She found Michele's number and pressed the button. Michele picked it up on the third ring.

"Hey, Mom, what's up?"

"I guess since you answered this, you're not teaching today, right?"

She heard Michele sigh over the phone. "No, I'm not. So far I've only taught twice in the last week."

Marilyn remembered Michele telling her they had started a baby fund in their savings account. All of Michele's school money would go into it.

"So, what's up? Are you home or at work?" Michele said.

"I'm at work. I'm here with Christina. We're about to open in a few minutes. The problem is, it looks like today's the day. I think she's starting to go into labor."

"Really?" Michele squealed into the phone. "She's in labor now? Has her water broken?"

"Yes—and no, to the second question."

"I'll be right there. I just need to get a few things together."

"No need to rush. I just wanted to give you a little heads-up, that it definitely seems like it's going to happen today. We thought you probably don't need to come down until the contractions are ten minutes apart."

"Where are they now?"

"Closer to fifteen." She looked over at Christina, whose face was all contorted. "Are you having one now?"

"Feels like it."

"We still have a ways to go," Marilyn said into the phone. "I just wanted to call you so you'd be ready and not go out shopping or anything. If it's in the next three hours, I can't go with her. There's no one else to watch the store."

"Well, I'll start getting ready so I can leave as soon as I hear back from you."

They said good-bye and hung up. Marilyn looked at Christina and wondered if she felt excited or something closer to dread as this moment arrived.

She had one more phone call to make on Christina's behalf. Something Christina had asked her to do as a favor— to call the adoption agency for her when the labor pains started. Marilyn was happy to do this and understood why it might be a challenge for Christina to do it herself. But there was another reason, a much bigger reason, for this phone call.

Typically, this was the day when most birth mothers who consented to adoption changed their minds. They may have wanted to place their baby in a stable home and may have even agreed to do this on paper. But the truth was, the counselors had to be very careful not to pressure the young mothers into feeling this was their only choice, even after they'd made it. The laws were written to protect the mothers' freedom to change their minds after the baby was born. Marilyn didn't know the statistics, but it happened a lot.

Christina had insisted that she would not change her mind. She believed God had made it clear that the couple she had chosen from the files to adopt her baby were the ones God had picked to raise the baby as their own. She was so certain of this that she wanted to break protocol and have the agency call the parents when she was brought to the hospital. They couldn't take the baby home right away, but she wanted them to know it was happening, so they could get ready. She had learned a lot about them, though she didn't know their names or even where they lived.

She hoped they lived in Florida or somewhere close, so they could see their baby right after she was born. And then be able to take her home the moment the law allowed.

Marilyn walked up to the counter and looked at Christina. "Want me to make that other call, the one to your adoption agency?"

"What?" Christina said, repositioning herself on the chair.

"Michele can join us as soon as we give her the word. But I wondered if you wanted me to call the adoption agency now, to let them know what's happening?"

"I forgot all about that. Definitely call them, if you don't mind."

"You sure you're ready? You don't have any doubts at all, now that the contractions have started?"

Christina looked directly in her eyes. "I'm totally sure, Marilyn. God's put total peace in my heart about this. I know this is the right thing to do."

"Okay, then, if you're sure." And she dialed the number.

— 36 —

Michele had just hung up the phone a few minutes ago, after a quick conversation with her mom. Now she was in the car and so nervous. Christina's contractions were ten minutes apart. It was happening. Today really was going to be the day.

She said a prayer for Christina as she backed out of the garage. They had become very close over the last four weeks, and Michele's respect for this young woman had grown deeper. She had never known anyone in a "crisis pregnancy," had never really pondered the physical and emotional challenges they faced. It was a scary time.

So many young women of her generation, millions, had chosen the easy way out when they had gotten pregnant unexpectedly. Michele had forgotten how many abortions were performed each year, but the number was staggering. There were so many, because it was so easy.

But Christina had said no. No to herself and yes to her baby.

A few days ago, Michele had asked her, now that things were getting so close, did she have any regrets about going through with the pregnancy. "Not one," Christina said. "I won't lie to you, it's been a lot harder than I expected. But my baby's not gonna pay for my dumb mistakes."

No, she wasn't. And Michele had no doubts, either, about Christina changing her mind today, once the baby was born. She would put that baby in the arms of a nurse, and they would take her away. Christina would probably cry, but then with a heart full of faith, she would entrust her baby's future to a young couple not that much different from Michele and Allan, and entrust her daughter into the hands of God.

Michele felt emotional now as she thought about it.

Lord, help me be a good friend. Help me not to lose it completely when I see Christina. Help me to share with her your encouragement and a sense of how very proud you are of the young woman she's become.

◆ ◆

Michele pulled into the parking lot of the River Oaks hospital and stopped her car under a section of shady tree limbs. The hospital was an attractive facility built with a Mediterranean flair. Theme-park-worthy landscaping lined the walkways. She was hurrying through the front door to get directions on Christina's whereabouts in the building when she bumped into her mom heading the other way.

"How's she doing?" Michele asked.

"Pretty good for someone in labor. I wish I could stay."

"How far apart are the contractions now?"

"I think I heard about eight minutes. She's in there now, getting a pep talk from one of the nurses. They've got a great staff here. No one's treating her like, well . . . you know."

"How's she doing . . . emotionally? Now that it's really happening?"

"Very well, as far as I can see. I'm sure it'll be hard when the moment comes to actually . . ." Her mom paused, as if she couldn't bear to say the words. "Let's just say, I think Christina's got a lot more courage for something like this than I would have. Have you called Allan?"

"I have, but he can't get off work. He wanted to, but he's got a job out in the field. He was driving there when I called."

"So you're going to be by yourself?"

"I'll be fine."

Marilyn looked at her watch. "I better get back. Harriet's all alone in the store, and it's almost the lunch hour. You call me if anything happens."

"I will."

"I get off at five. I'll come right over after that."

They hugged and parted ways. Her mom had given her directions to Christina's room. When she got there, she was told Christina was still talking with the nurse. She mentioned she was there as Christina's birthing coach, and they led her to a comfortable chair next to the bed. A chair Michele figured was normally used by anxious husbands.

She probably wasn't as anxious as they were, but now that she was here, she was feeling pretty tense. She wondered how Allan would do when the time finally came for them to share a room like this.

They had been doing well over the last four weeks. Allan especially so. He had made good on his decision to shift his focus from all-things-Africa to supporting their efforts to start a family. She knew he was serious when he had moved all the money from his mission's savings account to a new "Our Child" account he'd set up to cover the significant expenses they would incur. And he agreed that all of Michele's teaching money could go into the fund. Every single penny.

That wasn't all. They had agreed he would devote only one evening a week to the new orphanage project for Ray. Several times, Allan worked on his computer until well after midnight, but he kept that boundary line in place. She was proud of him, and this restriction didn't seem to hurt his ability to fulfill his commitment to Ray. That morning at breakfast, he'd told her he had finished the orphanage proposal and sent it off to Ray for final review.

He was so pleased. Not just that he'd finished the proposal but that he had been able to keep his heart in check this past month. He'd gotten everything done for Ray and had still kept their relationship in first place the whole time. "I have, haven't I?" he'd said.

It was so sweet. This little boy look came over his face when he'd said it. Michele was glad she could say, "You definitely have, hon. I'm really proud of you."

Her cell phone rang, startling her. She looked at the screen. It was Jean.

"So Christina's in labor? I just read it on Facebook."

"Who posted it?" Michele asked.

"Christina. Looks like from her phone. Maybe twenty-five minutes ago."

"She definitely is," Michele said.

"Are you with her now?"

"I haven't seen her yet. But I'm in her room. She's talking with the head nurse in another room. I guess she's explaining everything to her. They told me they'll be bringing her in any minute."

"How far apart?"

"The contractions? Mom said eight minutes."

"Is your mom there?"

"No, just me. And Christina. Mom just dropped her off.

She had to get back to the store. She won't be back until after five."

"You think she'll have the baby before then?"

"I guess it's possible. You'd probably know better than me. You've done this three times."

"It's hard to say," Jean said. "The first one's always the hardest to predict. You could be there all day today and still be there tonight."

"I hope it's not that long."

"Wish I could be there with you, but Mom's usually my babysitter during the day."

"I'll be all right. Christina's the one with the hard part."

"Well, call me if you have any questions. And definitely after the baby's born."

"I will."

"And tell Christina we love her. The kids and I are praying for her."

Michele hung up and was just about to put the phone back in her purse when it rang again. This time it was Doug. Why was he calling?

"Hey, Michele, it's Doug."

"I already knew that."

"So Christina's gone into labor. I just saw it on Facebook."

"It definitely looks like today is the day."

"You know how much more time she has left? Before the baby comes, I mean?".

"Not really. It could be a couple of hours or anytime between then and sometime tonight."

"Good. Then I've got time."

"What do you mean?"

"I'm coming down. Christina and I have become pretty good friends on Facebook, and we send each other emails every now and then. I just want to be there to support her. I think it's a pretty brave thing she's doing."

Wow, this was unexpected. "I think so too. Are you hoping to get here before the baby comes?"

"Not so much then. But after, when, you know . . ."

"She has to let the baby go?" Michele choked up saying it.

"Yeah, then," Doug said.

— 37 —

It was almost five o'clock. Allan was getting ready to go home, then he realized Michele wouldn't be there. She was at the hospital with Christina. He picked up his phone to call her.

"Hello? Allan?"

"It's me. Just calling to check on things, see how you're doing. How's the labor coming along?"

"I'm with Christina now. The contractions are a lot more painful than they were, and they're about five minutes apart."

"That means it's getting close, doesn't it?"

"Closer, but they told us it still could be several more hours."

Guess that meant he'd be eating dinner on his own. "Are you hungry? Can I bring you something to eat?"

"Thanks, but we already have that covered. Mom gets off at five, and she's going to pick up something on the way."

"You need anything from the house?"

"I don't think so."

"How's Christina doing, you know, emotionally?"

"Amazing so far. Hold on a minute. Let me just step out-side into the hallway." Allan heard the phone rustle then a pause. "It must just be God's grace. I think I'd be a wreck if I were in her shoes. But she seems to be doing fine. Are you on your way home?"

"Almost. I'll be leaving in a few minutes."

"Sorry I won't be there."

"Me too, but it's for a good cause. I'll pick up something on the way home. Don't worry about me. I'll be praying for you guys."

"Especially for Christina."

"Right. Love you much."

"Love you too," she said. "I'll call you when I have news."

After he said good-bye and hung up, the phone icon on his cell indicated a missed call. He clicked it and saw it was Ray. He clicked again, and the phone began ringing. "Hey, Ray, it's Allan. Just calling you back."

"Thanks, Allan. About quitting time for you, isn't it?"

"I'll be heading out the door as soon as we're done talking. What's up?"

"Just wanted to thank you for that proposal you sent this morning. It was perfect. I mean that literally."

Wow, perfect. Literally perfect. Allan wasn't sure he'd go that far, though. "Glad you liked it."

"I spent all morning on it, then used it during several phone conversations this afternoon. But I'm not kidding about the perfect remark. When I got to your bottom line, I could hardly believe my eyes."

Allan wondered if Ray thought he'd come in too high. Ray was looking for a specific figure showing how much they'd need to operate the orphanage the first two years. That was the amount the government of Ethiopia wanted to see before they'd give their full permission. "Did the amount make you happy or disappointed?"

"Extremely happy. You're not going to believe this. You know our church is getting behind this in a big way. Just last night I got the final tally from the other churches. Guess how much it came to?"

"Are we close to my bottom line?"

"Not close. We surpassed it. By four thousand dollars."

"We raised thirty-nine-thousand dollars?"

"Can you believe it?" Ray said. "I just got off the phone with Henok in Ethiopia. I've never heard him so excited."

"So it's official," Allan said. "We're really going to do it?"

"I believe we are. Isn't God great?"

"He certainly is." Instantly, Allan pictured little Ayana's face. They had only budgeted for six orphans initially. Eventually they hoped the project would grow to include hundreds. But Ray had already said he would do everything he could to make sure Ayana was one of those first six children. "What's the next step?"

"Well, now that we have your budget proposal, which proves we've already raised enough money to get started, job one for me tomorrow is to plan another trip over there. When Henok got over the shock of hearing all the money we raised, I asked him what he thought the next step should be. He's been interacting with his contact person in the government constantly. He told me he's using the persistent widow approach to keep this thing in front of them. He said they would definitely need to see somebody from America over there soon, someone who could confirm everything he's been saying. To prove the money's real. I told him to go ahead and set up that meeting next week, and as soon as he had the dates confirmed, I'd book a flight."

"That's wonderful, Ray. I imagine they're going to want to see some of that money, not just hear you talk about it. Have you thought about that?"

"No, that's a good point. I'll shoot off an email to Henok, see if he can get them to nail down some specific amounts for some of the up-front fees and expenses. I see you have a category for that in your proposal. How confident do you feel about that number?"

"It's a pretty solid guess. I contacted several other mission groups working in Ethiopia. Those numbers are based on an average from what they told me. The one thing that's not included is a bribe fund. No way to come up with a number for that."

"Is that something we're likely to run into?"

"Hopefully not. Only one of the groups I talked to did. It's hit or miss over there, depends on the people you wind up working with."

There was a pause. "Well, we're just going to have to pray God gives us officials with integrity."

"Where are the monthly pledges at so far?" Allan asked. According to his figures, they needed to reach two thousand dollars a month for the first year. A shockingly low amount if the same project were undertaken in the States. They might need to raise that much each week.

"We're there," Ray said. "And one of the churches still has another presentation to make this Sunday. I know we need to start small, get all the bugs worked out, all our legal ducks lined up in a row. But I don't think we'll be stuck at six children for long."

"That's great news, Ray. You've really made my day."

"Well, you made mine when you sent me that proposal this morning. Know how you can make my day even better?"

"How's that?"

"Say you'll go to Africa with me next week."

Why hadn't Allan seen that one coming? He took a deep

breath, steeled his resolve. It was so hard to say no to Ray. Part of him really wanted to go. "I can't this time, Ray. There's just no way."

"Can't get the time off so soon from the last trip?"

"No, it's more than that. I should've talked to you about this sooner. We probably need to grab a lunch together for me to explain it properly. It has to do with me and Michele. You know we talked about how hard it's been for us to get pregnant."

"You been trying for over year, right?"

"Yeah. It's hard to explain. But Michele's been feeling kind of . . . well, *unsupported* might be the right word. I've been giving all my energy and interest to these Africa trips, really, since we got married. I've been spending a lot of money on them too. It turns out, a lot of the infertility things we may need to do aren't insured, so we're going to need to start tucking money away for that."

"I get it, Allan. No need to apologize. You're doing the right thing. I just love your company, and you've been such a part of this thing from the beginning."

"I'd love to come, Ray. Take some pics for me."

"I will."

"No, I'm serious. Me or one of the guys usually takes pics on these trips. If you go by yourself, you'll forget. It's not just for me. This is a historic moment for the orphanage. We've got to get some pictures."

"Okay, I'll do it."

Allan thought a moment. "Maybe you should teach Henok how to use the camera."

38

Marilyn arrived at the hospital around 5:30, carrying some takeout from Giovanni's for her and Michele. For most of the afternoon, it had been hard for Marilyn to keep her mind on her work. She wanted to be here. As she walked the halls toward the birthing room, she felt as tense as she had for all three of Jean's babies.

She was also carrying a small wrapped box tied with a pink ribbon and bow. Just a little gift for Christina she'd bought with her employee discount at Odds-n-Ends. Something to ease the pain Marilyn knew she'd be experiencing a few hours from now when it came time to release the baby. Although she totally agreed with Christina's decision, she couldn't imagine being able to go through with it, if she were facing the same challenge at that age. Or any age, really.

Before she'd left to come here, she and Jim had prayed for Christina over the phone. Both of them had cried a little. It was hard to accept the fact that they would never see Christina's baby girl, or hold her, or even hear her cry. But now she needed to be strong for Christina.

She found the room and knocked gently on the door before going in. The room was pleasantly decorated. Gave the appearance of a large River Oaks bedroom more than a hospital room. Except, of course, the hospital bed. Christina appeared to be blowing or panting in response to Michele's instructions. Beads of sweat gathered across her forehead. "How far apart now?" Marilyn asked.

"Still five minutes," Michele said. "But they're more intense now." She reached for a washcloth, rinsed it in some water, then wiped Christina's forehead. "You're doing just fine."

"I brought you some fettuccine alfredo. But you're busy. I'll set it over here on the nightstand. You can nibble at it when you get a break."

"Thanks. I really am hungry. We won't make you sick if we eat, will we?" she asked Christina.

"I don't think so. I'm not hungry at all. You won't even tempt me."

Marilyn set her to-go carton down with Michele's. She didn't feel right eating by herself.

After Christina finished her heavy-breathing episode, Michele held a styrofoam cup up to Christina's lips. "Take a few ice chips. We don't want you getting dehydrated."

"Did they give you any idea how much further you had to go?" Marilyn said.

Christina shook her head. "I hope it's not too long. Everything I read said your first labor is the longest."

"It was for me." Her first, Tom, took almost twenty hours. But she didn't want to tell Christina that.

"All I know is, there's no way I'm going through this again unless I'm married and bringing the baby home. This really hurts. I can't imagine the pain getting worse."

Oh, it will, Marilyn thought. It was time for the distraction. "Here." She pulled the gift out from behind her back. "Just a little something for you."

Christina's eyes opened wide, and she smiled, no trace of pain on her face for the moment. "What is it?"

Marilyn handed it to her. "Open it, before the next contraction comes."

Christina reached for it and quickly began to unwrap it. Beneath the paper was a white cardboard gift box. She slid her finger across the front, breaking the Scotch tape. She gasped with delight as she looked inside. "I can't believe you got this." She lifted out a Precious Moments porcelain angel figurine. "It's way too expensive."

Marilyn had watched Christina pick up this angel many times in the store with obvious desire. Then she'd turn it over and look at the price and instantly set it down. A few days ago she had asked, "Know the next time the Precious Moments figurines go on sale?"

"I love it, Marilyn. Thank you so much."

"It's so cute, Mom," Michele said.

Christina spun it around slowly. "Here," she said, handing it to Michele. "You better take it. I may fling it across the room when the next contraction hits."

"I have something else that I hope will cheer you up," Marilyn said. "Jim and I talked about this several days ago. I've been meaning to talk to you since then, but we kept missing each other. And now you're here."

"And now I'm here. What is it?"

"How would you like to keep renting the garage apartment, for good?"

"You mean, I don't have to move out when I come home from the hospital?"

"Nope. You can stay and live there as long as you want."

"Really? But what about Doug? Won't he want to come back and live there himself?"

Marilyn shook her head. "Already called him. Since Tom and Jean moved into Audrey Windsor's house last week, he said he'd be fine staying in one of the upstairs bedrooms when he comes home."

Christina smiled. "You sure about this?"

"We're sure. Christina, you're like family now. I haven't thought of you as my 'client' for a long time. I know a few days from now, we'll wrap up our official relationship at the Women's Resource Center. But I hope we keep meeting as friends for years to come, and I hope you feel free to talk to me about anything you're going through, big or small."

Christina didn't say anything. "Could you hand me that box of tissues?" she asked Michele. "I'm crying way too much these days for a New Yorker." After she dabbed away her tears, she said, "Marilyn, you're like a mother and a good friend all wrapped up into one. After Megan left to take care of her mom, I was actually thinking of quitting the center. I didn't think I'd ever meet anyone I liked as much as her. But now I think meeting you might be the main reason God brought me to that center in the first place." Suddenly, Christina's face contorted in pain. "Here comes another one."

"Breathe," Michele said, reaching for Christina's hand. "Just like that. Breathe with me."

~39~

Michele was exhausted. Five hours had gone by, the last three spent coaching Christina through hard labor. But the baby was born strong and healthy—a little girl, weighing seven pounds, four ounces. The nurse had just taken her out of the room for some reason. Michele had forgotten why. But the baby was okay. Everyone was saying she was just fine.

Christina looked totally spent. She had done a marvelous job. As hard as the labor was, God was kind to allow the baby to come so soon. Two hours ago, when she learned this was Christina's first child, one of the nurses said they should be prepared for this to go all night. Michele didn't see how either one of them could have made it that long.

She patted Christina's hand, and she opened her eyes. "Will you be okay in here for a little bit, if I go out and see Mom and Jean?" Both of them had been in the birthing room right up until the actual delivery began. Then they had to go to the waiting room.

"I'll be fine. You go ahead. And thank them for coming." Her eyes closed as she was talking

"You just rest now." Michele slipped out.

The waiting room was just down the hall. When she walked

through the doorway, her mom and Jean stood. Michele had already texted them right after the baby's first cry.

"How's she doing?" Jean asked.

"She's resting. I wouldn't be surprised if she falls asleep."

"Where's the baby?"

"Down the hall in the other direction. The nurse told me what she was doing, but I forgot. Mind if I sit down? I feel like I'm going to fall over."

"You look awful," her mother said. "Not awful. You know what I mean. Wiped out."

"That was the hardest thing I've ever been through," Michele said. "And I wasn't even the one in pain."

"When your time comes," Jean said, "I think that'll become the new hardest thing you've ever experienced. After Tommy was born, I remember telling Tom that I would never go through that again. After a while, you forget about the pain and you've got to have another one. I said the same thing right after Carly was born. Right there in the delivery room. 'Tell me we're done, Tom,' I said. 'Promise me we're done.'"

They all laughed. Then something Jean said repeated in Michele's mind. *When your time comes.* Would her time come? When? In a month? In a year? Two years? Five? No, she had to stop this. It was just the exhaustion talking.

"Do you know what the plan is?" Jean asked. "I mean . . . with the baby? Is Christina going to see her, or will they take her right away? That's an awful thing to say, but . . . do you know?"

"I don't know," Michele said. "We didn't really talk about it."

"I know," Marilyn said. "I don't think Christina would mind me telling you. She doesn't have any other family here."

"Speaking of family, did you call her mom in New York?" Jean said.

210

"I asked her if she wanted me to," Marilyn said. "She said no. I don't think she's bitter. It's just that her mom is totally out of the picture. It's hard for me to fathom a mom writing off her child like that. But it doesn't sound like they've had any contact since Christina moved to Florida. Christina said she sent her a bunch of letters in the first few months, but her mom never got back with her. It's a really rough situation. She mentioned once she had an older brother. He moved out to California, but she hasn't seen him in years. She's not even sure he's out there anymore."

Michele couldn't imagine what Christina's childhood must have been like. Not to mention going through the ordeal she just experienced without any family to support her. "Well, she's got us now."

Just then, their pastor, Ray, walked in. "How's Christina doing? Allan texted me a little while ago that she just had the baby."

"She's doing fine," Michele said. "So's the baby. I'd take you in to see Christina, but she's sleeping. She had a pretty rough time."

"I'm sure she did," he said. "Poor thing. I don't want to disturb her. I just wanted to stop by, see if there's anything I could do. Besides pray, I mean. We're already doing that."

"I think we're okay for now," Marilyn said. "We'll tell her you stopped by."

"Do you know what will happen with the baby? Will Christina be able to see her? I've never been involved on this side of an adoption before."

"I was just about to tell Jean and Michele. Christina asked to see her just one time after the dust settles, alone. Of course, that's allowed. She could see the baby much more than that, if she wanted to. But she thought it would be too hard to see her more than once. She asked that the adopting couple be allowed to take the baby home with them as soon as the doctors give the okay."

"Can they do that?" Ray said.

"In Florida they can. Different states have different laws on this. But from what I understand, the adopting couple is here in the hospital, in another room. I'm pretty sure they know the baby's been born. If the doctors approve, they'll probably get to hold her very soon. Christina can't sign the consent forms until she's ready to be discharged. They want to make sure she's free of any medication. But she's told me, she wants to do it as soon as they say she can."

Jean sighed. "I can't even imagine the pressure she's going to feel when they give her that form."

"I'm not sure she will," Michele said. "Every conversation we've had about this, she's been totally settled about it."

"I agree," her mom said. "She's shown amazing resolve. But that doesn't mean it won't be incredibly difficult to say good-bye to her baby."

"I'm sure you're right," Ray said. "We'll really need to keep her in prayer and give her lots of encouragement, especially over the next few weeks. Well, I guess I'll go then. Please give her our love and tell her if she'd like to get with us, with Julie and me, we'd be happy to meet with her."

"I will, Ray," Marilyn said. "Thanks again for coming."

Ray was barely out the door when they heard a commotion in the hall. Ray was talking with someone in a loud but friendly tone. After a few moments, Michele heard him say, "Well, it's good to see you again. Let me get out of your way."

A moment later, her little brother Doug walked into the waiting room.

40

"Doug, what are you doing here?" Marilyn asked.

"Is that a problem?"

"No, of course not. I just wasn't expecting you." She hurried over and gave him a hug.

"He called me earlier," Michele said, "and told me he was coming. I forgot to mention it."

"Has she had the baby?" he asked.

"She did, a little while ago," Marilyn said. "Everyone's fine."

"Where is she now?"

"She's in her room, just down the hall," Michele said. "The baby's in with a nurse. They're just doing some routine things."

"Come on over and sit down." Marilyn led the way, and everyone sat in the padded chairs.

"Has she seen the baby?" Doug asked.

"For just a moment, right after she was born," Michele said. "But they're going to bring her back in a little while, I think, so Christina can say . . . good-bye." Tears formed in Michele's eyes. In the next moment, everyone got a little teary, even Doug. But he turned his head away, just once, as if willing the tears away.

"That's going to be so hard," Jean said.

213

Times like this, it was nice being a guy, Michele thought. It was so much easier for Doug to gain control of his emotions. She looked at her mom. "I'm not sure what to say when I see Christina. Do I tell her what I'm really thinking or do I try to think of something distracting to talk about? Did they give you any training on this?"

Her mom thought a moment. Regained her composure. "I think the best thing is just to take our cues from Christina. None of us really know what she's going through right now. But it seems obvious God is giving her grace for this. I don't think it's a good idea to try and guess how she's doing, then think of comforting things to say based on those guesses. Let's just let this play out a little, let her help us be the kind of friends she needs right now. If she says she doesn't want to talk about something, just let it go and give her some room."

"That sounds like great advice," Jean said.

"Yeah, thanks, Mom," Doug said. "When can we see her?"

"I don't think we can go in as a group. That'll probably just overwhelm her. Let me go find out where things are at now. I think they'll tell me because I'm her mentor at the Resource Center. You can come with me, Michele, since you're her birthing coach. We'll come right back after we find out some news."

They walked down the hall toward the nurses' station on the right. Michele stopped briefly when they got to Christina's room. She peeked in the little window. Christina was there, but not with the baby. Her eyes were still closed. Michele said a quick prayer and rejoined her mom, who had begun to talk with one of the nurses. By the time she reached her, the conversation had ended.

Her mom stepped away from the counter and turned toward Michele. "Apparently everything is all set. The doctors have checked the baby out, and she appears to be perfectly normal and healthy."

"Thank God."

"And Christina is doing very well too, considering all she went through. It was actually a fairly short labor for a first baby."

"It didn't feel very short. So what's going to happen now?"

"They're going to bring the baby back to Christina for a few minutes, so she can . . . you know, be with her for the last time."

"Should one of us go tell her? I peeked in the window. She might be asleep."

"You can go ahead. I'll go back to the waiting room and tell Jean and Doug what's going on." They started walking back down the hallway. Her mom said, "I asked the nurse to let us know when Christina was done visiting with her baby, so we could go in and see her."

When they got to Christina's door, Michele said, "Pray for me."

"You know, you don't need to say very much right now."

"I know," Michele said.

She opened the door quietly. As soon as she walked in, Christina's eyes opened.

"Hey, Michele."

"How do you feel?"

"Beat up. I feel all beat up. But they told me to expect that."

"You don't look beat up. My mom and Jean are in the waiting room. Doug's here too."

"Doug came?" She instantly started messing with her hair. "Oh crap. I don't want him to see me like this."

"Why? You look good."

"You know lying's a sin, right?"

Michele laughed. "I mean for someone who just delivered

a baby." She looked around the room, saw Christina's purse on a short counter in the corner. "You have a brush in there?"

"Yeah. Will you get it for me?"

Christina brushed her hair as best she could. Michele had suspected that Christina had feelings for Doug, and this pretty much confirmed it. Doug had denied he had any feelings for her in a conversation with their mom, insisting they were just friends. But Michele had to wonder, considering that Doug would leave school in the middle of the week and drive here at night to see her. They could barely get him to drive home most weekends.

"He's not coming in now," Michele said. "I'm just checking to see if you're ready to see your baby." *Please, God, help me say the right things.* She took a deep breath.

"So soon?" Christina said. "I thought it would be awhile before they ran all their tests."

"I guess that's a good thing. It means she's perfectly healthy."

"That's a relief." She finished brushing her hair. "Could you take this?"

Michele took the brush and walked it back to Christina's purse.

"I guess I'm ready. As ready as I'll ever be."

"Then I'll go tell them." She smiled feebly and walked toward the door. Christina looked so small and frail and young. Michele stopped, her hand on the doorknob. "We'll be praying for you down the hall. People in the church will be praying too. Ray stopped by while you were—"

"The pastor?"

Michele nodded. "He said he and Julie would be praying for you tonight."

"That was nice of him to do that, come all the way here to see me."

216

They looked at each other for a moment. Michele was glad to see how well Christina was doing, but she was also trying to suppress a tinge of jealousy in her heart. She'd give anything to switch places. Not to be going through what Christina was facing, but to have a baby she had just delivered right down the hall.

Christina sat up a little straighter, evened out the wrinkles in the blanket and sheet. "Guess you better go get them, tell them I'm ready to see the baby."

— 41 —

Michele had just left. Christina was alone.

She closed her eyes and prayed for strength. She needed to do this. Not for legal reasons. She didn't have to see the baby again. When they had taken her away at birth, things could have ended then. She could have begun shutting down her emotions, shifting her focus forward. Trying to pretend this whole ordeal had never happened.

People did that. They called it denial. It was a powerful thing. Just keep lying to yourself long enough and hard enough and you can silence all the emotions connected to anything you didn't want to deal with.

But she knew that wouldn't do. Not for her, anyway. This was a moment that needed to happen. A memory she needed to make.

There was a knock on the door. She tensed, opened her eyes, and looked up. The door opened and a nurse walked in. Christina glanced at her arms. She wasn't holding the baby. Christina breathed again.

"Are you ready for . . . your special visitor?" the nurse asked.

"Trying to be. No, I am. You can bring her in."

"She's right out here in the hall. Another nurse is holding her. Just wanted to make sure you were ready."

Christina shifted in her bed. "Okay."

The second nurse came in holding the baby. Christina could just see the pink crown of her head poking out of the blanket. The nurse was also holding a white envelope.

"Here she is." She came around the bed and placed the baby in Christina's arms.

For a few moments, she didn't look at her baby but at the two nurses' faces. Afraid if she did, she'd start crying in front of them.

"How much time would you like?" the nurse asked.

"Just a few minutes."

"Well, here's the remote. Just press that button and one of us will be right in. I'll set this envelope here on the nightstand."

"What is it?"

"It's a letter from the baby's new parents. You can read it now or later. Even take it home and read it if you'd like."

"They're here, right?"

The nurse nodded. "Down the hall, in a different waiting room."

"Did they get my letter?"

"They did."

"Have they seen the baby?"

"They have. That's what you wanted, right? That's what we were told."

"Yes, definitely. That's what I wanted. Were they excited when you brought her in?"

"Excited, thrilled, speechless . . . lots of tears."

The other nurse added, "The mom said she couldn't believe this day had finally come."

The mom. She called her the mom. That was good. That's

who she was. Christina was glad they were so excited. She thought about Michele and how excited she would be when her day finally came.

They stood there looking at each other. Finally, the nurse said, "Well, we'll leave you two alone. Just push that button when you want us to come back."

"Okay."

And they left.

For the first time, she registered the weight and warmth cradled in her arms. She looked down into the baby's precious face and just stared, taking in every feature. Her eyes were closed. Her cheeks pink and pudgy. Her tiny left hand was pulled up under her chin. Christina reached her finger down and touched each of the baby's miniature fingers. The baby instantly grabbed hold of Christina's finger and squeezed.

"Look at your little fingernails," she said. "They almost don't even look real."

It was hard to believe this tiny little person had been living inside of her up until a short while ago. She reached down along her legs until she could feel the balls of her feet through the blanket. How long was she? She'd forgotten. "No bigger than a breadbasket," she said aloud.

That phrase floated up from somewhere deep in her memory. It was something her older brother was supposed to have said the day she was born. He'd walked around their neighborhood on Long Island, telling it to housewives out hanging their clothes on clotheslines. Her mother had told Christina this years ago, back when they used to talk to each other. "You probably won't ever meet your uncle," Christina said. "Or your grandmother."

Then she thought a moment about the Andersons. She had prayed her baby would go to a family like theirs. She looked at her daughter again. "I bet God's going to give you lots of uncles and lots of aunts. Nice ones. Ones that will hug you when they come over, and pick you up and spin you around. Ones that will remember your birthday and bring you presents and cards that play funny songs when you open them. You'll have lots of cousins and live in a nice neighborhood. A safe neighborhood. One where your mom won't have to worry about you all the time."

She had just said "your mom." She was looking at a baby she had just given birth to and thought of someone else as her mom. But that was a good thing, wasn't it? She glanced at the white envelope on the nightstand. Her baby's mom had written it. She felt an urge to read it, to connect with this woman she was about to give her baby to. She wanted to make sure everything she had just promised her baby was true.

Tightening her hold with her right arm, she reached for the envelope with the left. It was a little tricky, but she managed to break the seal and tear it open. She began to read.

Dear Christina,

I know we haven't met, and based on your wishes for a closed adoption, I realize we may never meet. But my husband and I wanted you to know how incredibly happy you've made us, entrusting us with this precious little girl. We've been trying to have a family for so many years. It's a long and complicated story, so I'll just say this . . . I had almost given up hope that I'd ever become a mom. But you have made our greatest dream come true. We already love this little girl with all our hearts, and we'll do our very best to care for her and provide for everything she needs.

We both come from big families with lots of brothers

and sisters. My husband and I are the only ones on both sides who don't have children yet, so she'll already have plenty of cousins to play with. All four of our parents are still living (they even live near us), so she'll be properly spoiled by them. A huge party awaits our arrival home.

We also want you to know we've done lots of reading and had lots of conversations with people who were adopted and are now adults. Looking for the best way to handle this information with our little girl as she grows up. The best advice seems to be to raise her with the knowledge that she is adopted and help her realize how special her story is, but also to let her be the judge of how much or how little detail she wants to know, when she's old enough to make that decision.

We've already picked out her name. The agency has asked us not to mention her first name in this letter, but they said it would be okay to tell you that we've decided to give her your name, Christina, as her middle name. So, in a way, you will always be a part of her life. Considering the age we live in, we both think your decision to have this baby and to place her in a home like ours is such a brave and courageous thing to do. We will raise her with the knowledge of the amazing sacrifice you have made.

> *With God's Love*
> *in Our Hearts,*
> *Your Baby's New*
> *Mommy and Daddy*

Okay, reading this letter now may not have been the greatest decision. Tears were pouring down Christina's cheeks. She dropped the letter and wiped her eyes so she could see her baby clearly, and talk to her one last time before she pushed the button to get the nurse.

She bent down and kissed her baby on the forehead. "Did you hear that?" Her words were halting and broken through the tears. "Did you hear how much they love you, my little darling, and what a big family you're going to have? See, I couldn't give that to you, but they can. That's what you deserve. A mommy and a daddy who are ready right now to love you and take care of you. I'm not ready to be the mommy you need. One day I hope God gives me another chance. I've made so many mistakes and so many bad decisions, but I know God has forgiven me . . . for all of them."

She kissed her baby again. "But you're not a mistake. You are a treasure. You're proof that God can make beautiful things even when we get everything all wrong. He's made you, my sweet little girl, just the way he wanted to."

She decided to pray for her. "Lord, thank you for letting my baby be born healthy and safe. Thank you for answering my prayers about the family she'll be going home with. I put her in your hands now. Take good care of her. I know you will. In Jesus's name, amen." She wanted to say more but knew she'd fall apart if she did.

Wiping her eyes again, she kissed her baby's forehead one last time and held her close. "God picked out the perfect mommy and daddy for you." She couldn't say any more, so she reached for the remote and pressed the button for the nurse.

42

She had to stop crying.

The baby had been gone for almost five minutes. She'd asked the nurse to let Marilyn and Michele have a chance to see her before taking her to her new parents. That would also give Christina a little time to pull it together.

The thing was, she wasn't really sad. She wasn't sure where the tears were coming from. She'd actually felt something pretty close to peace inside. From within that peace, she felt a sense of assurance that everything would be fine, that her baby was in good hands and that God would take care of her from now on. It was like the tears had a mind of their own, like they were going to come and keep coming until they were done.

As she reached for another few tissues, she decided to stop trying to shut the tears down. A knock on the door. She looked up. A head popped in. A hand waved.

It was Doug.

She didn't want him to see her like this.

"Okay if I come in?" He was still standing by the door in the shadows.

How could she say no? She sat up straighter, dabbed her eyes again, tried blinking her tears away. "I guess so."

"If you're not ready, I can give you a few more minutes."

To feel good about seeing *him*, she would need a few hours. She looked down at her stomach, still big under the blanket. No, she would need a few weeks.

"I asked if I could go first," he said, still standing by the doorway, "since everyone else had already seen you. But if you'd feel more comfortable starting with one of the ladies, I'm okay with that."

"You can come in. I'm sure I look like a complete hag, but if you don't mind—"

"You look fine. You just delivered a baby. I've never been in a delivery room right after a baby's been born, but I've seen it in the movies plenty of times. You look better than most of the moms in the movies."

She laughed, then winced. "Don't make me laugh. It hurts."

He approached the bed, stood to her left. "I wasn't joking. Your eyes are kind of red and puffy. Your hair's a little messy, but that's really about all."

She began fiddling with her hair. "How bad is it?"

He reached up and gently pulled her hands down. "You look fine, Christina. After what you've just been through, you look great."

There was such tenderness in his voice, and in his eyes. And his touch. She knew they were just friends, but in that moment, how she wished they were something more. She instantly relaxed. The beat-up feeling was still there, but just barely.

"How are you doing?" he asked. "How did your time go, you know, with . . . the baby? If you don't want to talk about it, that's okay."

"It was a little hard. But not traumatic. I guess God prepared me for it. I've been praying about it a whole lot, especially the last few weeks. I cried more than I thought I would, but look, I've already stopped."

"That's because I'm here."

Just as she began to wonder what he meant by that, he said, "You know, to take your mind off it."

Yes, you did. "It's really not a depressing thing." She pointed to the note sitting on top of the white envelope. "That's the letter from the couple adopting the baby. They are so excited, and she's going to such a great home. It sounded like their family is bigger than yours."

"That's cool you have something like that already, so you don't have to wonder about what's going to happen to her."

"They even made the baby's middle name Christina," she said.

"Really?"

She nodded, felt tears beginning to form. *Change the subject.* "It was so nice of you to come."

"I had to," he said. "What kind of friend would I be if I let you go through something this difficult all by yourself?"

She couldn't help it. That made her cry. She didn't care that he used the word *friend*. Or if that was all he was, or might ever be. He was that, her friend, the best kind. The kind that drops everything and runs to your side when they knew you were hurting. The kind who couldn't bear to see you suffer alone.

"I'm sorry. I didn't mean to make you cry." He reached for the tissues and pulled out a few. "Did I say something wrong?"

She wiped her eyes. "No, dummy. That might have been the nicest thing anyone has ever said to me."

"Oh."

When she regained her composure, she reached for the letter on the nightstand. Seeing her stretch, Doug got it for her. "Would you like to read it?" she asked.

"Do you want me to?"

"Only if you want to."

"Sure."

He took it from her and began to read. She watched his eyes crisscross back and forth across and then down the page. When he finished, he said, "Wow. That's pretty amazing."

"Isn't it? That's why I have no reason to be depressed. God has given my baby a wonderful home, and he's given me such wonderful friends to help me make a new start."

He put the letter back in the envelope and set it on the nightstand. "To my folks, you're more than a friend, Christina. They talk about you like family. You may not look like an Anderson or talk like an Anderson, but you're pretty much an Anderson now."

She wanted to ask him, in the worst way, was she more than a friend to him? But she already knew the answer. Why spoil such a beautiful moment? "Thanks again for letting me stay in the garage apartment."

"You're welcome. But it's not much of a sacrifice, since I'm not sleeping on the sofa anymore. Now that Tom and Jean have moved into their new place, I got the whole upstairs to myself when I come home from school. Oh, I forgot to tell you. When this new semester starts, I'm moving out of the dorm and getting my own apartment. I've already picked it out. It's smaller than the garage apartment in River Oaks but a lot bigger than the dorm room. I should have a lot more freedom there too."

She wondered what he meant by that. Something in the

way he said it made her a little concerned. No way she was going to ask.

"Well, I better go get my mom, Jean, and Michele," he said. "Are you still up for seeing them?"

"Sure. I think I can manage that."

— 43 —

It was Friday morning, four days since Christina had her baby. Michele was as nervous as she could be. Today was the big day. Her first doctor appointment totally focused on their infertility problem. She had no idea what to expect. Allan was taking off work and was supposed to meet her there. She grabbed her purse and headed out to the garage.

After pushing the garage door button and turning on the car, she pulled her phone out of her purse to call Allan. He picked up after a few rings. "You remembered our doctor appointment, right?"

"I've already left the office."

"Then you should get there before me," she said. "Why don't you sign in for us?"

"Actually, you'll still get there before me."

"Why? Your office is closer to the doctor's than our house."

"It is, but I have a quick stop to make first."

"Allan . . ."

"Don't worry. It'll be quick."

"Where are you going?"

"Just a quick stop to Ray's house. Remember? Last night he called about that report."

She didn't remember.

"The orphanage report, remember? The rest of the pledges came in from the other churches, so I updated the report."

"I remember you saying something about it. But I thought Ray was going to Africa later next week."

"He is."

"So why does he need your report now? Couldn't you just send it to him as an email attachment?"

"He has some time this afternoon and wants to look it over before tomorrow. I think he's working on something he wants to share with the whole church this Sunday during the announcements. I did send it to him as an attachment, but he's working at home today trying to finish some chores before the Africa trip. He said his printer's broken."

"But if you stop at Ray's, you guys will start talking, and you'll be late. The receptionist told me this doctor is very punctual. He doesn't like making patients wait in the waiting room."

"I won't be late. I'll just drop it off and come right over. He can't talk anyway. He's going to be pressure cleaning his house. Don't worry."

◆ ◆

With the report resting in a manila folder on the passenger seat, Allan drove the familiar ten-minute ride to Ray's house. But when he turned onto Ray's street, he could see that something was wrong. Halfway down, a red fire truck with flashing lights blocked most of the road. Parked next to it was an ambulance, its emergency lights also flashing. A small crowd had gathered in a huddle on the sidewalk.

"What in the world?"

They seemed to be at Ray's house.

"Oh no." He closed the distance slowly, keeping an eye out for Ray's neighbors. There wasn't any smoke or evidence of a fire. No police cars. He pulled up as close as he could, parked the car by the curb, and got out, leaving the report on the seat.

When he reached the crowd, it was now obvious; the emergency vehicles were parked at Ray's house. "Do you know what's going on?" he asked an elderly man.

"I think it's the guy who lives in that house. I'm not sure what happened to him. Some kind of accident."

"I think he got electrocuted," the woman next to him said. "See that big pressure sprayer over by the side of the house? Ray, that's the man who lives there, he was using that a little while ago. I saw him earlier when I walked my dog. Water and electricity don't mix."

"Has anyone seen him?" Allan asked.

"I think they're over there working on him now," the man said, "behind those bushes. I went over there, but they asked me to move back and give them some space."

Allan didn't wait. He headed right for the bushes. As he stepped around them, he saw Ray wrapped in blankets from the waist down, being strapped to a gurney. His face was racked with pain. Allan rushed over. "Ray, what happened!"

Ray looked up. "I'm such an idiot. Fell off the ladder. Pretty sure I broke my legs."

"Both of them?"

"Are you family?" the paramedic asked.

"Just good friends," Allan said. "You think that's true?"

"Could be," the paramedic said.

"One of them's definitely broken," the other paramedic said. "Compound fracture. The other leg might be."

"Oh Ray, I'm so sorry. Is Julie here?"

"No. She'd be worried sick if she saw this. She's out shopping with the kids. Thankfully, I had my phone in my pocket, so I called 911. What are you doing here?"

"I brought over the report with the new figures. Our call last night?"

"Oh yeah." His face contorted with pain. "Man, this hurts."

"We need to load him up." The paramedic signaled for Allan to step back.

"You want me to call Julie, let her know what's going on?"

"She knows. I called her while I was waiting for help to arrive. She's going to meet me at the hospital." The paramedic started pushing Ray toward the ambulance. "One thing you could do, though."

"Anything," Allan said.

"Could you follow us to the hospital, see where they take me? Then meet Julie in the waiting room and show her where I'm at."

"Sure, Ray."

"And maybe on the way, could you call the church office, so the secretary can let the guys on staff know what's going on? Obviously, I'm not gonna make it to church on Sunday."

"Right, I'll call them. Don't worry about it."

"We've gotta go," the paramedic said.

They lifted him up and slid the gurney into the back of the ambulance. As the doors closed, Allan remembered the report. What should he do with it now? Then he realized, it didn't matter. Ray couldn't do anything with it. With a compound fracture, they'd probably have to do surgery. With both legs broken, he might have to be in a wheelchair for a while.

Then another realization hit as he ran back to his car. The Africa trip. Ray couldn't go to Africa now.

The ambulance drove by. Allan pulled his car right behind it.

— 44 —

Michele stepped out of the doctor's office and began walking toward her car in the parking lot. She was an emotional wreck.

First, there was the absolute annoyance and irritation at Allan as she waited alone in the waiting room, alternating between being worried sick that something had happened to him and angry that he had gotten distracted by something and had forgotten their appointment. Then, just as the nurse ushered her—alone—into the examination room, a quick text from Allan saying Ray had been in some kind of terrible accident and was being rushed to the emergency room.

She was relieved that Allan was okay but was now worried sick about Ray. She couldn't stay angry at Allan for missing their appointment over something like that. On the other hand, she hated having to meet the doctor alone, especially after hearing what her nurse had to say about her infertility situation.

As she opened her car door, Allan pulled up beside her. A look of dread was all over his face.

"I'm so sorry I wasn't here for you," he said as he got out of the car.

"Me too."

"I thought it would just take a minute to drop that report off." He walked toward her.

She sighed. "I know it wasn't your fault." They hugged. She felt like crying but held it in.

"It was awful, Michele. I've never seen a compound fracture before."

She pulled back and looked into his face. "Allan, I don't really want to hear the details. You know how I am about things like that."

"I know. I couldn't see very much anyway. He had a blanket wrapped around his legs. But the angle of his leg on the gurney—"

"Allan . . ."

"I'm sorry. I'll stop."

"Is he going to be all right?"

"Eventually. But I'm pretty sure he'll need surgery on that leg. Julie's with him now. That's really why I was late. As they were putting Ray into the ambulance, he asked if I could meet her there at the ER, show her where he was. I didn't see how I could say no."

"I don't either." Poor Julie. What a horrible thing to have to go through. "Can we at least go to lunch together now, so I can fill you in on what the doctor said?"

A long pause.

"What's the matter?"

"I can't," Allan said. "My boss called on the way over. A big client is complaining about something one of the other guys did, and he wants me to drive right over there and try to straighten it out."

She sighed again. This day was going from bad to worse. He hugged her again. "I'm so sorry, Michele. I really do

234

want to hear everything the doctor said. Can we talk about it over dinner?"

"I guess we'll have to."

"Was the news mostly encouraging or discouraging?"

"Discouraging," she said. "I'm not sure I heard anything encouraging."

◆ ◆

Michele had just arrived home. Allan had prayed with her before he'd driven to work, which helped for a little while. As she pushed the garage door button and got out of the car, she felt unsure if God had heard Allan's prayers. The feeling of gloom and discouragement had returned.

She walked through the garage and across the short side-walk that led to the back of their townhome. As she unlocked the patio door, she heard the doorbell ring. Must be Jean, her sister-in-law. Michele had called her just after she and Allan had parted and invited her over for coffee. Maybe Jean could help her get unstuck from the pit she had fallen into.

She set her purse down on the counter and hurried to the front door. "Hey, Jean, thanks for coming over. Where are the kids?"

"Your mom said she wasn't doing anything for a couple of hours, so it's just me."

Michele was glad. She loved Jean's kids, but it would be nice to talk without constant interruption. She closed the door behind her and walked toward the kitchen. "I thought we'd just use the Keurig, if that's okay. I put some fresh water in it this morning." She pointed to a rectangular ceramic bowl filled with single-cup coffee containers. "Pick whichever one you like. The half-and-half and hazelnut creamer are in the fridge. I'll be right back. I just want to change into something more comfortable."

"Which coffee do you want?" Jean said. "In case you're not back when mine's done."

Michele walked over and picked out the one she liked. "I won't be a minute."

She came back to find Jean fixing her own coffee. She had just gotten Michele's started. "It's a little humid out there. Want to just sit in here?" Michele pointed toward the living room.

"Definitely. I walked over here, and I still feel pretty sticky. The A/C feels nice." Jean picked out the chair she always sat in when she visited.

Michele walked her coffee over and sat across from her.

"So I take it the doctor visit didn't go too well."

Michele sipped her coffee, shaking her head no.

"Did they find something wrong already?"

"No, it was nothing like that. I wish it was that easy. The problem is, it's very involved and complicated trying to di- agnose this kind of thing. I just saw my new primary care doctor today, and she did a fairly basic exam. But from what she told me and what her nurse said before she came in, we've got a pretty long road ahead. And an expensive one. That's really the most discouraging thing I'm dealing with right now, the money."

"But I thought you guys had insurance through Allan's work."

"We do. Pretty good insurance, I thought."

"But it won't cover this? All these infertility expenses?"

"It doesn't sound like it. I've gotta do a lot more checking, but it sounds like the insurance may only cover the diagnostic side, figuring out what's medically wrong with Allan or me. If it turns out something is, most of the time, the infertility treatments themselves aren't covered. And they're not cheap. Most of the cost is out-of-pocket."

Jean didn't say anything for a moment. "You poor thing."

"She had some brochures to give me with a bunch of websites to look up. But I guess she's had enough patients come in with this problem, so she's looked into what they'd be facing. Apparently, there are a few work-arounds that might force the insurance companies to cover some of it. But she told me, we really needed to be setting lots of money aside if we're serious about this."

"Like how much?"

Michele took another sip and set her coffee on the coffee table. "Thousands. Depending on what's wrong and how long it takes, could be tens of thousands."

"Oh my gosh. I had no idea," Jean said. "And adoption's even worse. A cousin of mine adopted a little girl, and they spent almost twenty-five thousand dollars."

"This isn't working."

"What isn't?"

"Having you over. You were supposed to cheer me up."

"I'm sorry." She shook her head. "I don't know what to say. I don't understand why people make having babies so expensive. And why insurance won't cover it."

"Me neither." And that was so frustrating to Michele. If she and Allan could get pregnant the old-fashioned way, the whole thing would be covered by insurance right off the bat. She wondered if she and Allan had missed God completely when they turned Christina down. "It almost looks like a closing door at this point."

"I wouldn't say that," Jean said. "Don't give up yet."

"I'm not giving up. I just don't know what to do or what to tell Allan when he gets home."

"Did the doctor give you any ideas?"

"She did, for now. The insurance will still cover the first part, all the tests Allan and I need to take. So we'll start there. I guess it will help some to know what the problem is. If we do get that far. But it sounds like sometimes, you don't even know after you run all the tests. We could go through all this and still come up empty-handed, not sure what the problem is." The look on Jean's face wasn't helping. If anything, Michele had just ruined her day with all this.

Neither one said anything for a few moments.

"We'll just have to start praying more," Jean finally said. "Being helpless isn't always a bad place to be."

Being helpless. That reminded Michele of something she'd read in the children's ministry notebook a few mornings ago. She set her coffee down, got up, and walked back into the kitchen.

"Where are you going?"

"To get this." She picked up the notebook. "Something you said reminded me of something I read in this a little while ago." She brought it back to her chair and opened it up, then began scanning the first few pages.

"Is that the notebook Julie gave you for the children's ministry?"

"Yes. I just remembered something when you talked about being helpless, about it not being a bad place to be." She read a few more paragraphs. "Here it is. Not in the lesson for the kids but in a section for the parents. The author says you can't really help your kids if you're not walking in the things you're trying to teach them. So he takes the first part of each lesson and talks to the parents. The whole premise of the book is that there are four basic beliefs every Christian needs to own, and that all of Christ's commands tie back to one of these four beliefs. We talked about the middle two. Loving God and loving others."

"So what's this one?" Jean asked.

"The first one, humility. Well, 'Humble yourself.' That's how he puts it." She found the paragraph and read it again. "He says humbling yourself means thinking of yourself as a helpless person, like a spiritual beggar who has nothing to give."

"Feeling helpless is a kind of humility?" Jean said.

"In a way, it is. He's saying we can't fix ourselves or our situation. So we're supposed to come to God aware that we need him for everything. And if we ask for God's help with that attitude, he always will." Just rereading the words began to stir something in Michele's heart.

"I like that," Jean said. "And it definitely describes your situation right now."

Michele closed the notebook. It definitely did. She was helpless. Her situation was helpless . . . and hopeless unless God intervened. But she also saw how proud she had been. It had never dawned on her that God might be resisting her for being so self-sufficient. "Maybe we should do something about this. Would you pray with me?"

"You mean right now?" Jean asked.

Michele nodded.

"Okay." Jean leaned forward. They held hands and prayed, acknowledging how big this thing was. Too big for Michele to carry. The more she prayed, the lighter Michele felt. When they were done, she looked up at Jean and felt something else inside.

Hope.

45

Allan arrived home after work that evening feeling a little tense. Michele seemed to be doing better when he'd left her in the parking lot of the doctor's office, but he wondered what kind of shape she'd be in after having all afternoon with nothing to do but think. Then there was his concern about Ray in the hospital. On the car ride home, he'd spoken to Julie. Ray was asleep, thanks to some heavy sedation. Allan had guessed right about the surgery. She'd mentioned they had scheduled an operation on his leg for tomorrow morning.

After setting his things down, he walked into the kitchen. Worship music was playing in the background. That was nice. Whatever she had going on in the oven smelled wonderful. He didn't see her downstairs, so he walked to the stairwell. "I'm home, hon. You up there?"

"I'll be right down."

He walked back into the kitchen to get some ice water out of the fridge. That's when he noticed a number of Scriptures handwritten on index cards, mounted with magnets to the freezer door. They hadn't been there that morning when he'd left for work. Curious, he read each one.

God opposes the proud but gives grace to the humble. (James 4:6)

Blessed are the poor in spirit, for theirs is the kingdom of heaven. (Matthew 5:3)

Apart from me you can do nothing. (John 15:5)

Clothe yourselves with humility toward one another. (1 Peter 5:5)

"I wonder what brought this on," he said quietly. He poured the water, rereading the Scriptures. Clearly, humility was the prevailing theme. That, and needing God's help. Nothing wrong with that, he thought. Still, he didn't know what to expect as she came down the stairs.

Michele almost bumped into him when she stepped into the kitchen. "Oh, there you are." She reached her arms around his waist and gave him a hug. "So glad you're home."

This wasn't the greeting he'd expected. "You seem . . . upbeat."

"I am." She turned the oven light on and bent down to check her dish's progress. "Looking good. Maybe another ten minutes." She turned the light off, grabbed his hand, and began tugging him toward the living room.

"What's for dinner? The smell's killing me."

"Meat loaf."

She made the best meat loaf. Because she did, he never ordered it in restaurants anymore. She sat on the couch, so he sat next to her. "What's going on? I was thinking that since your doctor visit didn't turn out so well, you might be kind of down."

"I was. In fact, I was pretty much a wreck right after. Jean came over, and even she couldn't cheer me up."

"Obviously something did. And I want to hear it. But first, tell me what the doctor said."

So she did. And it *was* discouraging. The more she explained, the more discouraged he became. The process the doctor had described seemed like it could go on for months and months, if not years. Costing thousands, maybe tens of thousands of dollars. She also shared the tidbit about Jean's cousin adopting a little girl, and how much that cost. What he'd heard was right: almost twenty-five-thousand dollars.

What a racket, he thought, but didn't say it. He didn't want to diminish the unusual joy she seemed to be experiencing. But a new concern began to build in his mind as she talked. About money. About how much discretionary cash they had each month after expenses. So far in their marriage, he'd been able to assign a decent portion of this to his mission activities. With Michele's permission. From what he was hearing, this would have to stop when they began pursuing these infertility solutions.

He found his anticipation growing to hear about whatever was responsible for her positive outlook. He could use a sip of whatever she was drinking.

She finished her update with, "Now, that's the bad news."

"Yeah, that's . . . pretty bad. But you're doing way better than you should be after sharing all that."

"I know, it's weird, isn't it?"

Weird was one way to describe it. "I'm guessing it has something to do with those index cards on the freezer door?"

"You saw them? Good. Yes. Isn't it wonderful? I learned something today about humility. Something I never knew before. Maybe I never really understood humility. But after the things I read, my outlook completely changed."

"So, what did you read?"

She leaned across the couch and picked up a notebook sitting on an end table. Allan had seen it around the last few days.

"Isn't that the notebook Julie gave you?"

She opened it on her lap. "It is. I've been reading it every morning this past week. After I got home from the doctor's, I was a mess. Totally deflated."

Probably like I am now, Allan thought.

"Jean came over for coffee, and we talked. But that didn't really help. The whole situation seemed so big and out of my control. I felt helpless. I couldn't imagine how we could ever get all that money together. And even if we did, there are no guarantees I'll get pregnant after we spend it."

"So you don't want to pursue this infertility thing anymore?"

"No, that's not it. I still do."

"Then I'm not getting where you're going here."

"Jean said something about being helpless, that it's not always a bad place to be. Then I remembered something I read a few days ago in this notebook. It says when you're helpless and you know you don't have what it takes to make your situation work, it's kind of a gift. That's where humility comes in. Humility's all about realizing how much we need God's help. According to this, we turn to God as a last resort, only after we've tried everything else we can do ourselves. But the truth is, we need him all the time, we just don't realize it. As long as we think we can handle our problems, that's what we do. We handle them, or at least we try. We don't trust God. We don't even turn to him. We just . . . try to figure it out on our own. Then a trial like this comes along, and we find out just how helpless we really are. It's so big, it overwhelms us. We realize we can't fix it no matter how hard we try."

This was actually making sense.

"All Jean and I did was pray. We surrendered the whole thing to God and said, 'Lord, this is too big for us to carry.

We need your help. We need to know what you want us to do. Please take away all this fear and anxiety.' And he did. I have no idea how this is gonna work out. Where the money's going to come from, but that's okay. According to this notebook—well, the Scriptures in here about humility—my part is simple. Humble yourself."

Allan looked down at the notebook, which had suddenly increased in value. "I've read a lot of things about humility. But I think I've learned more from what you just said than from anything I've read."

"Isn't it simple? It's like, after seeing it broken down this way for children, the lights came on for me. God's not expecting me to do big things for him or try to impress him with my great faith. He wants me to depend on him . . . for everything. And if you think about it, that's exactly how Jesus lived in the Gospels. Totally dependent on the Father."

"So why all the index cards on the fridge?"

"I guess the idea is memorizing Scripture. This chapter on humility says our minds drift through thousands of thoughts each day. Many of them draw us away into doubt and fear. Our minds need something better to hold on to. So the author suggests putting Scriptures together that speak about the very thing you need the most help with. Well, we're supposed to teach kids to do this, but he says adults need it just as much. One of the ideas for helping you memorize them was writing them down on little cards. So that's what I did."

Allan reached for her hand. "I'm really proud of you, hon. I expected to come home and find you totally down and depressed. But look at you. I'm actually encouraged. How about you and I pray like you and Jean did, then we'll get up and eat that incredible meat loaf."

— 46 —

The following morning, Saturday, Michele texted Julie to see if there was anything they could do for her. It was hard to know how to handle something like this. Ray and Julie had plenty of family in town and tons of friends in the church. Julie would probably be bombarded by people expressing concern. Michele didn't want to pile on. She sent just a quick text, telling her no need to reply if things were crazy.

She stood near the patio door as she sent it, in time to see Allan's car pull into the driveway. He had just made a quick run to the store to solve their coffee emergency. A few moments later, he walked across the connecting sidewalk holding a bag of half-and-half in one hand and a manila folder in the other.

Her cell buzzed, a reply from Julie: *Thanks for praying. Just got to the hospital. Haven't even seen Ray yet. Will call you if I think of something. Right now, job one is trying to keep the kids from freaking out about his surgery. LOL. Just pray. Talk soon.*

The patio door opened.

Allan stepped past her and into the kitchen, set the cream on the counter. "I had an idea on the way home. Why don't I put this in the fridge, and we go out for breakfast? Then we can swing by and visit the hospital."

She walked toward him. "We can go someplace that has good coffee. How about Panera?"

"Sounds great. Are you ready to go?"

"I can be. Just give me a few minutes." She headed toward the stairs. "By the way, I just texted Julie. She just got to the hospital. From the sound of it, she's alone."

"Then we should definitely go. And I'll give her this," he said, holding up the manila folder."

◆ ◆

They were almost to the hospital now. Michele glanced toward the backseat at the folder. "Is that the report about the orphanage?"

Allan nodded. "I know Ray won't be in any shape to look at it today, but I'm guessing they'll be keeping him a few days. He'll probably be bored stiff."

Neither one of them said anything for a few moments. Allan didn't want to bring up what he was thinking. He'd been working on not talking about the orphanage very much. Every time he did, he'd use it as a reminder to take an interest in their baby challenges. It was starting to work. Now, only about half his daydreams took him back to Korah and to thoughts of little Ayana.

When he did go there, he'd see the same thing: an image of her squatting by a pile of garbage three times her size, poking through it with a stick. She'd hear him call, turn, and look up at him with those big brown eyes and bright smile.

"What do you think is going to happen now?"

Allan turned toward her voice. "What?"

"Wasn't Ray supposed to leave for Africa on Tuesday?" she said.

"Yeah. He was. No chance of that now."

"Wasn't this kind of an important trip?"

Ridiculously important, he wanted to say. In fact, he had no idea what they were going to do now. "Pretty much. Ray was going to set everything up. Sign all the forms, pay all the up-front fees. Even get with Henok to select the first six children for the orphanage."

"Is that little girl supposed to be one of them? What was her name?"

"Ayana."

"Yeah, Ayana."

"I hope so, but we put Henok in charge of selecting the children. I don't think he's talked to any of their legal guardians yet, including Ayana's grandmother. He was waiting for Ray to get there." They pulled into the hospital parking lot. "Wonder where we should park?" Signs pointed to the ER.

"Isn't he there, in the ER?" Michele said.

"I don't think so. That's probably where they brought him at first. But I don't think they'd do surgery there."

"Well, it's not that big of a place."

"I'll just park near the main entrance. Won't hurt us to walk a little." They parked, got out of the car, and headed toward the door.

"Allan, your folder." They stopped walking. "You left it in the backseat."

"Oh, right." He headed back to the car, leaving Michele on the sidewalk. He wondered why she was suddenly taking such an interest in Africa.

47

A woman at the information desk had given them directions to the surgical waiting room. They were heading there now. Michele wasn't sure where she was going with all these questions about Africa. Since their big talk a month ago, when Allan had agreed to shift his focus toward starting a family, she had tried to help by not taking an active interest in the orphanage plans.

But she was still using the children's ministry notebook in her devotional time. This morning she was writing down memory verses about loving others. One that stuck out to her was from Philippians 2. She forgot which verse but not what it said: "Let each of you look not only to his own interests, but also to the interests of others."

That pretty much contradicted her plan to avoid any discussions about Africa. It was definitely something Allan was interested in. And he'd shown he really did care about her and her desire to focus more effort on starting a family. She didn't feel alone anymore. Based on what that verse said, it was time to care about Allan's world a little. He had been working so hard on this orphanage proposal, trying to help Ray get ready for this trip.

Up ahead, she saw the waiting room sign sticking out above a doorway. When they got inside, the room was mostly empty. A scattering of people here and there, some watching the news on a television hanging in the corner, others reading magazines or talking quietly on their cell phones. Julie was in the far corner by herself.

"Good thing we came," Allan whispered. "She's still alone."

They held hands and walked toward her. She looked up as they came near. Michele could tell she had been crying. She sat beside her and gave her a hug. "How are you doing?"

"I guess I'm okay. They took him into surgery a few minutes ago. I know this isn't a life-threatening thing, but it still got me when they wheeled him away."

Allan sat on the other side. "They give you any idea how long he'd be in there?"

"They said maybe a few hours, if they didn't run into any complications." She sighed. "I wish they hadn't said that last part."

"It doesn't mean anything," Allan said. "I'm sure he's going to be fine. I'll bet the whole church is praying for him by now."

"That's what one of the other pastors said. They're all on their way here."

"Did the kids get to see their dad before surgery?"

"Just for a minute, before they rolled him away. They were so worried. All they wanted to know was how much it hurt." She smiled. "He said, 'I'm feeling *no* pain.' They had already given him some kind of sedative. After they took him, my mom took the kids home for me."

"I'm glad he's not suffering," Allan said.

"You saw the break?"

"By the time I got there, he was already on the gurney, his legs wrapped loosely in a blanket. But you could see—" He looked over at Michele. "I'm sorry, she doesn't do well with these kinds of conversations."

Julie reached for Michele's hands. "That's okay. Before Ray and I had children, I was an RN. Ray always wants me to be careful how I talk around the kids."

"I don't know why it bothers me," Michele said. "It's like nails on a chalkboard. I can't even watch those scenes on *CSI*-type shows."

"Ray can't either. We have to watch them on the DVR, and he fast-forwards through them."

No one said anything for a few moments. Michele wanted to keep Julie's mind distracted. "Oh Julie, I almost forgot. I never got back to you about the children's ministry notebook."

"Oh, that's okay. We still have awhile before we need to order anything. Did you get a chance to look it over?"

"I read it all the way through."

"Really? So, what did you think?"

"Mostly, I loved it. I started reading it just thinking about the kids, but I really get what you mean about the section for the parents. I'm not a parent yet, but I learned a lot. I'm still getting a lot out of it."

"Did you think the parts for the kids were too complicated? Think it might go over their heads?"

"No, I don't think so. I think maybe the only weakness, if you're thinking of it for a Sunday-morning curriculum, is you might need someone to come up with some creative games and activities that tie back to the material. But I'm sure there are all kinds of creative people in the church who could work on that."

"I was thinking the same thing. But the content seemed so good to me. I figured we could work out something to make it fit the age group we have in mind."

"Definitely," Michele said.

Julie turned a little in her chair. She looked at the manila folder in Allan's hand. "Is that the orphanage report?"

"You know about that?" Allan said.

She nodded. "Ray told me that's why you were at the house yesterday. To give him some kind of report."

Allan held it out. "I don't know when he'll get to look at it, but I thought I'd bring it over anyway."

"I'm sure he'll want to see it, but you might want to hold on to it for now. At least until you can make a copy."

Allan didn't seem to get what she meant.

"He asked me to ask you—and he made sure that I tell you, you don't have to do it—but he was wondering if you might share what he was gonna share with the church tomorrow."

"What?"

Oh no, Michele thought. Allan hated talking in front of large crowds.

"He wants me to talk with the whole church?"

"That's what he said. He knows you prefer to be a behind-the-scenes guy, but he'd really like the church to get this up-date."

"But I wouldn't know what to say."

"He said you'd say that. He said to tell you he already wrote out everything last night. He just had a few blanks to fill in once he got your report."

Poor Allan. He was trying to look open-minded, but Michele knew better.

"Is that really a good idea now?" he said. "I mean, with this accident . . . the trip's going to have to be postponed now anyway, isn't it?"

Julie looked at him. Then she reached into her purse, pulled out a handwritten note that was folded in half. "He asked me

251

to give you this. The handwriting's a little shaky. He wrote it before they gave him the pain meds."

Michele's eyes instantly locked on the note. Where was this leading?

Allan took it from Julie and unfolded it.

Michele stood up and walked over to Allan's side so she could read it along with him.

Allan,

Hate to bring this up, my friend, but with this accident, I'm kind of stuck. As you know, I'm supposed to get on a plane this Tuesday and head over to Ethiopia, make this presentation to the government and get everything all set up. I doubt that can happen now. But we can't cancel this meeting in Addis Ababa. We just can't. Too much riding on it. I'll explain why when I get out of surgery and I'm thinking straight again. In the meantime, would you please pray about taking my place? Maybe talk to Michele about it, see what she thinks? Maybe it can't work, but I had to ask.

—Ray

— 48 —

Michele tensed up as she read the note over Allan's shoulder. She noticed his hands gripping the note tighter by the time he was through. They both stood there a few moments.

Julie broke the ice. "Ray asked me to read the note before I gave it to you. I don't think he expected Michele to be here when you got this." She looked at Michele. "I'm not sure why, but I got the impression he thought you wouldn't be too happy about the idea. Is it because the last trip wasn't that long ago? I know it's really hard when they go. It's still hard on me, and Ray's been on a bunch of these trips."

Michele walked back to the chair. "Allan's been on five since we met. But that's only part of it." This didn't seem like the time or the place to have this kind of talk.

Allan spoke up. "I explained a little of this to Ray last month when he asked me to go with him. Did he tell you I said I couldn't go?"

She nodded. "But he didn't get into why."

"I guess it's really more a question of timing and priorities."

"You don't need to explain, Allan. That's really between you and Michele. I know Ray wasn't upset when he said it, so I'm sure he understands."

Maybe so, Michele thought. But here he was, asking Allan to go again. She dreaded the thought, but she also felt the tug from that passage in Philippians this morning, about looking out for others' interests not just your own. "There isn't any way they can postpone this trip? Seems like they have a great excuse with Ray's accident."

"They may have to. But I could tell, the thought of cancelling was causing him more stress than the surgery on his leg."

"Any idea why?" Allan asked.

"You'll have to ask him for the details. He said something about losing the facility Henok picked out for the orphanage. Apparently some local businessmen are ready to buy it, even willing to pay more for it. He's afraid the government will give it to them if someone doesn't show up for that meeting."

Michele looked at Allan. "That sounds pretty serious."

He rubbed his hand through his hair. "Ray and I didn't talk much about this. I thought it was a done deal. All my budget figures are based on this facility."

Just then they heard some noise behind them. She turned to find two of the pastors and their wives coming into the waiting room. They rushed over toward Julie, hugged her, and greeted Allan and Michele.

"Well, look," Allan said, "we'll let you guys visit awhile together. I'll check in on Ray in a few hours. Julie, you let us know if there's anything we can do."

"I will. And thank you guys so much for coming."

Allan and Michele started walking toward the door.

Julie called out, "And Allan, don't worry about that note. You guys just talk it out and pray. Ray will be fine with whatever you decide."

They held hands but didn't talk much on the way out to the car. Allan felt backed into a corner by Ray's note. Especially reading it with Michele standing right there. Obviously, he would have told her about it, and they would decide together how to respond. The way it came about just added an extra layer of tension he didn't need.

They got in the car. Allan turned it on. "That was a little awkward."

"Are you okay?" she asked.

The gentleness in her voice surprised him. He pulled out of the parking space. "I'm fine. I have no idea what to do. What we should do."

They drove out of the hospital parking lot. She reached over and massaged his right shoulder. "I guess it's not possible for one of the other guys on the team to go?"

He didn't want to answer this too strongly, but the truth was they couldn't. The guys were completely committed to this vision, but none of them had been involved in this thing as much as him or Ray. "I wish they could. Don't get me wrong, they're great guys. But they've only been doing things like fund-raising so far. It would take more time than we have to get any of them up to speed enough to take Ray's place."

"But you're ready now, aren't you? You could go there Tuesday and take care of everything, just like Ray."

Allan looked over at her. She was serious. "Well, not just like Ray. He's way better with people than I am. Especially people he doesn't know. On this trip, that would pretty much include everybody except Henok."

"But you could do this if you went, couldn't you?"

"I guess so. To be honest, I'm more nervous about the thought of getting up in front of the whole church tomorrow to talk about this."

They drove in silence the rest of the way home. Allan turned on some pleasant, romantic music. One of Michele's favorite CDs. He couldn't believe her reaction to all this. It sounded like she was seriously thinking he should go. He hadn't let his mind go there as he read the note. He wasn't even sure what *he* thought about it. He'd never been to Africa without Ray. He'd never been there alone. Certainly sounded like he'd be alone on this trip if he went. And the stakes were so high.

They pulled into the one-lane road that ran behind the townhomes.

"Does the thought of doing this alone make you nervous?" she asked.

Man, did she know him. He pushed the garage door button. "Totally. On all these trips, I've been like the sergeant. But Ray's not been the lieutenant, more like the general. He handles everything." He pulled the car in, he stopped, turned it off and looked at her. "Are you seriously thinking I should do this?"

"I'm seriously going to pray about it. I don't want you to go. I really don't want you to go. But, I also don't know what God's doing here, why he allowed this to happen."

"What if I mess it up, Michele?"

"I don't know, Allan. If God wants you to do this, we have to believe he'll go before you and give you the wisdom you need when the time comes. Can we get out of the car? It's starting to get stuffy."

When she was halfway across the sidewalk, she said, "Do we have enough money for you to go? You do the bills. Is there enough in the new baby account?"

He couldn't even believe his ears. "You're amazing, you know that?"

"What? Why?"

He found the key to unlock the back door. "Because you know we don't have money for both of these things, and having a child means more to you than anything else in the world. We've just started building the fund, and just like that, you're offering it to me for another trip to Africa?" He was actually getting a little choked up. He left the keys in the doorknob, put his arms around her, and drew her in.

After the hug, she said, "Well, do we?"

"I'll have to crunch the numbers, but . . . I think so." Mentally, he did a few quick calculations. If he was adding it right, they did have enough. But this trip would use up almost all the money they had saved. At most, there'd be a few hundred dollars left.

— 49 —

Allan was driving back to the hospital a few hours after dinner. Julie had texted him, saying Ray's surgery had gone well. He was recovering nicely and was actually asking to see Allan. She'd added she was just conveying the message, not trying to pressure him in any way.

Off and on over the last few hours, he and Michele had continued talking about this Africa trip. To his surprise, her support of the idea never wavered. She had even suggested he look at the financial picture before meeting with Ray, in case there was a gap and they needed a little help from the church to close it.

As he pulled into the hospital parking lot for the second time today, he thought again about Michele's generosity in this situation. He already loved her with all his heart, but through this, his love found a way to grow even more. He walked into the lobby to the information desk to get Ray's room number. A few minutes and a few hallways later, he stood at the doorway. The door was closed.

He knocked gently. "Come in." Julie's voice.

He found Ray propped up slightly on the bed, both legs covered by a blanket. Looked like quite a lot of activity going on underneath. An IV tube stuck out of his arm. Two racks of monitors stood on either side of the headboard. But Ray was awake. Allan could tell by the look in his eyes, he was still pretty sedated. "Wow, didn't expect to see all this."

"It's because of the surgery," Julie said. "You don't normally get all this attention for a simple fracture. Because the bone broke the skin, it involves . . . a whole lot more. For one thing, there's a real danger of infection. So they have him on some serious antibiotics. Fortunately, the doctor said for a compound fracture, it wasn't near as bad as it could've been."

Allan looked at Ray. "What's the pain level?"

Ray smiled. "What pain?" He pointed to the morphine drip hooked up to his IV. "Thank God for pain meds."

"Are you even going to remember this visit, or anything we say?"

"Why?" Ray said. "You plan to share any secrets?"

Allan laughed. "I don't think so."

"I can take notes if you want," Julie said.

"I don't think that'll be necessary." Allan pointed to Ray's legs. "Are they both broken?"

"No," he said. "The left one is, but I'm sure you knew that. The other one's just badly sprained."

"Julie said you were asking for me. I'm guessing it's about the trip to Ethiopia."

"Yeah. By the way, thanks for bringing that report by. I can't read anything right now, but I'm hoping that'll clear up soon. The main reason I wanted to see you was to apologize."

"Apologize? For what?"

"I don't know what I was thinking, writing you that note. Especially at a time like this. Julie told me Michele was with you." He rubbed his eyes and his forehead like someone massaging a headache. "I should have realized with Julie here, she would've come too. I didn't mean to pressure you like that. I hope I didn't cause any friction between you guys."

"Don't worry about it, Ray. It's okay."

"No, it's not okay. I'm sure I was just reacting to the moment, not thinking clearly. Everything for this trip was coming together so well. Everything on Henok's end, all the funding, the pledges. I'm all set to go Tuesday to get everything set up and finalized, and then this." He pointed to his legs.

"Ray, it's okay. I understand. You were under a lot of pressure. Julie told me about the local guys wanting to buy the orphanage building. I didn't know about that. I thought we had the deal locked up."

"We did, but just with Henok's signature and a phone call from me promising I'd be there Tuesday with the money."

"Are you guys going to lose it now?" Julie asked.

"Probably," Ray said. "But if that happens, we weren't meant to have it." He turned to Allan. "Anyway, I forbid you to feel any guilt over that. I should never have asked you the way I did."

"Yeah," Allan said, "but you did. And like I said, it's okay. I didn't think it would be okay, especially with Michele reading your note right over my shoulder. I guess God did some kind of work in her heart this morning to prepare her, because she didn't get upset. Just the opposite. As soon as we got in the car, she started asking me questions about it. Not challenging questions. She just wanted to make sure this trip was as important as it seemed, and that none of the other guys could take your place. After that, she actually started suggesting that I should go."

"Really?" Ray said. "So, you'll go?"

"We're praying about it. Pretty much ready to say yes. I was just waiting to talk to you here, make sure there weren't any other options. I can already tell, there aren't. So yeah, I guess I'm saying . . . I'm going."

"Allan, that's wonderful. I totally didn't see this coming."

"Me neither."

"And you guys aren't doing this because of any pressure from me?"

Allan shook his head no. "To show you how far Michele is stretching here, we started a new baby fund just over a month ago. I moved over the money I had left in my missions fund. Between that and what we saved, it'll just cover this trip. Michele didn't even flinch. She said go ahead and use it."

A strange look came over Ray's face. Allan couldn't interpret it, but it wasn't the reaction he expected.

"What are you talking about, Allan? You're thinking of using your own money for this trip?"

"Well, yeah."

"That's not the plan," Ray said. "Never was. You guys keep that money in your baby fund. The church was planning to pay for my trip. I haven't asked them yet, but I already know what they'll say. You're doing this for us, for the church, for the entire team. We're going to cover all your expenses."

Allan was stunned. This thought had never crossed his mind. "Really?"

"Yeah, really. It might cost us a little more for your ticket, since we're buying it on short notice but, yeah, you guys aren't paying for this. For the sake of time, we'll need you to purchase the flight on your credit card, but the church will reimburse you 100 percent."

A big smile came over Allan's face. He couldn't wait to tell Michele.

50

Allan's joy at the news the church would be paying his way to Africa diminished somewhat by the time he'd arrived home from the hospital, displaced by the growing realization that he would be making the trip all alone. What if he got there and they were all set to make the deal, then something changed? What if they decided to rethink things or wanted to negotiate? He was no good at that. He didn't even like to dicker at the flea market. What if some government official drew him aside after the meeting, looking for a bribe? What would he say?

Allan had certain skills and a good measure of confidence when those skills were called upon. But he also knew his limitations. He believed it was both humble and wise to live within them. Everything about this trip called for skills he either didn't have or possessed in meager amounts. That was why he'd always traveled to Africa with Ray.

He got out of the car and hit the button to lower the garage door. As he walked toward the back of their house, he recalled Michele's encouragement from their conversation earlier that day. *If God wants you to do this, then we have*

*to believe he'll go before you and give you the wisdom you
need when the time comes.*

Michele greeted him as he came through the patio door.
"How's he doing?" she asked as they hugged.

He set his keys and phone on the hutch. "He's pretty banged
up. They had to do some serious surgery on the broken leg."

"So he didn't break both of them?"

"The right one's just badly sprained. But because of the
surgery on the other one, it's not in a cast yet. They're giving
him heavy-duty antibiotics. He didn't seem to be in any pain.
I'm sure that's because of the morphine drip. I think he'll be
in the hospital at least a few more days."

They sat in their normal spots in the living room. "Did
you find out anything more about the trip?" she said. "Why
it can't be postponed?"

"It's the facility thing like Julie said. There might be other
reasons, but that's the biggie." He explained what Ray had
said about the very real possibility of losing the facility if
someone from their team wasn't there on Tuesday.

"So . . . are you definitely going then?"

"Are you still okay with that?"

"Okay's the right word. It seems pretty clear God wants
you to go. The need is real, and we have the money."

"Oh wait, the money."

"What about it?"

"We don't have to use ours. Ray said the church was planning to pay his way, so they'll definitely do the same for me.
We don't have to touch our new baby account."

Michele's face lit up at the news, and she hugged him again.
"That's wonderful, Allan. You get to go, and we get to keep
growing our baby fund. I actually prayed about this."

"You did?"

She nodded. "I didn't want to say anything, but it seemed only fair to me. It's not like you're going there on vacation. You're going there to take Ray's place."

"Ray almost seemed shocked that I'd even think they'd expect me to pay my own way."

"I'm so glad."

Allan forced a smile. He really was glad. But crouching at the door were all those anxious thoughts about making this trip alone.

"I guess you'll have to call your boss tomorrow, get next week off."

"You're right."

"Is that going to be a problem?"

"I don't think so. We've got plenty of work, but none of it's late. And I won't be taking off two or three weeks like before."

"How long will you be gone?"

"I asked Ray before I left the hospital. He said he had only planned to be there three or four days. So I'm thinking about coming home next Saturday." He stood up.

"Where are you going?"

"To get my laptop. I've got to book my flight."

She stood up too. "Are you okay about all this?"

"What do you mean?"

"I don't know," she said. "You don't seem that excited. Usually when you're heading to Africa, you're all jazzed about it."

"I'm glad to be going." The words had barely come out of his mouth when he realized it wasn't the truth. "This time is just so different. Do you realize I've never gone on one of these trips without Ray? Even the ones before we were married."

"I know."

"And he's not just not going, he's stuck in a hospital bed. Probably looking at several months before he's well again."

"But it's not just because Ray won't be there, is it?"

Sometimes Allan wasn't sure he liked how perceptive Michele was about his emotional state. Like right now. He would prefer not having to share the honest answer to her question in hopes that, given a little time, he might get to a better place. "No, but I think you already know what I'm struggling with."

"Doing something this big on your own? Worried about what will happen once you get there if you make a wrong decision?"

"Things like that," he said. "Ray said maybe I could come by the hospital tomorrow afternoon, after he gets some time to rest, and he'll try to brief me on everything he thinks I should expect."

"That should help, shouldn't it?"

"Should help some. It would help more if the cell phone connections were better. You know how hard it is for me to call you on these trips. I wish I could call Ray if something big comes up. Between the lousy phone reception, the nine-hour time difference, and the fact that he's laid up in a hospital bed . . ." He stopped and rubbed his head. "I'm sorry. Not quite the man of faith and power, am I? More like Eeyore."

She came close and hugged him, rested her head on his chest. "I know it's gonna be all right. Look at all God has done already. He provided all the money, not just for you to go in Ray's place but for everything you guys needed to launch this thing. He provided Henok over there to set everything up. He helped you all find a place within your budget. I know he's gonna keep helping you once you get there. You're doing his work, caring for widows and orphans."

This was definitely helping. Having her here, talking like this.

Then, he got an idea. A crazy one. He almost blurted it out

but caught himself. But it was a wonderful idea. Something they had talked about before, many times. A dream of Allan's that she had always refused. They stood there together in silence a few moments as he prayed about what to do. Should he bring it up? What should he say? She might say no. But what if this time she said yes?

A voice in his head simply said, *Ask her.* He pulled back from the hug, far enough that they could look at each other as he spoke. "Michele, I just had a thought. It may not be from the Lord, but I feel like I'm supposed to ask. Don't feel any pressure to answer right now."

"What is it?"

"Would you come to Africa with me?"

"What?" A puzzled look on her face.

"Would you come with me on this trip? You know how much I've always wanted to share this experience with you. This would be a perfect time. You always seem to know how to help me through tough decisions. You were willing to spend our baby money to send me before. Would you be willing to use it instead so that we can go together?"

A new look on her face. The reality of his request was sinking in.

— 51 —

It was Sunday afternoon.

Michele sat at the Starbucks in the downtown area of River Oaks, waiting for her father to join her. He had just texted, saying he was on the way. She hadn't slept well last night and was fairly distracted throughout the service that morning.

Would you come to Africa with me?

That moment and that question kept replaying in her mind. She definitely hadn't seen it coming. She hadn't said an outright no to Allan, though she was tempted to. She was still functioning under the influence of that passage in Philippians 2, the one about looking out for the interests of others. Yesterday, it had already stretched her in a big way when she had encouraged Allan to take Ray's place on the Africa trip. She had even conceded to allowing him to use the money from their baby fund.

Wasn't that being stretched enough? Go to Africa? With Allan?

God had even set things up so that Allan could go and they could keep their baby fund intact. Wasn't there some kind of limit to this idea of looking out for the interests of others? There had to be. Otherwise, Christians would wind up becoming doormats, living their entire lives at everyone else's beck and call.

For the longest time after Allan had asked her the question, Michele had just stood there staring back at him, unsure how to respond. He had bailed her out, quickly taking it back, saying he never should have put her on the spot like that. The idea had just come to him that moment. But she didn't want to close the door on it completely, not without giving it some thought or at least asking for God's guidance. Besides, she genuinely felt sorry for Allan and hated the thought of him facing this situation all alone.

They had agreed to pray about it over the next twenty-four hours. Allan had checked the ticket situation on his laptop. There were still a few seats left on all three of the connecting flights, enough room for both of them to go. Allan was excited by this news. As he'd researched it, Michele had stood behind him, secretly hoping there might only be one seat left, closing the door on the matter for good.

"Deep in thought?"

Michele looked up at her father standing there holding his coffee cup.

"I walked in, saw you sitting over here staring out the window. It was going to be my treat, but I see you've already got yours." He was holding a big oatmeal raisin cookie. Noticing her eyes on it, he said, "Want me to get you one?"

"No thanks, Dad. I'm still a little full from lunch."

He sat across from her. "So what's up? It's been awhile since you and I did something like this, just the two of us."

"I know. I've got a big decision to make. Well, Allan and I do. But he doesn't want to pressure me into something, which I appreciate. But it means I'm kind of on my own. It's such a big decision, and we don't have a lot of time. I told Allan I would give him my answer this evening. I prayed about it last night but didn't seem to get anywhere. When I woke up this morning, I had a strong feeling I should bounce these ideas off you."

"Okay. Why don't you fill me in a little bit? I talked to your mother on the way home from church, and she didn't have any idea what this could be about."

"That's because all this just came about yesterday afternoon." She took a soothing sip of her latte. "We really haven't had a chance to talk to anyone yet."

She spent the next fifteen minutes giving him an update while he ate his cookie. As she did, she was grateful for how much her father had changed in the last year or two compared to the man she had known growing up. He was such a good listener now, and he really looked in her eyes as she talked. When she was through, she really wanted to hear what he had to say.

His first words were, "So sorry to hear about Ray. That's terrible. They announced it this morning in church, but I didn't know all the details. Do they know how long he's going to be in the hospital?"

"At least a few more days, but we're not sure."

"You could tell he was a little nervous," her father said, "but I thought Allan did a good job this morning on the announcement about the orphanage. That's some great news. He didn't say anything about taking Ray's place, though, on this trip. Are they keeping that quiet for some reason?"

"I think he just forgot," she said. "He went over his notes with me this morning, so I know he intended to share it. He was even supposed to ask the church to pray."

"Well, he still did a good job. I know he doesn't like talking

269

to a crowd. And I'm proud of you too, Michele. That shows real maturity, setting aside something you deeply care about like that. And you did it before you even knew the church was paying for the trip."

"But now we'll be paying for it anyway, if I go with him."

"That's true."

"So, I need you to tell me what to do."

"Michele, I can't do that."

"Why can't you? I'm giving you permission."

Her dad smiled. "Can I ask you a few questions?"

"I guess."

"Do you know what your main hesitation is, what's keeping you from saying yes? I know Allan's been hinting at you going on one of these trips for quite a while. Is it the money?"

She sat back in her chair. "I don't think so. It may be a part of it. But I really was willing to spend it when I thought we were sending him. And there's a part of me that wants to go. Well, that's not exactly true. I don't *want* to go. But I don't want Allan to have to go alone, either."

"Do you think it's fear? It's not something you've ever done before."

"I'm sure that's part of it. Maybe a big part. Most of the places we've been to together have been nice places. Vacation trips. I've seen the pictures and videos Allan brings back from Africa. Korah is not a nice place. Even by African standards. This place really got to him, more than all the other locations he's been to . . . combined. I couldn't get the stink out of his clothes. If he had a hard time there, what's it going to do to me?" She sighed. "I'm just not wired like Allan. For some reason, I can't seem to take seeing people in horrendous suffering. Especially children. It makes me feel so helpless and depressed."

"And maybe a little guilty?" her father said.

"Yeah, some of that too, I'm sure."

"That's perfectly normal, Michele. I think most Christians in America feel the same way about missions, especially when extreme poverty is involved. We have so much, and they have so little. And we don't understand why. The emotions can get overwhelming pretty quick. They do for me when I'm exposed to the situation, and I've never actually been there. I know you've been able to avoid most of this so far. Except for a week or two after Allan gets back from one of these trips. But maybe God wants to change that."

"You mean . . . change me?"

"Maybe. I don't know what he has in mind here, but it does seem like he's orchestrating things in this direction. Definitely seems to be stretching you. But if it is God, he will give you grace for it. This far away, it may seem like too much for you to deal with. But if he wants you there, with Allan, God will give you plenty of grace to make it work. You'll see. I think it will be like Peter walking on water. He couldn't tell what it would really be like as long as he was sitting in that boat."

But Michele liked being in the boat. She was definitely an in-the-boat kind of Christian. "The other eleven disciples never walked on water."

"That's true."

They both sipped their coffee, looked at each other.

"The question is," her father said, "what is God calling you to?" He smiled. "I don't know if this will help, but for some reason, I just had a flashback of you and Tom on Christmas morning, before Doug was born. You know how kids look forward to Christmas? They're totally focused on all the toys and presents they're going to get. That's what Christmas is all about. But for the parents, it's different. They might get a present or two, but they're not focused on what they're getting that day. For them, their joy is the look on their kids' faces, their reactions to what *they're* getting. You know that saying, it is more blessed to give than to receive? Jesus said that. What he's saying is that the happiest person is the one giving the gift, not the one receiving it. The one giving is the one who truly gets blessed."

It dawned on her that this was the joy she saw in Allan about Africa and these mission trips. He never thought about the money he spent, or the vacation time he lost, or the hopeless situations he was forced to leave behind when he came back to the States. Because he wasn't going on these trips to get something but to give. He gave his heart away. And in the giving, God blessed him so much, Allan immediately wanted to do it all over again.

"I want to experience that," she said.

"You mean . . . you'll go with him?"

"I think I will."

"I think that's a good decision," her dad said. "And I predict that by the time you return home, you'll have no regrets on any of the money you spent. The reward you will feel deep inside will be like a gift from God, a much bigger prize than anything you could possibly lose."

She reached her hand across the table and squeezed his. "Thank you, Dad."

— 52 —

They had finally made it to Addis Ababa, the capital of Ethiopia. It had been a long and trying day. Because of the nine-hour time difference and how long the trip was, they had to get up at 3:00 a.m. and be at the airport by 5:00. When they'd finally landed and had their first conversation on the ground, both had agreed they should unpack the mouthwash first. She wasn't sure what time it was now. She was too tired to even pull out her cell phone and check.

They had just checked into the hotel and were walking to their room on the third floor. It was mostly dark when the airplane landed, completely dark outside now. She'd get a better look come daylight, but she could already tell this city looked nothing like any city in America. The cars were different, smaller, odd-looking, and there were a lot less of them for a city this big. But the exhaust fumes were horrible. The buildings looked very different. But it appeared more modern than she had expected.

"Here we are, hon." Allan opened the door with the hotel key.

The hotel wasn't bad. Nothing fancy. Like a low-budget hotel you might find in the States. Old but fairly clean. At least it looked clean in dim lamp lighting. "Do I need to worry about bugs?" she asked as they walked through the door.

"Wasn't a big problem for me the last time. Maybe an occasional fly." He set their bags on the bed.

"Not a good idea," she said. "I plan to collapse there in about two minutes."

Allan laughed. He turned and took her hand and led her to a chair in the corner. "How about you sit here a few minutes? I'll just unpack the things that wrinkle, not that it matters too much in a town like this. But I know how much you hate wrinkled clothes. I don't think this room comes with an iron."

"You are so nice to me." He really was. He must've thanked her for coming a dozen times since they left the house.

"You're easy to be nice to."

She watched him work, amazed he had any energy. "It wouldn't take much for me to fall asleep sitting here."

"I'm almost done." He pulled her last blouse from the suitcase. "Think you might like to take a shower before bed?"

"That sounds nice. How's the hot water?"

"It works. The showerhead's nothing fancy. But it might relax your muscles, make it easier to sleep."

"I don't think I'm going to need any help with that. I could sleep on a wood floor right now."

After finishing his chore, he zipped the suitcases back up and moved them to a nearby table. "I think I might take one. My back's pretty stiff from all that time on the plane."

She got up and checked the curtain, adjusting it to make sure there were no cracks. Then walked over to him and began massaging his shoulders.

"A little lower, between my shoulder blades."

"You go ahead and take a shower. I'm just gonna change into my pj's. But maybe you better pray with me first." Ever since their wedding, Allan had started a habit of praying together every night before they fell asleep. "I don't think I'll be awake when you're done."

He turned and drew her close, said a short prayer. Once again, he included thanks for God making it possible for Michele to be there with him. Michele knew that all of Allan's anxiety and stress about the trip had completely disappeared the moment she told him she was coming.

He was tired but very happy.

She was just tired.

Michele woke up the next morning, surprisingly refreshed. They had both slept almost ten hours. On this part of the journey, the jet lag slanted in their favor. The opposite would be true on the way home.

Allan had gotten up a little earlier and was already showered and dressed. "There's a little café just a couple doors down the street. The team ate there almost every morning as we planned out our day. The food's not terrible. The coffee's actually pretty good. How about you start getting ready, and I'll go down and get two cups to go? Bring them back up here."

"I could definitely use some coffee. Speaking about planning out the day . . . what is our plan?"

"We're supposed to meet Henok back at that same café in about" —he glanced at his watch—"forty-five minutes from now."

"Forty-five minutes? Allan, you know I like more time than that to get ready."

"I know. But you were completely zonked thirty minutes ago. I didn't have the heart to wake you. But you'll be fine. Everything is casual today. Besides, look at you now. You just woke up, and you're already beautiful. Most women take an hour just to get where you're at now."

She laughed. It was a total lie, but it worked. "Go get the coffee."

He came back about fifteen minutes later. The coffee was surprisingly good; then she remembered one of her favorite Starbucks coffees had Ethiopia in its name. This actually tasted similar.

He picked up his cup and took a sip. "Guess who I saw in the café? Henok. He was already there, drinking coffee and writing in a notebook. So how about this? You finish getting ready and I'll go down and meet with him. See if we can get some of our business out of the way. And then you come down and join us when you're ready."

"By myself?"

"It's really close. You just walk out the front door of the hotel, turn right, and go three doors down. You don't even have to cross the street. You can even see the café sign from the front door of the hotel. It hangs out right over the sidewalk."

That didn't sound too bad. She just felt insecure. Of course she would, she was halfway around the world. "I guess I could do that. How much time do I have?"

"Doing it this way, you can take another fifteen or twenty minutes if you want. We'll be at a table along the right wall. I won't order breakfast until you get there." He came over and kissed her on the cheek.

◆　◆

When Allan got back to the café, he found Henok where he'd left him. Henok looked up from his notebook; a big smile came over his face as he stood.

"You don't need to get up," Allan said.

"Of course I do, my friend. I am so happy to see you."
They shook hands. "You have come such a long way, and on
such short notice. I was so sorry to hear about Pastor Ray. Is
he in very much pain?"

"He would be, but he's taking some strong pain medication."

"I saw some pictures on Facebook of him in his hospital
bed," Henok said. "He was smiling. He sent me a lengthy
email also, explaining everything. Which I found amazing
considering the accident was just Friday."

"Well, he's very sorry he couldn't come himself. And I'm
sorry for him. He's the one who's done most of the work
getting all this together back in the States."

"That's not how he explained it in his email," Henok said.
"He talked about all the work you have done. You are the
one who figured everything out and put the budget together.
I have been studying it carefully. It will be my job to make it
work once you leave."

Allan couldn't believe the change he was seeing in Henok
from the last time he was here. His eyes were so bright, and he
was so confident now. "We know you'll do a great job. So tell
me, what can we expect in our two meetings this morning?"

Ray had already briefed him that there would be one meeting with the government officials to pay all the necessary fees
and sign some papers, and one with the building landlord
to sign the lease. Henok explained these events in a little
more detail. It didn't sound like either meeting would take
very long. Henok said he wasn't expecting any surprises and,
thankfully, there didn't appear to be any worry about bribes.

After he finished the briefing, Henok said, "When will I
get to meet your wife? She's with you, isn't she?"

"Yes, she is. She should be down here very soon to join us

for breakfast." He turned for a moment to look at the front door. "Before she gets here, I wanted to ask you about Korah. Will we have time to go there this afternoon?"

"I was planning on it. The facility we have picked for the orphanage is on the edge of the city closest to Korah. That's where we will meet the landlord and sign the lease. After he leaves, I'll give you and your wife a tour of the facility, show you some of our plans. After that, we'll drive out to Korah."

"How long before we'll be ready to let the first six orphans start living there?"

"We can start now. It is very basic, but it will seem like a king's palace to the children."

— 53 —

Michele sat in the very plain lobby of a government office, reading her Kindle. Allan and Henok had been gone about twenty minutes for their meeting with the local officials. Hopefully they were signing papers to set up the orphanage. She could tell Allan was nervous on the car ride over, but Henok seemed confident the meeting would go well. He had already met several times with these officials, bringing them printed copies of the email exchanges with the "wonderful men from America" who were providing all the funds to make this a success.

As Allan and Henok walked into the office and before they closed the door, she heard Henok introduce Allan as "one of the men I've been telling you about."

She liked Henok right away and, during breakfast, was fascinated by stories of his childhood growing up in Korah. It had been an unimaginably hard life. As he spoke, she had decided not to press him for details. Otherwise, she'd lose her appetite for sure. She'd also loved his accent, although she couldn't quite place it. He spoke with such great diction.

The drive here from the café had given her a clearer picture of the town. It was close to how she had imagined it, both from Allan's stories and the handful of videos she had watched on YouTube about Addis Ababa. It didn't remind her of any city in the US. She saw evidence of new construction and modern buildings but mingled in were so many structures that were old and poorly maintained. They hadn't driven past a single block that would've passed the commercial building codes in River Oaks. But here, none of the buildings seemed out of place.

She had seen plenty of signs of poverty but nothing close to the things Allan had shared about Korah, or what Henok had described at breakfast that morning. That would soon change. They were heading to Korah after lunch.

She was just about to reconnect with her book when the office door opened. Henok came out first, followed by Allan. As soon as he saw her, his face lit up with a smile.

It had gone well. She was so relieved.

He waited until they were completely outside before talking. "We got the approval to launch the orphanage right away. As soon as we sign the papers with the landlord."

"Which is where we're going now," Henok added.

"Once the first six children are brought into the orphanage," Allan said, "and their paperwork is settled, the orphanage can begin to make adoptions to couples a reality."

They reached the car. Allan opened her door. Henok went around to the driver's seat. "We already have a lawyer from our church who has agreed to work with us on this."

"How far is it to the orphanage from here?"

"Less than ten minutes," Henok said.

◆   ◆

The landlord had just left, his copy of the signed lease and a check representing the first three months' rent in hand.

Henok was walking Allan and Michele through the facility, showing the work they had already done and discussing plans for the weeks ahead. It reminded her of a smaller version of a daycare center. There were no decorations on the walls, nothing to indicate little children would live here. And nothing Henok had shared so far seemed to indicate that correcting this was part of his future plans.

"Allan, is there any money in the budget to buy some things to make this place seem a little . . . happier? You know, stuff kids would like."

"I'm sure we could fix that," he said. "Henok, do you know of any stores where we could buy fun things for children?"

"Not at the moment, but I know someone I could ask. I have hired two women to care for the children full-time. They are coming later this afternoon while we are at Korah. I will ask them when we get back."

They walked past two open doorways to small bedrooms. Three child-sized beds lined the walls in both rooms. "Do we know who the first six children are?" Michele asked.

"Yes, I've picked them out," Henok said. "All of them are children in Korah that I think would fit in well here. I haven't talked to them or their guardians yet."

"Are their guardians the children's relatives?" Michele asked.

"Most are. Grandmothers, aunts, cousins."

They walked through the kitchen. Adequate, but no bigger than you'd see in an average apartment.

"Here's one benefit of doing business in Ethiopia," Allan said. "If we tried doing something like this in the US, we'd probably have to put in huge commercial appliances, as if we were opening a big restaurant."

Henok looked confused. "For six small children?"

281

"I know," Allan said. "Crazy, isn't it?"

Henok walked them out through the back door into a large fenced area. Barbed wire lined the top of the fence. It was bigger than a courtyard but smaller than a backyard. There were no swings, no slides, no playthings at all. Not even any grass, just dirt.

Allan looked at Michele. "We'll work on this too."

"Can we do it while we're still here?" She would have to talk to him about this later; she didn't want to embarrass Henok in any way. Clearly, his mind had been on other important things.

But this place needed a woman's touch.

As they finished the tour, Allan said, "Henok, what you've done here in such a short amount of time is simply amazing."

Michele was stunned.

They had finished their lunch and were now on the outskirts of Korah. She had tried to prepare for this moment, forcing herself to look over Allan's pictures and some additional material about Korah she had found on the internet. Seeing it up close was dramatically different. They were on their way to meet Ayana's grandmother but were not at the dump yet, where people all gathered to scrounge for food. Already, she could smell it. And so many people walked by on both sides of the road, carrying dirty white bags and sticks. They had just passed another group of young people. "Those bags they're holding, that's where they put the food they find, isn't it?"

"It is," Henok said over his shoulder. "And those sticks, they use them to move the garbage around as they search. Another thing to notice, something I hope we can address in the future. Look at their feet. Hardly any of the children have decent shoes. They are either ripped or torn, their toes are sticking out. Many get cut as they walk through the garbage. Broken glass or even HIV needles. Used needles." He turned the car down a narrow dirt street.

"Do some of them get infected because of this?" she asked.

"Or worse," he said. "Last week I was here doing some research on which children should be on our list. Living next door to one of the children was a young boy who had just come home from the hospital, his leg amputated below the knee. His aunt told me he had cut his foot on a piece of glass. Just a small cut. But there were no doctors, no hospitals nearby. The cut became infected, the infection grew, and . . ." He sighed. "All for the want of decent shoes."

How heartbreaking. Back home, they would have cleaned the cut, applied some Neosporin and Band-Aids. Maybe a quick trip to the urgent care center for a few stitches.

"Ayana's grandmother's home is just up ahead through that break in the wall." Henok pulled the car over and turned it off. A long wall made of rusty corrugated steel separated a row of shacks from the muddy dirt road.

"Follow me. She lives a few homes ahead on the left."

Homes, she thought. How could these be homes? She looked down the long dirt walkway separating two rows of tiny shacks. A flash in her mind, of a landscaped street in their townhome complex in River Oaks. Like the difference between heaven and hell. Small children came out from dark doorways, gazing, no doubt, at the spectacle of this white couple walking through the neighborhood. All of the children were dressed in rags. She looked down at their feet. It was just as Henok said.

Then she looked into their faces filled with smiles. As if they hadn't a care in the world.

— 54 —

They stood at the doorway as Henok knocked. A huddle of children had formed a half circle around them. He said something loudly that Michele did not understand. Moments later, an old woman's voice said something in reply.

"She said we can come in."

It took several moments for Michele's eyes to adjust. When they did, what she saw broke her heart. The room was smaller than her laundry room back home. Dark and dreary. Low ceiling, dirt floor. "This is where Ayana lives?" she whispered to Allan. He nodded.

From the shadows, a short, elderly woman emerged, holding her arms out toward Henok, a smile with very few teeth in her mouth. They hugged and exchanged three kisses: on the right cheek, left cheek, and right cheek once more. After, the woman turned to face them. She smiled politely at Michele, but when she saw Allan, her eyes widened, and so did her smile. She reached for him the same way she did for Henok. She looked at Henok, said something, and Henok replied. Then she gave Allan a big hug.

"She remembers you," Henok said.

He said something else to the woman, none of which

Michele understood except the mention of her name. The woman reached up both hands and grasped Michele's and squeezed gently. "Tell her I'm very happy to finally meet her," Michele said. Henok did.

Allan looked around. "I don't see Ayana anywhere. Is she at the dump?"

Henok spoke with the grandmother, who nodded her head as she replied. "She has already left with some other children to find food. But it's probably just as well, so we might speak with the grandmother in private."

"You're right," Allan said. "It wouldn't be good for her to overhear this conversation. Do you mind if I explain the situation to her and you interpret? I know you could do it fine without me, but I think it might help for her to hear it coming directly from me."

"Not at all," Henok said. "Just begin talking."

Allan stepped closer to Michele but looked at the grandmother. "The other man who was with me the last time hurt his leg and couldn't make the trip. But he wants you to know he wishes he could be here, and his prayers are with you. I have come representing him and the people of many churches back in America." He let Henok interpret. "Has Henok mentioned our plans to establish an orphanage here?"

Through Henok, she said, "Not directly to me, but I've heard exciting rumors. He's made several trips here since you left, and each time he's come in to see how we are doing."

"Well, the rumors are true. We have just signed the papers with the government and with the landlord. The orphanage is ready to open . . . today."

After Henok related this, a startled look came over her face.

"This is why we're here, why I've brought my wife here

all the way from America to help me. We have permission to welcome six children from Korah into the orphanage."

The words had barely left Henok's lips when the grandmother started trembling. Tears filled her eyes. She backed up until she reached her tiny bed, where she braced herself as she sat down.

Henok asked her something, probably trying to find out what upset her. She said something back in Amharic. Henok listened, a serious look on his face. He nodded and said something in reply. At that, the grandmother's smile returned even wider.

"What's going on?" Allan said.

Henok briefed them. "Ayana's grandmother said God must have sent us this very day. Since the last time we were here, her health has deteriorated badly. She's been concerned she could die any day and has been terrified about what would become of Ayana. She asked if we would consider letting Ayana come to live at our new orphanage."

"What did you say?" Michele asked.

"I told her it would be my honor to take her in. That I've been praying about that very thing." He looked back at the grandmother. "Now she is very happy," Henok said.

The grandmother dabbed her eyes with a cloth from a small table. Still crying, she managed to say some things that Henok understood. "She said God has been very good to them, bringing you back here to Korah. She has prayed for this very thing every day since you left. She asked how long before Ayana can come to this orphanage?"

"As soon as she is ready," Allan said.

"Today?" the grandmother said through Henok.

"Yes," Allan said, wiping tears off his face. "I would love to bring her there today."

She said something else. Whatever it was, it took Henok a moment to regain his composure. He turned to Allan. "She wants to know how far away is this orphanage, and will she ever see Ayana again after today?"

"Go ahead and tell her whatever you want to say, Henok. You are the orphanage director."

Henok took a deep breath, took a step toward the grandmother, and squatted down to be at face level. He said several things through many tears, and when he finished, the grandmother leaned forward and hugged him. She looked back in Henok's face, said something else, then cried even harder.

When the grandmother stopped crying, she let go of Henok. He straightened up again.

"What did you say?" Allan asked. "And what did she say back?"

"I told her the orphanage is not far from here. It's in the city but as close to Korah as we could make it. And I told her, of course she will see Ayana again. I will have many occasions to come back here. I can bring Ayana with me to visit her when I come. She said again that God has shown her that she will die very soon, but now she can die in peace knowing Ayana will never have to go to the dump for food after today."

— 55 —

After leaving Ayana's grandmother, Henok led them back to the car and drove them closer to the rear entrance of the dump. Allan said this was the way he and Ray had come on their last trip. For Michele, the bad smell had suddenly become unbearable. Allan had tried to warn her, but it didn't help. She wanted to turn back for the city, at least get far enough away to catch a fresh breath.

She couldn't imagine these poor people breathing this odor even for a few minutes, or imagine how they could eat food in the presence of this putrid smell. Then she realized their food was *part* of this smell. There were hundreds of people all around her—so many of them children—doing this very thing. None of them seemed even a little concerned.

Allan held her hand. He leaned over and whispered, "I know the smell is horrendous, but do your best not to show it on your face."

She understood what he was getting at. "Do we know where Ayana is?" Henok was a few yards in front of them, leading the way.

"He thinks he can find her," Allan said. "The main thing once we get to that hill is to stay in his footsteps as we

288

climb. There's all kinds of dangerous things hidden in the garbage."

"Like HIV needles," she said.

"Right. Henok has a good eye for stuff like that. Once we get to the top, you'll get quite a view of the dump. It's a shocking sight. Ayana will be somewhere in the crowd of people. Just stay close to Henok, especially on the way down."

Michele wasn't sure whether his warnings were helping or hurting her outlook. She did her best to stay close and keep inside his footsteps. When they reached the top of the first hill, they caught up with Henok, who stood surveying the scene below.

It was just as Allan had said. She had seen snippets of these scenes on YouTube, but seeing it for herself, the full panoramic view, was almost overwhelming. She had no reference point for any of it. The thought that all these people, including so many children, followed behind all these garbage trucks, searching freshly dumped piles of dark gray garbage for their daily food, was tragic. Heartbreaking.

"Oh, Allan," she said, squeezing his hand. She realized then how much he had been holding back.

"There she is," Henok announced. "I see her." He hurried down the hill.

Allan and Michele followed at a much slower pace.

◆ ◆

Allan kept his eye on Henok but mostly focused on Michele, making sure she didn't trip or fall. Things got a little easier when they reached level ground. He looked beyond Henok to see if he could catch a glimpse of Ayana. For almost a minute, he followed blindly. Then he saw her about fifty yards ahead at the bottom of a fresh pile of garbage.

She was with that same little boy Allan had seen her with the last time. A bunch of older children were climbing the new pile, rummaging through its contents. Ayana and the little boy picked through the clumps that had fallen from the older boys' efforts.

"Ayana!" Henok yelled, hurrying in her direction.

She looked around as if she didn't know where the sound came from.

"Ayana, over here," he said again.

This time when she looked, she saw him. So did the little boy. She stood up, dropped her bag and stick.

"You go on," Michele said. "Catch up with Henok. I'll be okay."

They didn't seem to be in danger of falling now, so Allan let go of Michele's hand. As he walked, he pulled three Hershey's Kisses out of his pocket. He'd brought them on purpose this time, thinking they might help Ayana remember him.

With about twenty-five yards left to close the gap, Ayana began running toward them. She yelled out something in Amharic. Allan saw her face; she was so excited. Then she saw him coming up behind Henok. Her eyes grew even brighter. She recognized him! He didn't need the Hershey's Kisses after all.

Henok slowed his pace, but Ayana kept running, her eyes fixed on Allan. "Be careful, little one," Henok said.

Ayana tripped over a small clump of garbage and fell flat on the ground.

"Ayana!" Allan shouted.

◆ ◆

Without a thought, Michele ran toward the little girl. By the time she arrived, Henok had already lifted Ayana off the

290

ground. She looked more startled than hurt. Then Michele saw something precious. Ayana stared at Allan. He had one hand resting on her shoulder; with the other, he brushed the dirt off her legs. She reached her little arms around his neck and began hugging him for all she was worth.

Allan immediately hugged her back. "You remembered me," he said, standing up with her. She released her hug but kept her left arm around his shoulder and neck. "It's so good to see you again." He looked at Henok. "Did you see that? She remembered who I was."

"I saw it," Henok said.

Allan held up the three Hershey's Kisses. Ayana's face looked like Christmas morning. "You remember these too," he said. "Go ahead, eat one."

She removed her arm from around his neck and began unraveling the foil wrapper.

Michele noticed a little boy walking up, the one Ayana had been with. "I think someone else would like a Hershey's Kiss."

Ayana saw the little boy too and, without hesitation, handed him one.

"Look how sweet she is," Allan said.

The little boy took the candy, but as he stepped back, he suddenly looked concerned. He was staring at Ayana's foot. He said something to Henok, then pointed.

Henok stepped over and looked. "Uh-oh. She's bleeding."

"What?" Michele said. "Where?" She reached down and gently lifted Ayana's foot. "She is bleeding."

"Use my shirt," Allan said.

Michele took the bottom of Allan's shirt and carefully wiped off the blood. It wasn't a deep cut, not the kind that would need stitches. But she instantly remembered what Henok had said about the little boy who'd lost his leg from an infected cut. "We've got to get her out of here. Can I hold her?"

"Sure," Allan said. "Henok, would you tell Ayana who Michele is? And that we're bringing her back to her grandmother's?"

Henok handed Ayana over to Michele. She went willingly.

Michele walked quickly back the way they had come. "We can't bring her back to her grandmother's. It's too dirty. We need to take her back to the orphanage. I saw a first aid kit in the bathroom cabinet." Allan and Henok began to follow her.

"Michele, wait up."

"We can't. We have to get her back and clean this cut."

Allan caught up with her. "Michele, slow down. It won't do any good if you fall holding her."

"But you heard what Henok said about that little boy who lost his leg."

"I did." He put his hand on her shoulder. "But hon, we don't need to panic. That cut got infected after several days, not a few minutes. We've got time. We'll get her taken care of. That's why we're here, to take her out of this place. For good." They reached the bottom of the hill they had climbed to get here.

"We really need to get her back to her grandmother's," he said, "so we can explain to her what's happening, and she can say good-bye. Then we'll bring her to the orphanage and get this cut all cleaned up. If you want, we can take her shopping with us when we buy some of the fun kid things for the place."

She stopped walking and turned around. Allan was right. They didn't need to rush. Henok caught up with them. The little boy wasn't far behind. Michele felt so bad for him.

"Where are we going next?" Henok asked.

292

"Back to Ayana's grandmother," Allan said. "Maybe there you can explain everything to Ayana, and she and her grandmother can say a proper good-bye. Then we'll get her to the orphanage and clean up this cut."

"Perhaps after that," Henok said, "we can buy her some new shoes."

"That's a great idea, Henok," Michele said. She looked up the hill. "Why don't you lead the way?"

"You want me to take her?" Allan asked.

"I'm okay. She's very light."

"Look at the way she's looking at you," Allan said.

Michele looked down into the most beautiful set of dark brown eyes. Ayana smiled, then rested her head against Michele's shoulder.

The little boy was standing back about fifteen feet, watching them. "I feel so bad leaving him," Allan said. "He and Ayana seem so close."

"It won't be for long," Henok said. "He's one of the five other children on my list."

"That's great," Allan said. "I'm so glad." Henok started climbing the hill. Allan said to Michele, "I'll go last this time. In case you slip."

They began making their way carefully up the hill. About halfway, Michele felt this intense peace come over her. Then a clear thought, almost like a voice speaking gently in her mind.

This is the child I have for you.

It took her breath away. She suddenly felt weak. Her legs almost buckled.

Allan steadied her with his hand. "Are you okay?"

Tears began to well up in her eyes. "Yes, I'm fine. We're . . . fine." She looked down at little Ayana again.

She was sound asleep.

— 56 —

They carried Ayana back to the car. She woke up at some point along the way. But she remained perfectly calm, content to let Michele hold her. Henok drove the car slowly on their way back to the grandmother's hut. All the while, Michele's excitement grew. She was convinced that the thought—that she was holding the little girl God meant for her to have—did not come from her own imagination. It was something she'd never experienced before but heard others talk about: the still small voice of God.

She didn't know how it would all work out, but she was sure it would. She looked at Allan in the front seat, wishing they could be alone so she could tell him what had happened.

He turned in his seat toward her. "How's she doing?"

"She seems fine. I can't believe how brave she is. Most children would be crying. I think the bleeding stopped. I'll still feel better when we can get it cleaned up properly and bandaged."

"Perhaps we shouldn't mention the cut to her grandmother," Henok said. "She will want to care for it using the best means she has, but we have much better medical supplies at the orphanage."

Michele looked down at Ayana. Her big eyes roamed all about the car. "Do you think she has ever been in a car before?"

"I doubt it," Allan said. "This would be like our first ride in an airplane. Or maybe even a spaceship. Have you ever flown in a plane before, Henok?"

"A few times. But only small two-seater planes. Never a big airliner. I have never been out of the country before."

"We'll have to see what we can do about that," Allan said. "I wouldn't be surprised if someday in the future God makes that possible."

That got a big smile from Henok. He pulled the car over. "Here we are." They got out of the car.

"You want me to take her?" Allan said.

"Just until I get out," Michele said. "Do you mind if I carry her a little while longer?"

"Not at all."

Once out of the car, Michele wasn't sure Ayana wanted to come back to her. She was squeezing Allan's neck so tight. But when Michele reached for her, the little girl let go of Allan and reached back. Michele picked her up and followed the two men through the dirt walkway that led from the muddy street, through the fence, and into the row of shacks and huts. Ayana's eyes instantly locked on to the doorway where her grandmother lived.

She knew where home was.

Michele couldn't help but recall their neighborhood in River Oaks, the view from the sidewalk to their front door. Or even the view coming in from the garage through the courtyard and back patio. *Lord,* she prayed, *someday let that be what Ayana thinks of when she thinks of home.*

Henok led them into her grandmother's hut. The old

woman greeted them warmly. When she looked at Michele holding Ayana, she said something.

Henok interpreted. "She likes you, her grandmother said."

Michele hugged her gently. "Tell her I like her too." Henok did.

Then he spoke to both Allan and Michele. "With your permission, I'd like to explain to her grandmother the situation and our plans. I think it's best if she explains everything to Ayana herself. Of course, I will interpret what I'm saying as I go."

"We're fine with that, Henok," Allan said.

"Perhaps you should let me hold Ayana for a moment," he said, "so that she can be looking into her grandmother's eyes as she speaks." Michele handed Ayana to him. Looking at both the woman and the child, he said in their language: "Allan and Michele would like to do what they came here to do today, now, if you approve. But only if you approve. If you have any reservations, they can come back later this evening, or even tomorrow. They don't want to rush you in any way. They also think it might be wise for you to explain things to Ayana in your own words, since she knows you the best. If you'd like, you can do it now. Or if you'd rather, we can step outside to give you privacy, or even come back later."

Michele thought Ayana looked a little confused by this exchange. The grandmother seemed to grasp everything clearly. She said something to Henok in reply.

He looked at them and interpreted. "She has been praying since we left to find Ayana. She says God has put her heart at rest and has assured her she need not carry the burden of Ayana's welfare on her shoulders any longer. God has brought you." He pointed to Allan. "I think she means through the orphanage, to care for Ayana from now on. So she is ready to do this today. Even now."

"Great," Allan said. "Then let's do this."

Henok released Ayana to sit close to her grandmother, who held her chin as she spoke. Henok stood next to Michele and Allan, quietly interpreting what she said.

"My sweet Ayana, you have heard me pray many times since these men came to visit us a while ago. God has answered our prayers today. He has brought Henok and this couple from America to bring you to a wonderful new place to live. It is not far from here, so we will see each other again. You will have your own bed and clean clothes and never have to search through garbage for food again. And you will not be alone. Henok tells me he is bringing five other children from the village to this place. And two very nice women from the city will live there with you, to take care of you and the other children. Would you like to do this? Would you like to go with them?"

Ayana said something to her grandmother, the first words she had spoken. It caused tears to form in the grandmother's eyes. Henok did not interpret what the little girl said, but he did share the grandmother's reply. "Of course I love you still. I will always love you. It is my love and God's love that are sending you to this new place. My love will go with you. But you know I am very old and not well. Soon, God will come for me, to bring me to heaven where he lives. This way, you will never be alone and you will always be loved and taken care of. So will you go?"

There was a long pause. Then Ayana nodded her head yes and reached for her grandmother. They hugged each other tightly until, finally, the grandmother let go. When Ayana turned, she reached for Michele. Michele took her and held her close.

An unusual look came over the grandmother's face. She looked at Michele and Allan, then said something very quietly to Henok. Something she clearly didn't want Ayana to hear. The more she talked, the more concerned Henok looked. When she finished, Henok said something in a fairly serious tone, but just as quietly. It looked to Michele as if he also shook his head no. The grandmother smiled and continued talking to Henok, this time looking back and forth at Allan and Michele. Henok's expression changed, became softer. If Michele guessed right, he was conceding to whatever she said.

He looked at them and said, "I'm sorry. That must have seemed strange. It was a little strange for me. I will talk freely because Ayana doesn't understand English. Ayana's grandmother said something happened as soon as she finished talking to her granddaughter. She felt the Lord clearly show her that some of what she was saying to Ayana was wrong." Henok sighed. It was clear he didn't want to say what came next. "I did my best to talk her out of this, but it is no good. She is insistent that I tell you."

"That's okay, Henok," Allan said. "Tell us, whatever it is."

"She said . . . well, she said that God hasn't brought you here to bring Ayana to the orphanage. He has, but only for a time. He has really brought you here to bring Ayana home with you to America, to raise her there as your own."

Michele was stunned. She couldn't believe what she'd just heard.

"I'm so sorry," Henok said. "I tried to explain to her that—"

"I wish we could," Allan said, glancing at Michele, "but that really is impossible. That's not really why we—"

"Why is it impossible?" Michele blurted out.

"What?" Allan said. "Hon, do you hear what he's saying? Do you understand what Henok is—"

"I understand perfectly. And I understand what Ayana's grandmother said. I don't think it's impossible. I think it's maybe the reason why we came. The reason why I'm here, with you." She started to cry. "So that I could be here and see . . . all this. And see her." She looked down at Ayana. "See this beautiful little girl and be able to hear what I believe God wanted me to hear a little while ago."

Allan walked over and put both arms on her shoulders. "What are you saying? What do you believe you heard God say?"

Michele swallowed hard. She had to get the words out, just the way she'd heard them. "Do you remember when we began walking up the hill, and I almost stumbled?" He nodded. "I had just heard, well, I believe I just heard the Lord say, *This is the child I have for you.*"

Allan's eyes instantly filled with tears. "I can't believe it."

"So, you're okay with this?" she said.

"I'm more than okay. I've thought about adopting Ayana a hundred times since the moment I first saw her. But I never once allowed myself to think the thought came from God. It seemed like a completely closed door."

"It's open now," she said.

Allan hugged her, careful not to squeeze little Ayana in between them.

Henok turned to the grandmother, a shocked look on his face. "They are saying yes."

57

They were back at the orphanage now. Surprisingly, the good-bye scene with Ayana's grandmother was not a tearful one. Michele saw tears starting to form in the grandmother's eyes, but she blinked them away. She'd told Henok they were happy tears, that she was sincerely happy for this great blessing from God. But she couldn't even allow happy tears for Ayana's sake, because the little girl wouldn't know the difference.

It appeared to have worked, because Ayana seemed very content now. Michele had already cleaned her cut and dressed it with disinfectant and a Band-Aid. She was walking through the orphanage with a clipboard and pen—Ayana right behind her—making a list of things to buy with Allan once he arrived back from an important meeting. She couldn't wait to hear how it went, although the longer he was gone, the more nervous she felt.

He and Henok were meeting with some of the same government officials to discuss the possibility of adopting Ayana. Allan had already told her there was absolutely no chance of bringing her home with them this coming Saturday. Henok had agreed. There were too many details and legal formalities to work out. Not to mention agreeing on the costs. And that was just on this side of the Atlantic. She and Allan had never seriously considered adoption until today and didn't know what was required in the US, let alone the additional factors to consider for an international adoption.

But she considered all these just wrinkles to be ironed out. None of them diminished her happiness. The way God had brought this whole thing about had produced faith in her heart, and it was clear in Allan's too that God would finish this good work he had begun. She did find herself taking an even greater level of interest in decorating and outfitting this place before they left, seeing that it was now the temporary home for their daughter.

Their daughter.

She stopped, turned around, and bent down to face Ayana. The little girl looked up at Michele with those big brown eyes. Michele picked her up and, with a big smile on her face, said, "I can tell you one thing, little Miss Ayana, we're going to have to get Henok to start teaching you some English. And maybe teach us a few phrases in Amharic. If that's how you even pronounce it." She gently touched the tip of Ayana's nose with her index finger.

The playful gesture startled the little girl. But she quickly smiled back.

They were standing at the doorway to her bedroom. You wouldn't know it just by looking at it, because there was no distinction between the two bedrooms. But Henok had explained this bedroom was for three little girls and the one next to it for three little boys. "We're going to fix that, aren't we, Ayana? After we're done shopping today, no one will have to wonder which bedroom belongs to the little girls and which belongs to the little boys."

She set Ayana down on the floor. "Which bed would you like?" She knew Ayana didn't really understand what she was saying, so she made some gestures hoping the child would still get her meaning. Ayana stepped into the room and looked around. Even without decorations and frills, it was so much more luxurious than the dark hut she had known every day of her young life. Michele nodded, encouraging her that it was okay. Ayana walked to the bed in the middle along the back wall. First she swiped her hand across the blanket, then she patted it. She had probably never felt anything so soft.

"Would you like it? Would you like that one? You can have it. That can be your bed, if you want." She wasn't sure Ayana understood. She walked over, lifted her up, and set her in the middle of the bed. Ayana smiled as she sank into the mattress, just a little. Michele patted the mattress with both hands. "It's yours, Ayana. This is your bed now." She sat beside her, put her arm around her.

She thought about their upstairs back in River Oaks. She and Allan hadn't even talked about which bedroom would become Ayana's. Both were more than twice the size of this room. What would Ayana think when she finally came home with them and walked into her room for the first time?

She pulled Ayana close. "I have so many things to do now, because of you. Do you know that?"

Just then, a car pulled up in the driveway. Ayana heard it too. They got up and walked into the hall. Michele saw the car through a side window. Allan and Henok were back. She stood by the back door, waiting to see Allan's face as he walked in. Ayana stood next to her, reached for her hand.

The door opened. Henok came through. He was smiling. Then Allan walked in, and his smile was even bigger.

Michele's heart was exploding. "So it went well?"

"Better than well," Allan said. "Henok was simply amazing." He patted Henok on the back.

"God was good," Henok said. "He opened their hearts to hear what we were asking."

"So tell me what happened."

Allan walked toward the living area. "Let's sit down a minute." Ayana stood next to him. He picked her up, sat her beside him, and put his arm around her. "I can't believe how well it went. So much better than I was expecting."

"So they were open to the idea of us adopting Ayana?"

"At first they weren't. I could see they were becoming a little tense as Henok explained things. I guess they thought we were rushing things. But the longer he talked, the calmer they got. He didn't stop to interpret as he was speaking, so I had to just read their faces."

"I'm sorry about that," Henok said. "I thought that perhaps—"

"No need to apologize. Obviously, God was leading you. You accomplished so much more than I was even hoping for. Actually, why don't you tell Michele what you said? I might leave something out."

Henok sat on the edge of his chair. "They knew we were interested in seeing children adopted by American families. They just weren't expecting anything so soon. But I remembered one of their disappointments in our earlier meeting was that we were only taking six children into the orphanage at first, when there are so many who need our help. But I assured them we intended the number to grow as soon as we were able. But six was how many we could take at the moment. Once I remembered this concern, I pointed out one way to increase the number of children we rescue from Korah now is to streamline the path for adoption. Every child adopted from this original six opens a bed for another child to come into the orphanage."

"It was brilliant," Allan said. "But there's more. Wait till you hear what else."

"On the way there," Henok continued, "I asked Allan if you had been thinking of adoption already and were saving money for it back home. He said you had not, that you had used most of your savings to bring you here on this trip. Once the officials had agreed to streamline the adoption process, I suggested a rather . . . unorthodox idea. I pointed out how beneficial it would be if we could have one adoption happen as soon as possible, so that this child could serve as something of an ambassador back in the US, which would help encourage other couples to want to adopt these children, as well. Which, of course, would free up more beds in the orphanage, allowing more children to be rescued from Korah."

"You're not going to believe this next part," Allan said.

"When it seemed they liked this idea, I mentioned that you and Allan were interested in adopting a little girl, even now, as soon as it became legally possible. But that you lacked most of the funds. One of the men on the council spoke up before I could suggest it. He said after all Allan had done to start this orphanage, they should waive the normal fees and expedite this adoption. The other men agreed."

"So . . . what are you saying?" Michele asked.

"He's saying it's not going to cost us tens of thousands of dollars to adopt Ayana. They're waiving most of the fees. We'll have some legal expenses here and in the US, but nothing like the twenty-five-thousand figure people usually have to pay."

Michele couldn't believe it. She hadn't even allowed herself to consider the money side of all this. It was just too much to think about right now. But before she'd even been tempted to worry, God had tossed the mountain into the sea. "This is just so wonderful."

"Isn't it?" Allan said, giving Ayana a squeeze that made her smile. "I'm just . . . so incredibly happy right now." He looked at Henok. "It was like God gave you the wisdom of Solomon."

Henok smiled. "I'm just glad I could help."

"You did way more than help, my friend."

"So," Michele said, "do you have any idea how long it will take before we can actually bring her to the US?"

"I'm not sure," Henok said. "I'm afraid it still might take quite some time. If I had to guess, I would say . . . maybe six months, maybe more?"

"That long?" Michele said.

"Well, I'm sure it will fly by," Allan said. "We'll have so many things to do to get ready back home." He stood and picked up Ayana. "Who's ready to go shopping? Then let's go someplace nice to eat. Henok, you pick it out. Somewhere you and Ayana would really enjoy."

— 58 —

On Saturday morning, it was time to leave Addis Ababa and head for home. They were already at the airport. Allan and Henok were unloading their bags. Michele and Ayana stood on the sidewalk watching, holding hands.

The last few days had been extremely busy. Lots of shopping, cleaning, and setting up the orphanage. It looked totally different than it did when she'd first walked in. With each new purchase and each new item brought into the orphanage, Ayana reacted as any little American girl would at Christmas. She especially loved a doll Michele let her pick out in one of the local stores. She was holding it now. She had never owned a new toy before.

As tired as she was, Michele was torn about leaving. The love born in her heart when God first spoke to her about Ayana had only intensified in the days that followed. It was clear that Allan had experienced the same thing.

Henok had already taught them both some basic phrases. Ayana seemed to pick up English much easier than they were learning Amharic. Yesterday, Henok had explained to her in very simple terms the basic concept of adoption and that Allan and Michele wanted to adopt her and bring her back to

America to be their little girl. Before he'd even finished asking if she would like that, she yelled out "Yes!" in Amharic and began jumping up and down. The only disappointing part of the conversation came when he'd explained they had to leave for home this morning, but that for now, she could not go with them. She was ready to go now.

Henok said he had tried to explain when she would get to go home with them, but she was at that age when children don't clearly grasp the concept of time. But the conversation had ended on a high note when he'd asked her if she would like to call them Mommy and Daddy. Not in Amheric but English. She got very excited about that and instantly wanted to learn.

So, for the rest of the evening until her bedtime and all morning, Ayana had called them Mommy and Daddy, with the sweetest little accent. It had thrilled Michele's heart every time she heard it.

Allan and Henok had just given their bags to the porter. Michele knew what that meant.

"I'm afraid it's time," Allan announced. Henok extended his hand to say good-bye. Allan took it and drew him close for a hug. "There are no words to express our gratitude, my friend. I cannot believe all that's happened in just a few days. Pastor Ray will be so proud of you when I tell him all you've done."

"It's been my great honor. You all have changed my life. I feel like I'm living a dream."

Michele clutched her mini-iPad, which she'd pulled out of her purse moments ago. They had taken tons of pictures and videos over the last few days to show the family back home. But she would need to look at them herself as soon as they stepped onto the plane. Allan walked toward Michele and

Ayana. Michele turned and bent down to face her. "Henok, would you—"

"Of course, I will tell her whatever you say."

"Ayana, we are so glad God has brought us together. Meeting you has made me so happy."

"Me too," Allan said.

"We can't wait until we can come back again to see you. And one day soon, as soon as God lets us, we will bring you home with us for good, to America. You will have your own room, right next to ours. And you'll have lots of relatives that all live nearby. Remember the pictures I showed you in here?" She pointed to her iPad. "Grandparents, aunts and uncles, and cousins." Henok translated everything.

Ayana smiled, pointed to Michele's iPad, and said something. Henok answered her, then explained. "She really liked all the pictures you showed her. She had never seen pictures before. I wonder, could you possibly send some new ones every now and then, after you're gone? It might help prepare her for your return and give me some useful things to work with as I teach her English."

"Tell her we'll definitely send more pictures. You can get them over the internet here, can't you?"

"We can. They are very expensive to print, but I can show them to her on the screen. When the internet is working."

"Here," Allan said. He opened his wallet. "Most of my pics are on my phone, but I have one here I printed of Michele and me taken a few months ago." He handed it to Ayana.

She looked at it and smiled, then said something to Henok.

"Yes," Henok answered, "he's giving it to you. You can keep it."

She wrapped her arms around Allan's legs. Allan squeezed

back, then lifted her up to hug her properly. He looked at Michele. "We really need to go."

"I know." She took Ayana for one last big hug and kissed her on the cheek.

Allan leaned over and kissed her on the other cheek, then reached out to shake Henok's hand one more time.

Reluctantly, Michele handed her to Henok. As they walked away, Michele said, "We love you, Ayana!" And to Henok, "Take good care of our little girl."

"I will," he yelled back. "You have my word."

Our little girl, Michele thought.

She loved how that sounded.

59

Marilyn was so excited. Michele had just called. She hung up the phone and got everyone's attention. "Listen, everyone, they're on their way here." Everyone stopped, looked at her for a moment, then returned to their conversations.

Jim leaned over and said, "They'll get excited once Michele and Allan walk in the door."

"You're right." She was being a little silly. It wasn't like they were getting ready for a surprise party. The important thing was that everyone was here, including Uncle Henry and Aunt Myra, who just this week had gotten back from their long RV trip out West visiting their kids.

Doug was here too, sitting next to Christina. She was part of the family now. Christina seemed to be adjusting well, all things considered. Marilyn noticed how much she brightened up when Doug was around. Still, both had made it clear, they were just good friends.

They had all finished their big Sunday dinner and were now finishing up dessert. Allan and Michele didn't come to dinner. They had even missed church that morning. Both were too wiped out. Besides the flight time, they had lost nine hours in the exchange.

"So you really have no idea what this big surprise is all about?" Jim said.

"Not a clue," Marilyn said.

Aunt Myra sat across the table from her. "I've been looking on Facebook every day since they left for Africa, but I haven't seen a thing. Don't they have the internet over there?"

"They do," Jim said. "But the connection is pretty spotty."

"Used to drive Michele crazy," Marilyn said, "when he'd be over there for weeks without her."

"You think it has something to do with the orphanage?" Uncle Henry asked. "That's what they went over there for, right? Trying to get one set up."

Marilyn set down her coffee, glanced out the front window. Still no sign of them. "Yes. I'm sure things went well. Michele sounded pretty excited when she called last night." She looked around the table. Most of those seated had finished their dessert. She got up and began to clear.

"I'll help you," Jim said.

"No, you stay seated and finish. Keep Uncle Henry company. I just want to give folks some elbow room." She had barely set the first armload on the kitchen counter when she heard footsteps on the front porch.

"Think they're here, Mom," Tom said.

Right after that, the front door opened. Allan and Michele walked in. Everyone got up to greet them. They had only been gone five days. For some reason, maybe because Africa was the other side of the world, it felt like longer. Marilyn had to wait her turn to hug them both. When she hugged Michele, she held on especially tight.

When she pulled back to look at her face, there were tears in Michele's eyes. But the look on her face said they were happy tears. Very happy tears.

"I can't wait to tell you," Michele said.

"Aren't you going to tell us right now?" Marilyn said.

"We are," Allan said. "We were hoping everyone would be finished with dessert by now. We'd kind of like to tell you our big news with everyone sitting in the living room." He handed Michele's iPad to Doug. "Doug, do you know how to hook this up so videos and pics can show up on the TV?"

"Yeah." He took the iPad and walked around to the side of the big-screen TV.

"Could you just get it set up? Don't show anything until I tell you."

"Those of you who haven't finished your dessert," Marilyn said, "just bring your cup and plate over here and find a seat. Don't worry about making a mess."

"Tommy and Carly," Jean said, "that doesn't include you. Leave your plates and drinks on the table. You can finish them after." She looked at Marilyn. "I couldn't enjoy myself if they finished up in here."

Everyone found a seat, except Allan and Michele, who stood in front of the TV, holding hands. Marilyn couldn't wait to hear what they had to say.

Allan spoke first. "First, we want to thank you all for your prayers. Based on the things I'm about to say, it's very clear to us that God answered them. He even answered some things I didn't have the faith to pray for. This trip was kind of a last-minute thing, and I was pretty nervous about going. No, to be honest, I was terrified . . . until Michele agreed to come." He pulled the hand he had been holding to his lips and kissed it.

"Now, it's clear, to both of us, that her coming was the providence of God. The story we're about to tell you could never have happened without her. As you know, the main purpose of this trip was to try to get this orphanage up and running. That did happen. But something else happened there that was even more exciting . . . and totally unexpected." He looked at Michele.

She looked first at her father, who was standing next to Marilyn. "Dad? Remember before I left, when I came to you for advice, about whether or not I should go?" Jim nodded that he did. "You predicted that by the time I came home, I would have no regrets about any of the money we spent on this trip. You said the reward I'd feel inside would be a much bigger prize than anything I could possibly lose."

"Did I say that?" he said.

"You did. Well, God gave me an even a bigger prize than that. Bigger than I could ever imagine." Tears filled her eyes. "Mom and Dad, sometime in the next six to nine months, you're going to be grandparents again!"

"What?" Marilyn almost yelled. Everyone else reacted with similar shock. Marilyn was about to ask if Michele had found out she was pregnant on the trip, but that made no sense. Why would she say . . . six to nine months? "That's wonderful news," Marilyn said. "But how?"

Michele looked at Allan. Allan looked at Doug. "Is the TV almost ready?"

"Almost," Doug said. "Just a couple more minutes."

"Good. That's all I'll need." He turned to face everyone else. "I want to tell you all an amazing story. It's a story about a place called Korah and a little girl. A little girl named Ayana . . ."

Author's Note from Dan

We're so glad you joined us for book 3 in the Restoration series. Although the books have been written in a certain order, we've done our best to give each of them a "stand-alone" quality. But if *The Desire* happens to be book 1 for you, may I suggest you go back and read the first two books in the series (*The Dance* and *The Promise*)? You'll gain a richer sense of the characters you've already come to know and also explore some important lessons about family life.

Just as *The Promise* featured Jim and Marilyn Anderson's oldest son, Tom, *The Desire* features their second child, Michele, and her husband, Allan, in a primary way. We also spent time with each of the other family members and introduced a new character to the Anderson family story, a young lady named Christina. Christina has become a major character in the Restoration series and will play a prominent role in book 4, which will feature the Andersons' third child, their youngest son, Doug.

We hope you were touched by the powerful drama unfolding in the lives of Michele and Allan and also Christina. In many ways, this third story hits close to home for Gary and me. Some of the most significant parts of the book were drawn from our real-life experiences. For example, after trying to get pregnant for just over a year, and after wanting to be a mom for as long as she can remember, Michele begins to face the heartache of infertility. Something millions of couples struggle with every day. My wife and I faced this in the early years of our marriage.

Perhaps you have some experience with infertility or know someone who has. We tried for eight years before we had our first child through adoption. It took us six more years to adopt our second. But that was decades ago. To help me research the current challenges couples face today, I received lots of input from women struggling with infertility now or fairly recently.

During my research, I was saddened to learn that many of these women felt alone and unsupported by other Christians in their churches. Some church members reacted with real insensitivity to their struggle (similar to Michele's experience in the book). My wife and I experienced similar things back in the early eighties and nineties, when we went through these things firsthand. Part of the reason for including this theme in our series was to bring greater clarity to this important issue and stir fresh motivation for all of us to reach out with compassion and kindness to couples unable to conceive.

The issue of adoption was another important consideration for Gary and me as we explored the challenges Michele, Allan, and Christina faced in this story. We hoped through Christina's eyes you might see the unique challenges a young woman faces in a crisis pregnancy, and how much courage it takes to place a child in an adoptive home. To me, this choice is the opposite of abandonment. It's about placing a child's needs above our own, and thinking only about what's best for their future. Sometimes, as in Christina's case, the best thing is to entrust a child's care into the hands of a couple who are ready and willing to parent the child and raise them as their own.

My wife and I had the privilege of being on the receiving end of this blessing when we adopted both our children many years ago. Gary and Norma experienced this blessing firsthand as grandparents when their daughter Kari Gibson and her husband adopted a little girl from Ethiopia named Zoie. Two years later, Gary's son Greg and his wife adopted a little girl named Annie.

Actually, the entire story line surrounding Allan and Michele's desire to adopt little Ayana was inspired by Kari's real-life adventure. She and her husband Roger traveled to Addis Ababa and became missionaries to the poor people who lived in Korah.

As with the first two novels in the Restoration series, this book drew inspiration from one of Gary's earlier nonfiction books. This time it was *Guarding Your Child's Heart* (NavPress, 2011). You may recall in our story that Julie, the pastor's wife, handed Michele a children's ministry notebook to evaluate for their children's ministry. The notebook was fiction. But the content in the notebook was not. Remember when Michele began to share with Jean some of the surprising biblical truths about humility and love she had read in this notebook? Her reactions were my reactions as I read Gary's book *Guarding Your Child's Heart*. I had been a pastor for twenty-five years, had read dozens of books on things like humility, love, and rejoicing in trials, but as I read what God had shown Gary about these things, it was as if I'd read about them for the very first time. It's that good.

317

So . . . where do we go from here? What will become of the Anderson family in book 4? The next book will begin about seven to eight months after the close of this one. Sadly, Doug's time away at college in St. Augustine will increase the drift we've already begun to see, both from the Lord and from his family. The temptations of life in that environment coupled with a fairly shallow personal faith will prove to be too much for Doug. And it will put a terrible strain on everyone in the Anderson family, but especially his parents, Jim and Marilyn.

What will become of Christina, who has now been welcomed into the Anderson clan? Will the friendship and affection she feels for Doug grow into true love or be destroyed by his poor choices? Will Michele and Allan's long-awaited adoption of little Ayana finally happen or be held up by government bureaucracy and red tape? Be looking for book 4 of our Restoration series, due out in the spring of 2015.

In the meantime, as always, we'd love to hear from you, especially if the stories have blessed you or helped you in some way. You can reach me through the contact page on my website, or once there, by clicking one of the buttons to connect with me on Facebook, Twitter, or Pinterest. It's http://danwalshbooks.com. Also check out Gary's website, which is managed by his son Michael Smalley (himself an amazing author and counselor in his own right). It's simply, smalley.cc.

Dan's Interview with Gary
about *The Desire*

Dan: As with the first two books in our series, the spiritual themes in *The Desire* are drawn from one of your non-fiction books. This time I used a book you published in 2011, written to equip parents to teach spiritual truths to their children more effectively, called *Guarding Your Child's Heart*. This book seems different than most of the books you've written. What motivated you to write it?

Gary: It started thirteen years ago, when I turned sixty. I experienced a radical change in my spiritual outlook. God showed me that, for the most part, I tended to blame other people and other things for anything that went wrong in my life. He convicted me that I was just blame shifting. I saw that the Scriptures teach that I'm 100 percent responsible for my actions and my reactions to what other people do and say. Jesus said in Matthew 12 that "out of the heart" come evil thoughts and evil deeds, meaning out of our *own* heart. Other people can't make us do wrong things. And blaming them doesn't help anything; it just makes things worse and keeps us locked into destructive attitudes and behavior.

Seeing this was really liberating. Only God can cleanse my heart, but I realized to really experience the quality of life Jesus wants me to have, I was responsible for guarding my heart and renewing my mind. This led me into a study that totally changed my life. This book contains all the things God showed me from this time. I wrote it as a tool to help parents teach these truths to their children, so they can start their lives on this foundation.

Dan: When we first began this Restoration series, your staff sent me a box of your more recent books to help me create stories for our project. Initially I ignored this book because it looked like something written for children. But as I went through it, I was astounded by the depth and simplicity in the lessons and felt the advice you gave to parents before each lesson was priceless. Page after page was filled with so much practical wisdom and insight. Tell us a little more about the connection between obedience to Christ and experiencing genuine joy.

Gary: I've experienced more peace and joy since I began following these truths than I have my whole life. See, when we think our happiness is dependent on things going the way we want or on circumstances we can't control or on people doing what we want them to, we're unhappy all the time. But when we realize that joy comes from the Lord, that it's the fruit of faith and obedience, we realize that being joyful is something we can do all the time, every day. In Matthew 7, Jesus taught a parable about a house that either stands or falls when the storms hit, based on whether or not it had been built on rock or sand. Then he tells us what building on rock is like . . . it's simply hearing his commands and obeying them. Obeying Christ's commands brings incredible stability and peace into our lives.

At the Last Supper, he emphasized obeying his commands again, and this time he said he was telling us these things "so that our joy might be full." That's why God wants us to obey him, so that we can experience the fullest possible joy anyone can have in this life. And we can have it simply by trusting in him and doing what he says. No matter what happens, no one can take that kind of joy away from us. So I began studying Christ's commands, and I saw that we can actually obey all his commands if we'll obey these four: humble ourselves, love God, love others, and rejoice in our trials.

Dan: One of the main themes in *Guarding Your Child's Heart* is how our beliefs directly connect to the way we live. Could you explain a little more about how what we believe, whether true or false, dramatically affects how we live and the choices we make?

Gary: Everyone lives by what they believe, whether that belief is true or false. Our beliefs are formed by our thoughts, which is why the Bible teaches us to be careful about the things that influence us or our children, and why it's necessary for our minds to be renewed by God's truth. What we think really matters. If we think about something that's not true long enough, we will start to believe it. Once we start to believe it, our emotions get involved, and now it feels like the truth.

For example, if I believe I can't be happy unless my wife changes, then I'll constantly be focused on her, nagging her, pressuring her to change. And I'll stay unhappy. But this belief is based on a thought that isn't true. If I allow my mind to be renewed by God's truth, which says I'm supposed to love her as Christ loves the church no matter what, then my focus shifts from her performance to my own behavior, to the way I treat her, and the things I say. This new belief can radically change our relationship.

Dan: In our book *The Desire*, Michele is reading this children's ministry notebook and discovers some things about humility she never understood. I loved what you wrote about humility in *Guarding Your Child's Heart*, particularly the part about needing to become aware that we are all helpless without God and need to seek his help every day. What you shared were some pretty radical lessons for someone to be learning at your age. Why do you think pride comes so easily to us and humility is so hard to grasp?

Gary: I think pride is built into our nature. Then it is reinforced by our parents and the culture around us, which pushes us to succeed and emphasizes that it's all up to us. The focus is always on us. Pride makes us envious of others, so we're always striving to impress people or craving recognition. But Jesus shows us something brand new—humility. He lived a life of total dependence on God and taught his disciples that this is the way he wants them to live too. He tells us that true joy comes from being "poor in spirit."

The truth is, spiritually, we are all beggars. We're crippled. On our own, we can't produce things like love, joy, peace, patience, and the other fruits of the Spirit. We can try, but we can't pull it off. Humility is simply seeing this and admitting it, owning it. And God promises that when we do see ourselves accurately and look to him as our source, he pours abundant grace on us. But the Bible also says that God resists and opposes the proud. That really motivates me to want to cultivate humility.

Dan: In *Guarding Your Child's Heart* you talked about four major beliefs, or commands, we need to learn and live by as Christians. But in *The Desire* we didn't really have time to get to the fourth one, which is "Rejoice in Trials." Why do we need to embrace this command as essential, and why is this so important to our faith and even our own happiness?

Gary: It gets back to the idea about control. We don't have control over so much of what happens in our lives. Trials and troubles happen all the time. Christians aren't promised that we won't have them; we're promised that we will. But we're also promised that God is always in control, even in times of trouble. So we are commanded to rejoice in times of trouble, even to be thankful. It's an expression of faith that God is in control and that he can work all things together for good, even though it may take some time.

What we normally do is get angry or frustrated when trouble comes, or become afraid. This is a normal reaction, and it's not necessarily sin. Ephesians 4:26 says, "Be angry but do not sin." It's what we do with that anger that makes the difference. If we turn to the Lord and ask for his help (humble ourselves), he will help us. He'll give us grace to endure the trial and peace to guard our hearts. But Paul tells us in the next two verses in Ephesians 4 what happens if we *don't* resolve our anger properly, if we let "the sun go down on our anger." This unresolved anger gives the devil a foothold in our lives.

Many Christians go days, weeks, and months allowing this unresolved anger to contaminate their hearts. The light inside grows dimmer and dimmer until finally it becomes nighttime in their hearts. This is why it's so critical for us to obey God and rejoice when trouble comes.

Acknowledgments

In addition to our wonderful publishing staff at Revell, Gary and I would like to thank some very special people who helped us with the research of this book. At the top of that list would be Gary's son-in-law, Roger Gibson, and Gary's daughter (and Roger's wife), Kari. It's fair to say we could never have written this book without them. Most of the scenes set in Ethiopia came out of conversations and emails with them.

You can find out more about their story by watching the trailer for *Man Up and Go*, an award-winning film that actually features Gary sharing their experiences in Korah (manup andgo.com/trailer). Also, check out Kari Gibson's amazing blog at mycrazyadoption.org/blog/.

Gary and I would also like to thank three other women—all of them writers—for their invaluable insights about the current struggles women face with infertility. They are:

- Kym McNabney (find her at kymmcnabney.blogspot .com/)
- Elizabeth Maddrey (find her at www.ElizabethMaddrey .com)
- Marlo Schalesky (find her at www.marloschalesky.com)

Dan Walsh is the award-winning author of *The Unfinished Gift*, *The Homecoming*, *The Deepest Waters*, *Remembering Christmas*, *The Discovery*, *The Reunion*, and *The Dance*. A member of American Christian Fiction Writers, Dan served as a pastor for twenty-five years. He lives with his family in the Daytona Beach area, where he's busy researching and writing his next novel.

Gary Smalley is one of the country's best known authors and speakers on family relationships. He is the author or coauthor of sixteen bestselling, award-winning books, along with several popular films and videos. He has spent over thirty years learning, teaching, and counseling, speaking to over two million people in live conferences. Gary has appeared on national television programs such as *Oprah*, *Larry King Live*, *Extra*, the *Today* show, and *Sally Jessy Raphael*, as well as numerous national radio programs. Gary and his wife, Norma, have been married for forty years and live in Branson, Missouri. They have three children and six grandchildren.

CONNECT WITH THE AUTHORS

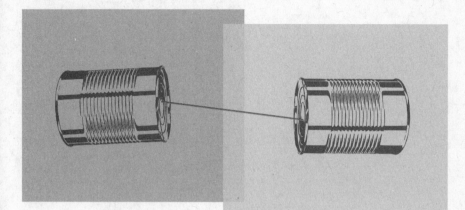

DAN WALSH

www.DanWalsh.com

CONNECT WITH DAN ON

 Dan Walsh • *DanWalshAuthor*

GARY SMALLEY

Smalley.cc

CONNECT WITH GARY ON

 Gary Smalley

Get to know the rest of the Anderson
family and don't miss any of
THE RESTORATION SERIES.

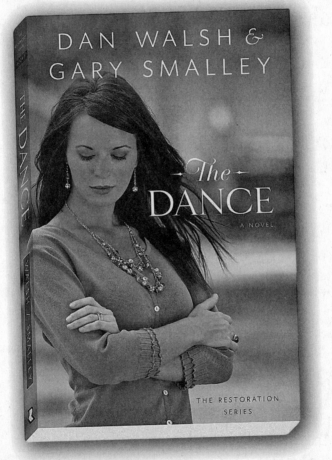

"Readers will definitely come away satisfied and
shedding tears at the end."
—*Publishers Weekly*

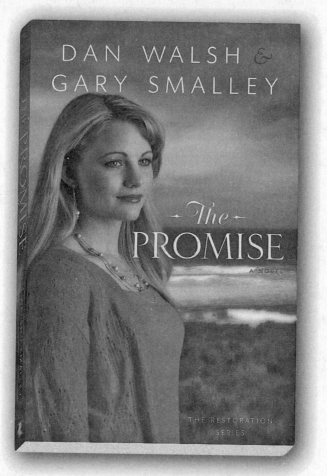

DAN WALSH & GARY SMALLEY

The PROMISE

A NOVEL

THE RESTORATION SERIES

"Authentic characters and challenges, beautiful and uplifting prose, and solid marital advice flourish. You'll find it very difficult to put down."

—*RT Book Reviews*, 4½ stars, Top Pick

In 1962, life was simple, the world made sense, and all families were happy. And when they weren't, everyone knew you were supposed to pretend.

"Dan is an artist who paints with words, and his canvas is the novel, where he uses different colors and hues of words to create a masterpiece. *What Follows After* is a marvelous old-school tale illustrating the importance of faith and family. It's a story that will surely touch your heart and soul."

—**John M. Wills,** *New York Journal of Books*